TILL DEATH US DO PART

Cristina Slough

TILL DEATH US DO PART

First Print Edition: December 2015

Limitless Publishing, LLC
Kailua, HI 96734
www.limitlesspublishing.com

Formatting: Limitless Publishing

ISBN-13: 978-1-68058-431-8
ISBN-10: 1-68058-431-6

DEDICATION

This book is dedicated to the man that I would choose in ten thousand lifetimes—my husband, Adam, and the life we created together—our son, Lucas.

PROLOGUE

Mimi
London, 2011

Mimi had been dreaming of a storm. Heavy rain, violent claps of thunder, and lightning flashing simultaneously.

She saw Joel reaching out for her, his body bloody and wet. She awoke in the darkened room. It was 2:17 a.m., 6:47 a.m. in Afghanistan, and the exact time she had woken up for three nights in a row.

She slipped out of bed, her pyjama bottoms loose around her ever-shrinking waist. The air was freezing. She dashed across the room to wrap herself in the fleecy dressing gown her mother had just bought her for Christmas.

Her stomach growled, begging for food. She couldn't eat. She clicked onto her Twitter feed to check for more updates about the suicide bombing in Kabul which had claimed at least six. Two were American Marines.

Mimi had contacted the Embassy several times, but nobody could tell her anything. The pain of not knowing was taking away her ability to breathe normally. The silence was too loud. She had tried to remember their last conversation. Did she tell him that she loved him? Words so quick to fall off the tongue to end a phone call. *Love you, bye*.

Often she had felt like being the wife of a Marine meant she was holding a grenade. She was always waiting for a letter, waiting to hear his voice, waiting for news that he was alive or dead.

She hadn't known how deeply this war would affect her. She remembered the morning she first learned of the Gulf War in 1991. Mimi's older sister, Larna, ran into her small bedroom in a complete meltdown. "Mimi, war has started!" She recalled the fear she felt. She was only eight years old. When she realised that the war wasn't in England, she'd cried with relief.

Somehow, throughout her life, Mimi knew war with the Middle East was going to directly affect her eventually. Her premonition was confirmed the day she met Joel Marcus.

In the bitter silence, Mimi was left with nothing but her own whirling thoughts. Memories flitted in and out. Knots kneaded together in her stomach, its grip tightening. She was stuck on a waltzer of panic.

"Why?" She had asked Joel many times. He had never met her gaze. He'd always change the subject in an effort to avoid giving her the answer she desperately craved.

She needed to understand. What was the driving force steering the man she loved to the front line?

Why did he choose to offer his life for a war that was never going to reach a peace treaty, a war full of bloodshed, a price too many lives had already paid with no signs of the bloodshed ending?

Then, one day, as they watched an anniversary special of 9/11 at Mimi's London flat, he asked her a question asked by so many before him when the subject of 9/11 was raised. "Where were you?"

She had told him that she was at work. It was one of those moments in history that people knew just where they were and just what they were doing. She recalled her colleague had delivered the news to her. Mimi remembered going into the break-out area, watching the breaking bulletin, and wondering, *was this really happening?*

She had recalled the images of that day. It was imprinted in her memory. She'd watched the play-by-play footage of the plane exploding on impact, demolishing at least six floors. Torrents of smoke appeared to be throwing out a backfire of orange fireballs. She remembered the very moment she saw a dark eerie shadow come into view. Then, when the second plane hit, it had occurred to her that what she was watching wasn't some tragic accident.

When Mimi's colleagues started filtering back into the office, the question on everybody's lips was, "have you heard…? Have you seen…?" Barnard & Millban, the company Mimi worked for, was American-owned. Calls were made to family members and colleagues overseas to ensure they were okay. Although the images were truly horrific, Mimi found herself hungry for more information. She wanted to know the ins and outs as to why such evil had been inflicted. And then…she wondered about the most morbidly, thought-provoking question.

Jump or burn?

Mimi understood why the people in the towers wanted to jump. She couldn't even begin to imagine the heat in those buildings, the intensity of those fierce flames. For Mimi, jumping indicated choice, falling into a final act of hope.

The next day, news of the terror attacks dominated the media. It was the first time Mimi had heard the name Osama bin Laden, the terrorist leader of Al-Qaeda. The papers printed a gallery of images of the doomed towers with the headlines: **"War Comes to America," "War on the World,"** and then the *Daily Mail's* photo of the dark, evil cloud of smoke with one word, one powerful meaning: **"Apocalypse."**

President Bush confirmed the terror attack. He called it "a mass murder." He said the American military was prepared.

There was a ripple of shock throughout the day. Many lives were changed forever. It was a day that changed history. The world was at war!

After she had shared her recollection with Joel, he rested his hands firmly on her shoulders. He surprised her by giving the answer to the question she asked him so many times before.

"Now you know why I'm doing this. It was all because of that day."

CHAPTER 1

California, 2010

Mimi's legs rested on the dashboard of the white rented Jeep. She was now Mrs. Marcus. She liked how that sounded and how her engagement ring and wedding band complemented each other, dazzling in the brilliant sunshine. Beside her, Joel was humming along to a country song blaring out from the radio. They had left the buzzing city of San Francisco, having done all the touristy things like visiting Alcatraz and watching the sea lions lazing around the decks on Pier 39.

Now they were headed to Yosemite National Park. Mimi felt nervous as they drove up and around the tight, winding bends. She'd gripped the handle of the passenger door so much her tanned knuckles turned as white as snow. Joel shot her a sideways look.

"Don't you trust my driving?" he teased.

"It's not about your driving, darling. It's that drop. We are six thousand feet above sea level!"

"I love it when you call me *darling*. It's so British."

"I am British. And I'll be keeping your American ass in check."

"Don't you mean *arse*?" Joel said in a terrible English accent.

A few miles on, the road finally evened out. They pulled over. Mimi stepped out from the car in her flip flops and inhaled the fresh air, closing her eyes. Joel leant against the car, holding his camera against his chest. He said, "This place is amazing."

"It really is."

"Do you want to explore a little?" Joel asked.

"I'd love to."

They walked through a trail off a beaten pathway. Mimi walked with caution, occasionally stopping to remove her flip flops and shake out some stones and gritty dirt.

"Wow, look at that," Mimi shouted over the pounding sound of a waterfall. There were flowers nearby that smelled like sweet honey.

Joel removed his vest, his body lean and muscular. He had several tattoos and a couple of scars. One was from childhood. He'd fallen off his bike and cut the top of his left arm. The other scar was from boot camp, where he was trying to look impressive by climbing the wall too quickly. He'd fallen backwards and ripped open his shoulder.

Mimi pulled her long dark hair into a ponytail. She watched Joel wander off.

"What are you doing?"

"Taking it all in," he replied, stretching his arms out wide.

Mimi dipped her toes into the bubbly water, which felt surprisingly warm.

"Hold on to this memory. Right here, right now," Joel yelled and smiled.

She knew she had to listen to him and savour this moment because in just a few short weeks, he would be deployed to Afghanistan. It would be his second tour. Mimi felt that going for a second stint would probably be more dangerous than the first because luck runs out. The first time he was deployed, she hadn't known him. She hadn't loved him.

I don't want you to go. She would never ask him not to because, by doing that, she would be asking him to be a whole other person. Joel was a military man. It was in his blood.

Joel had joined the US Marines when he was just eighteen in the wake of 9/11. He'd told Mimi that, at the time, he had been looking for a sense of purpose, somewhere to belong. Joel and his brother, Austin, had been raised by their mother. His father died in a ranching accident when they were both very young. Joel left in pursuit of saving the world, whilst Austin stayed to help his mother with the ranch.

Joel said he and his brother were once close, but Austin felt abandoned when Joel left to join the Corps. A few years later, his mother died. After this, Austin made very little contact. His letters became shorter and eventually they stopped. Joel said he had tried to reach out to him but he couldn't keep handling the rejection. The last time he had reached out to Austin was to invite him to their wedding, but Austin declined.

Joel and Mimi had chosen a small beach wedding with only Mimi's mother, father, sister, her best friend, Meg, and two of Joel's best friends and military brothers, Danny and Eric. It had been intimate and meaningful. Neither of them wanted a big, lavish celebration, but they both wanted an adventurous, memorable honeymoon.

"So, I need to ask you something," Joel said, hopping over some pebbles as he moved back toward Mimi.

"I'm listening."

"I know we have discussed this before, but you're a military wife now. You have an entitlement to stay on the base while I'm deployed."

"I know, and my decision has not changed. I want to stay with my family in London."

Joel took a deep breath. "And when I come back, where do you want home to be?"

"Where ever you are. The base, in the middle of a field—I don't care so long as I'm with you. But when you're gone, well, let's just say the days are going to feel like years, and I know I'll be counting the days 'till you come back to me. I just can't live in a place where I have nothing and nobody but time. Watching that clock, looking at the calendar on that wall…I swear that would kill me," Mimi said, her eyes beginning to water.

"I'm coming back, you know." He cupped her face and looked into her eyes.

"You better."

Mimi fell into his arms, stroking her hand against his dark shaven head.

"This…it's another life," Joel said with earnestness.

"I know," Mimi whispered.

"Not yet you don't, Mimi. There will be days, weeks even, when I can't contact you."

"Joel, I know. I don't want to make our honeymoon about you leaving. Actually, I don't want to talk about it. Take a look around." Mimi spun on her heel in a full circle.

"I see."

"You see with your eyes, but try to see it from within."

"I have no idea what you're talking about, but I'll quit talking about leaving. You're right, Mimi. Let's head to the hotel. My wife is waiting for me, ready for me to give her some lovin'."

"Better not disappoint her."

"Sergeant Marcus never disappoints!"

Later, after they'd checked into the hotel and showered, Mimi climbed onto the bed next to Joel. The sun had just set. The only light in the room was from the small crack of the bathroom door.

Joel smelt of mint and soap. She rested her head on his shoulder, making a small circle on his arm with her fingertip. There was no talking; they were happy enough to feel close to each other without the use of words to explain what they were feeling.

***

Mimi struggled to pull herself up any further. She'd considered herself to be above average in fitness. She had the hard, toned muscular body to prove it, but climbing was taking her body to places it had never been. She couldn't seem to meet the challenge of the strength and the endurance required for this task. On the plane to San Francisco, she had tried to read as much as she could on basic mountain climbing, but a book was never going to teach her what she needed right now.

She shifted her weight, but she could feel herself slipping. The heat of the sun was burning her neck. She tried to stay focused on the large rock jutting out above her. If she could just make it onto that, she'd be on the home stretch. Beads of sweat popped up on her forehead. She could almost hear her pulse thudding in her ears.

Keep calm.

"Shift your weight!" Joel yelled.

"I'm trying."

"Mimi, move your body to the right."

"I can't do this. I hate it."

"Yes, you can."

"No, I can't. I really can't."

Finally she pushed forward and made it to the top. She was once again on flat ground. She allowed her body to fall forward. She grabbed her knees, dropped her head back, and looked up to the perfect arena of the blue sky above her—not a cloud to be seen. The orange vest that she wore rode up, exposing her smooth, ripped stomach.

Another group of hikers walked past. They sounded German and attempted to ask Mimi and Joel for directions, but the language barrier was too great. They shrugged and walked away, annoyed.

Mimi and Joel continued to walk, aiming to find

a shortcut. Halfway through, Mimi had to sit down and take several sips of water. She felt like a flushed, sticky mess.

She remembered when Joel told her there were points during his vigorous training that he had to prove through his mind to his body that he could push himself further than he thought possible. There were even moments when he thought he had reached his limit, but then he powered through to go above and beyond, smashing that limit.

Although he was with Mimi here on their honeymoon, sometimes he would become detached from their immediate surroundings. Joel had told Mimi, more than once, that the Corps wasn't just a job. He didn't clock off at five in the afternoon, driving home and leaving it all behind. With conviction, he told her the Marines engineer their training and way of life to become a big part of who you are, who you will always be.

Mimi was a hardworking university graduate with a short-lived career in law. She had a lifelong passion for art, used her creativeness in the world of marketing, and didn't fall into the trap of becoming a starving artist, although painting was her dream.

Mimi and Joel met in London's Regent Park. They were both running in different directions. The collision of their bodies had knocked Mimi to the ground. Joel had extended his arm and given her his sweaty palm. The next day, they met again, but this time on purpose. They had breakfast at a small Italian café near the American Embassy in Mayfair. One expresso, two lattes, and two plain au chocolates later, it was clear there was chemistry between them.

They met again for dinner the very next evening. Joel wasn't looking for any romance during his time in London, but there was something about Mimi. He learned her father was a born and bred cockney Londoner called Simon who started out as a plumber in the East-End and eventually started his own business. Her Thai mother, Kanchana, meaning "gold," had immigrated to England as a child. Mimi and her sister, Larna, were raised in a modest three-bedroom semi-detached house in Finchley, North London.

In the year that followed, Mimi and Joel decided they wanted to take their breakfast dates, weekly serpentine swims, and Sunday lunches at the greasy spoon café to the next level, so they got married.

***

It was the first time that Mimi was about to jump out of a plane. It had been an ambition of hers for years. As the plane ascended, she watched the ground beneath them change into a sketchy landscape, like Google Earth view. The instructor teased her, pretending the straps tying her to him were loose. His dry sense of humour succeeded in making her relax and even laugh.

Back in London, Mimi had told Joel how much she would love to skydive. It was on her bucket list. When they had carefully planned their California honeymoon, he secretly booked the dive as a wedding present to her. She had been so excited, but as she looked out at the short wingspan of the light aircraft and compared it to that of a commercial jet, the contrast felt so great.

What am I doing?

Joel wasn't a dreamer. He was a go-getter. She had told him what she wanted to do, and he made it happen. If he hadn't booked the jump, Mimi wondered if she would have ever followed through with her bucket-list dream. That was the difference between the couple—they both had an appetite for adventure, but Mimi always proceeded with some caution, whereas Joel lived each day as if it were his last. He was fearless.

Mimi picked the skin on the side of her thumb until it bled, her nervous habit since childhood. She sucked the blood so it didn't stain the bright yellow rented jumpsuit she was in.

Joel was the first out of the plane. Her heart jumped out of her mouth. What if the parachute didn't open? Three others dropped. She heard the faint screams dim as gravity pulled them down, and then it was her turn. She was the last one to make the jump.

Mimi crawled to the open hatched door, her instructor edging her forward with his knee into the small of her back. She looked out to see nothing but sky. Her body felt tense with fear.

Before she could catch one last breath, she was free falling, plummeting through the wide open space. She tried to scream, but couldn't. Her mouth was open. She was gasping for air, but she couldn't catch her breath. It unnerved her. The instructor placed his hand on her forehead and pulled her head to rest on his shoulder. The sound of the whooshing air almost deafened her.

When the parachute sprung open, she was pulled back up with fast acceleration. Suddenly there was silence, and the scenery of the unspoilt, rugged landscape stunned her. The instructor steered them toward the ground. He had told her to keep her arms crossed in front of her chest and her legs together and elevated.

Mimi had expected to land with a hard thud, so she was surprised when her bottom touched the ground and it felt as if she had landed on a pillow. Her instructor high-fived her and told her he'd been a little worried, as she had fallen like a rag doll. Perhaps it was that dry sense of humour again. She wasn't sure.

Joel walked quickly toward her and took her in his arms. He picked her up, spun her around, and gave her a hard kiss on her cheek.

"How do you feel?"

"Oh my God, that was amazing!"

"Told ya."

"I can't believe I was up there," she said, pointing up with her index finger.

"You glad you did it?"

"Yes. Thank you so much, darling. Thank you so much. This was the best present ever!"

"I'm glad you enjoyed it." He pulled her static hair off her face. "So, what do you want to do now?" he asked as they walked back to the hub to change and get their transfer back to the hotel.

"After this, I just want to relax and be lazy around the pool."

"What, you don't want to do it again?"

"I do and we will, but not right now." She laughed

"Maybe we can get you trained so you can learn to free fall," he said in all seriousness.

"I don't think so."

"Why not?"

"Because it was one thing knowing I had an experienced instructor glued to my body. I couldn't actually get myself out of that plane. I'd die!"

Their honeymoon had been exactly what they hoped it would be—full of romance and exploration, discovering new places as they discovered each other. Mimi watched Joel. She watched how he moved and sometimes couldn't believe he was hers. She knew him, but she didn't really know where he had come from, only what he told her.

He was an orphan, which didn't seem a fitting title to give to a grown man, but it was true. She had never seen the place where he had grown up or sat at the table where he shared his meals with his family. He knew all of her. He met her parents and her sister, seen the old baby album pictures of her sitting in a pool of bubbles and in her highchair with tomato sauce all over her face.

Joel had told her about his father, how he was a pioneer who provided for his family, installing wisdom and morals into both of his sons. His memories of his father had become somewhat faded over the years. He remembered sporadic details, like the time he brought a new Arabian horse home. His mother had gone crazy, as he had spent all the money they had on that horse.

He remembered the winter that they had lost all the heating and electric in their home, so his father made a camp in the garden, lit a bonfire, and toasted marshmallows as they told one another ghost stories. His father taught him how to hold his first gun at the age of thirteen. He remembered how the heavy, cold, metal steel felt in his hand and thought about what the weapon represented, that by just squeezing the trigger hard enough, it was capable of ending a life.

Joel found in Mimi what he had been searching for, and in many ways she was home. Together they were traveling through the most amazing of places, becoming closer by sharing life-changing experiences. They had taken dozens of photos, smiling in front of the tallest of trees, looking like little people.

Toward the end of their trip, they had gone to a bar in LA and danced the night away, challenging one another to shots of vodka and tequila. Joel had let himself go that night. He let his feet move, his hips sway, and, for the first time since they had met each other, he was dancing.

Mimi giggled at her husband. She loved this new, carefree side of him. They nibbled on salted peanuts and the stale crisps that were in chipped, mismatched bowls left on the side of the bar. They woke up in a drunken haze the next morning and learned for the first time what it was like to look after one another as they both took turns throwing up.

They stayed in the hotel room for the entire day and didn't step into the smoggy city for some proper food until they finally felt ready. They promised themselves no alcohol would be involved. They ate in a small but trendy restaurant called Happy Buddha. It was here that Mimi taught Joel how to use chopsticks. She laughed as she watched his clumsy fingers drop chunks of sweet and sour chicken and flick grains of rice across the table.

She had worn little makeup that evening. She didn't need much since she had that happy newlywed glow. Joel had commented on the light, sprinkle of freckles that had appeared on her nose. She had playfully thrown a napkin at him across the table, hitting him in his face.

When they left the restaurant, they got caught in an unexpected downpour. Mimi hated to get her hair wet from the rain. It made it frizz. She would have to spend the next morning blow drying it within an inch of its life. They huddled together under a bus stop. Joel pulled Mimi close to him. She looked into his hazel eyes with specks of rich green emerald. He kissed her hard, open mouthed. Suddenly, Mimi pulled back.

"I don't want you to go," she sobbed.

"I don't want to go either, but you know and I know that I have to."

"What if you don't come back?"

"Of course I'm coming back. I promise."

"You should never make promises that you can't keep."

"I'm keeping this one."

"Joel, I watch the news. I see the death tolls. It scares the shit out of me. Are you not scared"?

"Of course I'm scared. Every Marine is. Some of

us admit it. Some of us don't. But I'll never show the enemy that."

The rain grew louder. It sounded like the glass ceiling above them was going to shatter into a thousand, tiny pieces.

"I can't lose you."

"You won't. Trust me."

Joel had always dived head first into situations of danger, like the time he heard a loud bang downstairs when he was fifteen. He grabbed his father's shot gun and crept down the darkened stairway. He was faced with an intruder. They had locked eyes with one another. The intruder had a bag, no doubt stuffed with cash his mother had stowed away under the mattress in the spare room.

The intruder had turned to run when Joel lunged at him and pulled him backwards, knocking him to the ground. He had his neck in the clutches of his powerful arms. His mother heard the altercation. She ran to the phone, violently shaking, and called the police. Minutes later, the uniformed officers were at the door. Their swift arrival had saved Joel from a very different future. If they hadn't arrived when they did, Joel was certain he would have shot the intruder dead.

There were key moments in everyone's life, moments which take you to a fork in the road, where the direction you take can define who you will become.

Joel was deploying just a month after their honeymoon. Now the real test for their love was about to start.

CHAPTER 2

Joel
Afghanistan, 2011

The tinted, beige, underdeveloped landscape with scattered shards of grass and sand was a view Joel could never get used to. He knew there were parts that were beautiful, but here, among the boxed stone buildings, the landlocked area and rugged mountains made him feel a million miles away from familiarity. It made him miss Mimi even more.

The special ops combat team had been out on a mission to rescue a wounded US Marine. He'd been shot in the face and had a punctured lung. A raid had taken place in Khataba Village. The list of civilian casualties was growing. There had been airstrikes and both enemies and bystanders were killed.

Joel had been there for three weeks. There was great variance in the Afghanistan weather, from day to night. He kept a photo of Mimi on the inside pocket of his camouflaged uniform. It made him feel like he was keeping her close to his heart. The days were made easier by the boys' constant pranks, guy humour, and laugh-out-loud humiliation they inflicted on the "new guy."

The hunt for Osama bin Laden was the key focus. Special intelligence worked relentlessly to find out his last known movement. President Obama made promises to withdraw troops and end this ongoing war. The procedure of getting information had changed since Obama had been elected into power. He stopped interrogation by tactics of torture. The mission, the beast, had taken on a new life force. The game was still the same, but the rules had changed.

Many people in the outside world condemned the troops for being out there. "What are we fighting for?" they'd say. "Bring our troops home."

Rumours had reached Joel's ears that finding bin Laden was just a matter of time. America was getting closer to defeating the man responsible for the murder of almost three thousand people. Joel had been briefed, along with his platoon, that they were on the edge of finding him. There were leads and information from the CIA.

Joel dreamed of being the one to hold the gun to Osama bin Laden's head and be the hero. He dreamed of taking down the most prolific murderer in recent times after the likes of Hitler and Saddam Hussein.

Joel was naïve when he was younger—gun-happy and prepared to fight in a war. When he got older, he learned not all Afghans were bad. He saw kind faces amongst the crowds of people walking through the dusty streets; he saw the innocence of young children running and playing simply with what they had, an empty plastic bottle used as a football, an old rag being tossed to each other in a game of catch.

Some things were really tough for Joel to deal with, such as the dark shadow of oppression surrounding women. He loved Mimi's dark, bewitching hair falling down her back seductively and he couldn't imagine ever asking her to hide it. The slight bump in her imperfect nose that made her so appealing…why should that be covered?

He loved all the things that made Mimi who she was. He loved how her hands would take on a life of their own as she dipped her paintbrush into the vivid colours on her pallet and created something so inexplicably beautiful. He loved that she couldn't ever fry an egg and transfer it to the plate without making it look like an insect splattered across a windscreen at eighty miles an hour.

All the little things made up the reasons why he loved her. She had the freedom to be the person she was meant to be, her true spirit. But here, women were suppressed, and their eyes were dull and lifeless as if they were already dead, or slaves, beaten and crushed.

***

"So, you reached Mimi yet?" Eric asked. He walked into their shared bedroom and flung his cap across the room, hitting the small lampshade.

"Yup, just now. She's good. She's going

shopping with her mother."

"Cool, cool." Eric nodded

"Have you spoken to Jessica?"

"This morning."

"How did her doctor's appointment go?" Joel asked.

"Good. Baby is growing ahead by two weeks."

"Doesn't surprise me with you as its father. Let's just hope he gets Jess's looks, not yours."

Eric smiled. He picked up a football and tossed it into Joel's hands. The room was dim, basic. There was a musty damp smell with a faint scent of cigarettes.

Joel opened a large brown envelope containing photos of Mimi—a mix of snaps from their wedding day and honeymoon. It was here, in his room, that he was able to really allow himself to miss her.

He, Eric, and the rest of his team had been selected by Special Intelligence to move 100 miles from the Afghanistan border to the far eastern side of Pakistan in the next seventy-two hours, where it was believed that the compound of bin Laden was situated in Abbottabad.

"You ready for this?" Eric asked.

"Ready as I'll ever be. You?"

"Yeah. You sure?"

"Yes. I said yes." Eric tugged at his hair; a nervous habit.

"You're lying," Joel pressed. He stood up next to his friend and looked at him face on, almost touching his nose. They locked eyes for a few seconds.

"I'm fucking scared, bro," Eric admitted.

"Me too. Me fucking too."

"Things have changed since Jess became pregnant. I think twice about every move I make. I wonder if I'm ever going to hold my kid." Eric sat down on the edge of his bed. The springs creaked with every slight movement he made.

"I think of Mimi. Who wants to be a widow before they are thirty?"

"Looking back, nothing mattered before. Do you almost wish you had nothing to care about?"

"In some ways, but I'm glad I have Mimi, and Jess is glad she's got you, although I don't understand why the hell she does."

"C'mon, this chick talk is making me sick. Let's shake this shit off and go for a run."

***

The sun was hot, the heat relentless. Joel and Eric pounded the ground hard and fast, driven by determination to win the race. They circled the perimeter of the barbed wire fence, the drilling sound of helicopters hovering above their heads. Their muscular bodies glistened with sweat and their cheeks were flushed.

They ran to ignore the storm inside of them. They were about to go to one of the most hostile corners of the world where nobody was their friend. They would have to fight for survival. There would be no mercy.

Joel pushed his torso forward which gave him that last bit of acceleration he needed to beat Eric. They ran under the tails and wings of several planes. They reached the finish line, where the rest of the team were sitting on the beaten and basic wooden tables, having food and drinks.

"Marcus by 1.4," Lieutenant Parker announced, looking at his black stop watch.

"Jeez, I had him. I almost had him," Eric complained.

"Almost, but almost doesn't push you over that finish line, my friend!"

Later that afternoon, they sat and discussed their mission to move into the Afghanistan border, to the far eastern side of Pakistan. "Listen carefully, men. We have been given orders to move you out at nineteen hundred hours."

"As in tonight?" Sergeant Danny Duran questioned.

"Affirmative!"

The projector showed an image on the wall of a group of Taliban with the sound of a baby crying in the background. A small army of men moving through the overgrown bushes were holding guns. Women were cowering their heads and clutching their knees.

"The objective of this mission is to capture and kill Achmed Sharma, senior Taliban. He's responsible for killing Marines in the western border. He's a Tier 1 target."

"Why tonight? We were told seventy-two hours," Joel blurted out.

"Because we just received positive information he's there. The CIA is certain bin Laden is just across the border."

Joel let himself take a long, hard breath. Mimi

flashed into his mind. He looked across the table at Eric with his head in his hands. He knew what he was thinking.

"Expect your usual comms problems, boys."

They were showed the rules of engagement. Each man was paying attention to what was expected from them and how they could survive this mission.

There were questions followed by silence, faces of bravery and of fear. That basic room held top secret information the world was not yet privy to. Today it was classified, but tomorrow it would be headline news. The images would be splashed on every newspaper, and the footage would be in every living room, displaying on millions of screens.

They knew this could only have two outcomes—they would live or they would die. Their hard training had led them to this fight. Every time they felt like their bones would break, their drill instructor had yelled, pushing them to go further. Every bruise that had appeared on their skin and every time they had screamed they couldn't do it—all the times they almost quit, but didn't—it was all for this. No matter how afraid they were, all that training had given them one thing. They were now ready for combat.

A few hours later, they walked like an army of ants in perfect uniformity, boarding the helicopter, one by one. Joel's mind flashed back to Mimi in her bright yellow jumpsuit before they skydived. Here he was now, ready to go into battle.

Isaac and Ryker, the military German shepherds, joined the team. The light of the night sky almost looked like it had a tinge of blue. The silence among them was eerie; the only sound was the chopping, the soft panting of the dogs, and the static on the radio with the odd voice command.

Since this mission was top secret, it was almost as though they had to keep their voices hushed, but in truth, each of them was saying a silent prayer. Nobody had time to reach their families before they departed, and if they had, they would have been forbidden to tell them where they were going.

Three hours later, they landed. They jumped out of the helicopter, moving like cats through the jungle. Their bodies moved with caution and agility, all of their senses raised as they listened for the smallest of movements—a footstep moving through the grass, the click of a gun, a foreign voice.

They crouched low. Eric directed them toward what looked like a large abandoned hut, using hand gestures to signal to the rest of the team he thought their target was in there, taking refuge amongst women and children. It was dark in most places, until they moved into the deeper part of the building, where there was a glow of oil burners.

"US Marines! Where are you hiding, Achmed Sharma?"

A woman screamed, her face and body hidden in layers of cloth. She threw her entire body at Joel. He pushed her backwards and pinned her to the floor. Joel felt himself switch into another gear, the determination of a warrior. His senses heightened to another enemy closing in on him, trying to attack him from behind. He used the gun across Joel's neck to choke Joel.

Then came the sound of a firearm, the splatter of blood. Joel looked up to see Eric lying face down. He didn't need to turn him around to know he was already dead because it was clear he had been shot in the head.

A few moments later, there was total darkness. Joel felt his head pulsate. His eyes couldn't adjust and he felt like he was falling. Then silence.

CHAPTER 3

Mimi
London, 2011

Mimi couldn't stand sitting in her tiny, rented one-bedroom flat any longer. She needed to get out, she needed to walk. She grabbed her coat and bundled into it, along with a hat and scarf. She knew that walking the streets at five in the morning wasn't the best idea. She would most likely encounter a few cats lurking the streets, darting in and out of the shadows, maybe late night shift workers returning home or a drunk staggering though the streets, mumbling and talking gibberish.

She needed to breathe. She had her phone fully charged and tucked safely into her inside pocket so she could feel the vibration of a phone call, email, or text message. She'd set it at full volume, a surefire way to assure nothing would be missed should news come. She didn't want to hear the voice of a stranger. She wanted to hear Joel's deep, Texan accent telling her not to worry, that he was just fine.

Mimi looked up to the early morning sky, which was deceptively black when she left her block of flats. She held tightly onto the black steel railings as she walked down the steps to avoid slipping on the ice that glistened on the ground like shiny crystals. The moon was glowing in its crescent shape. One single star twinkled in the blackness.

Please let Joel be safe. Please, God, let him be safe. Please!

Mimi walked for several miles 'till she was hot and tired. She had to be in the office in just a couple of short hours, but she already decided she couldn't face it. When she returned to her flat, she logged into her email on her laptop and told her boss she was sick and wouldn't be able to come in.

She sat quietly on her sofa, cradling a steaming cup of tea in her hand, checking her phone for information every five minutes, feeling irritated at news that didn't relate to what she was looking for. Unworthy reports—footballers caught cheating, two people arrested in a pub brawl, things that didn't matter to Mimi.

When dawn finally broke, Mimi had fallen asleep. The sound of her phone buzzing awoke her. She grabbed it, bleary-eyed, as she tried to focus on the caller ID: ***'Unknown.'***

Her heart stopped beating as she heard an American accent, a woman. *Bombing...Joel Marcus...regret.*

***

Mimi arrived at the US Embassy with her mother and her best friend, Meg. She wore a pair of ripped jeans, the first thing she could find on a pile of dirty laundry. Her skin was covered in goose pimples despite the room being hot and stuffy.

The women were ushered to a quiet office, out of sight of the office workers walking in with cups of takeaway coffee in their hands. She caught a glimpse of a Marine's shoulder. She felt sick, wanting it to be Joel. She had never wanted anything so much.

Two uniformed Marines finally walked in the room. They sat quietly, averting their eyes for a second longer than Mimi thought acceptable. She felt like she was in a dream, a bad nightmare that she would soon wake up from and feel so relieved when she did. Only this wasn't a dream; this was real and this was the horrible reality she feared ever since Joel had left.

"Mrs. Mimi Marcus?" asked the older of the two men. He had leathery skin and salt and peppered grey hair. He looked like he'd lived a thousand lifetimes, each wrinkle on his face marking a tale to tell. He kept his gaze on her but didn't look directly into her eyes.

"Yes," Mimi said. Her voice didn't sound like her own. She sounded like a little girl.

"We regret to inform you your husband, Sergeant Joel Marcus, was killed in the line of duty yesterday."

That word again—*regret*. Regret was a word used when an employer had to inform you that you didn't get the job.

She felt her mother's hand on hers. She was gripping Mimi's hand tightly, as if she could stop her from taking the fall. Somewhere in the room, she could hear the ticking of a clock. *Tick...tick...tick.*

Mimi was in a spin. She could feel bile in the back of her throat.

He can't be dead, Mimi told herself. He would have come to her. His ghost would have appeared to her; he wouldn't just leave her. When they had said "Till death us do part," she'd imagined them old and grey, dying together or within days of one another, but not now!

"His body, where is his body?" Mimi whispered.

"We have not been able to recover his body. We have confirmed information that Sergeant Marcus was captured and killed."

"Captured? What do you mean captured?"

"We can't give you all the information," the older Marine said.

"I'm his wife. I deserve to know!" Mimi yelled.

"I'm sorry, Mrs. Marcus. Truly I am. I know how difficult this must be for you."

"The hell you do!" she sobbed.

"This is really not acceptable," Meg interceded. "You need to give Mimi more information. She is his wife. Surely you can see that she has a right to know!"

"I'm sorry for your loss. Truly, Mrs. Marcus, I am."

A few months before, Joel told her that he was coming back. He had made a promise to her and he hadn't kept it. She was paralyzed by grief. She couldn't seem to lift herself off the leather chair she sat in. Meg wrapped her arms around Mimi and pulled her to her feet.

"Come on, honey, let's get you home." Her voice was motherly, full of sympathy.

"It's better for her to come back with me and her dad," her mother said to Meg. They were talking like Mimi wasn't in the room.

"No! No!" Mimi squealed. "His body, I need to know where his body is!"

"Mimi, please, don't do this to yourself," her mother pleaded.

"My husband is dead. Did you hear them, Mama? Dead. I am not doing anything to myself. I demand to know the details." She banged her fist into the desk so hard her knuckles felt like they would cut open.

"This is not right!" Mimi cried.

"We will find out the truth, Mimi, we will. I promise, but please let your mother and I look after you."

"I love him." Mimi let her tears flow. Her sobs got caught in her throat and her body trembled.

Meg took her friend in her arms and held her tight.

"I know you do. And he loved you." Mimi noticed the word *loved.* Meg was already using the past tense.

The rest of the day went by in a painful blur. Some information was passed on by the Embassy, but nothing that would explain the true details of Joel's death.

Mimi allowed her family to look after her. Her

sister had left work early and driven down from Yorkshire to London to be with her. They made her endless cups of tea which she left to go cold; made her food which she wouldn't touch; and held her to give her comfort which she couldn't feel. Even in the cocoon of her family home, she felt exposed to pain.

She had a million questions and no answers. She thought of the person that took her husband's life. Her heart filled with instant hatred for a person that had no face and no name.

She imagined how Joel died. Did he feel any pain? Did he fight back? Did he beg the faceless killer to spare his life?

"I need to go home." Mimi began rising from her father's armchair.

"We think it is better you stay with us, Mimi. Please let us look after you." Her father tightly gripped her shoulder and pulled her back. Her body immediately turned limp.

Dad was always Mr. Fix-it. When Mimi was younger, if a lightbulb had blown, her dad would fix it. If a tap kept dripping, her dad would fix it. But in this moment, her dad had a defeated look on his face. He knew he would not be able to fix this.

"Wilbur hasn't had anything to eat," Mimi said. "He can't be left alone."

"I'll get him. He can stay with me," Meg reassured her. "You know I love that black and white bag of trouble."

Mimi nodded.

"My clothes. I need my clothes."

"I'll go with Meg to your place and get them,"

her sister said, standing up.

Mimi let her body fall onto a cushion on her parent's sofa. It still had that new smell to it. She heard the clattering of pots and pans coming from the kitchen. Moments later, her mother returned to the room, holding out a small bowl.

"I'm not hungry." Mimi pushed the steaming bowl of chicken soup away.

"You must eat something, Mimi."

"I just told you that I am not hungry."

Mimi used the pillow to conceal the sounds of her shrieking sobs. Her father gently lifted her into his arms. He removed her hair from her hot, sticky, wet face and cradled her just like when she was a child. He rocked her back and forth as the grief poured out of her.

"Shhh. I'm here, Mimi. Daddy is here."

"He left me. He told me he would be back."

"He didn't leave you, Mimi. Not through choice. Joel would've never left you through choice."

Her father took a damp, pink cloth from her mother and wiped her head.

In the late hours of the evening, Mimi fell asleep. The sheer exhaustion of crying made her eyes swell and she had fallen into a slumber. She was still dressed in the same clothes she had worn when she learned Joel had been killed. Her mother brought down a single duvet and placed it over her. Meg and Larna had left to get her things and her cat.

"How will she ever recover from this?" Kanchana whispered to Simon.

"I don't know. I feel so helpless. I want to make this all go away, but I can't. He was everything to her, like you are to me."

CHAPTER 4

Two weeks later, rain fell heavy against Mimi's bedroom window. She kept her eyes closed. Her body felt heavy and achy. For a moment, she lay perfectly still and calm. Then she remembered.

Joel was dead and she had to live another day without him.

Thoughts of the faceless killer entered her head once again. Every day a different image, yet the outcome was always the same. The disturbing thoughts poisoned her mind. She didn't care that she was suffering; it was as if her tears were keeping Joel alive within her. If she cried, it meant the news was still recent. It meant she was closer to the last moment he had held her in his arms rather than time putting distance between them.

Beside her bed was a photo of Joel in his camouflaged uniform, his dog tags resting on his tanned chest. He was smiling in that photo, his sideways profile caught unaware in the moment. Every morning, she picked up the copper framed picture and rested it next to her pillow. She felt like a grieving widow holding onto every single memory of her deceased husband.

She knew she must get herself out of bed and into the world. She knew Joel would have disapproved of her living this way.

She finally pulled herself up and out of bed. She caught sight of herself in the mirror, but she had no idea who was staring back at her. Her long hair was tangled and dry, her face puffy and blotchy. She didn't like what she saw. Joel had loved how well she had always taken care of herself, but here, without him, everything seemed pointless.

She drifted into the shower. She let the hot water wash over her body and rubbed her raspberry shower gel into her skin.

She stayed in the shower long enough for the hot water to run cold. She stepped out and wrapped a heated towel tightly around her frail body. The mirror revealed another unfamiliar image. Every single one of her ribs was visible. She had barely eaten; food had lost its flavour. It all seemed so pointless.

She heard the sound of her buzzer. At first she ignored it until it became clear that the consistent noise was not going to go away.

"Yes," Mimi said into the intercom.

"Mimi, it's me. Let me in."

"Meg, I'm tired."

"I don't care. Let me up," Meg's static voice demanded.

Moments later, Meg was at the door. Her blonde hair was neatly pulled back into a bun, her makeup applied perfectly. She looked around Mimi's flat and didn't hide her disapproval at the mounds of dirty laundry, unwashed cups, and photos of Joel strewn all over the floor.

Mimi had spent her days walking the streets, wandering aimlessly with nowhere to go. The rest of the time she spent pulling out photos of them both.

"Mimi, we need to get this place in order," Meg said, her voice full of concern.

"Why?"

"Because living like this is not healthy." Meg sat on the arm of the sofa, pulling out a wet towel from underneath her.

"He wanted a photo of Wilbur. I was going to send it in my next letter to him, but I forgot."

"Don't punish yourself. These things happen."

"These things?" Mimi raised an eyebrow.

"You know what I mean, Mimi."

"I don't want to keep living. Not without Joel."

"I can't imagine what you are going through. Really, Mimi, I can't. We are all so worried about the way you are living right now. It's not good."

"It's been two weeks, Meg. Two weeks since my husband was killed. Am I not allowed to cry and live like a bum and, dare I say it…grieve?"

"Yes, of course you are, but not forever."

Mimi felt a wave of anger flush over her.

She looked at her friend and wanted her out of her sight, away from her. Meg had never had a relationship for longer than a few weeks. She flitted from man to man. She grew tired and bored of relationships easily, so how would she ever understand the feelings you needed to be so in love that you promised the rest of your lives to one another?

Mimi felt insulted that Meg was telling her to get it together after such a short time.

"Do you know he can't even have a proper funeral because there is no body?"

"Mimi, I'm sorry. You're right. I'm expecting you to snap out of something that just happened to you. I don't deal with death too well and I should be more supportive of you."

"Yes, you should," Mimi whispered.

"Come out this afternoon. Let me look after you. We can go for a drive to that little tea room in Hertfordshire that you love. Joel would want you to."

"I really don't feel like it."

"Come on, Mimi. For Joel."

"Okay, I will. Let me just get dressed and come back for me in a couple of hours."

"I'll call you when I'm outside."

When Meg left, Mimi looked around her. She knew she needed to get out and feel something other than grief. Her head was heavy. It felt like it had its own pulse. Her eyes felt as if weights were attached to them.

Just as Mimi was getting dressed, she saw a Facebook message pop up on her screen. The name "***Joel***" jumped out at her. Her legs felt like jelly. She clicked on the message from Austin. Joel's brother had gotten in touch.

***

Two perfect fine bone china cups were placed in front of Mimi and Meg. They sat in the far corner of the tea room located off a beaten track. Meg swirled the tea leafs around the pot and poured.

"So, how much do you know about Austin?" Meg asked. She took a sip of the tea and squeezed her blue eyes shut as it was too hot.

"Nothing. Well, only what Joel told me. They haven't spoken properly since his mother died."

"Hmm, bad blood?"

"From what Joel told me, Austin was a real homebody and he felt betrayed when Joel left to join the Marines. I guess he felt abandoned. I don't know."

"Do you want to know?" Meg said, moving forward.

"I always wanted to know about Joel's childhood. He knew all of me, but I guess I only knew Joel the US Marine. He always lived for the here and now, but I love memories. I loved how he knew Larna. Somehow, Larna and I sharing our adventures when we were younger came back to life when he sat at the dinner table with my family. I wished I'd had that with Joel."

"Did you ever ask to meet his brother?"

"I did. But Austin refused to come to our wedding. I think, after that, Joel let go."

"And now?"

Mimi looked at her friend, unsure as to what she was asking.

The waitress came and placed two warm scones with cream and jam in front of them. Mimi looked at them and picked one up. She took a small bite.

"Where does Austin live?"

"Still on the family ranch in Texas. He's always been there."

"I've saved up a shit load of holiday time. Actually, I have to take it by April. Use it or lose it."

"What are you saying, Meg?"

"I'm saying let's go and meet Joel's estranged brother, explore his home town, and see where he grew up. I know you will never get closure, Mimi, not without the facts. But maybe, just maybe, learning more about your husband will give you a little peace."

"And you would come with me?"

"Yes. I thought I just made that clear," Meg said with a smile.

Mimi sat back in her chair. She took a deep breath. For the first time in what seemed like forever, she smiled.

"Let's go."

"Brilliant! I really do think this is going to give you everything you need."

"Everything I need would be having Joel back."

"I know, darling. I know."

"Thank you for suggesting this. It means so much to me."

"Don't thank me yet. I'm a terrible traveller. Air travel makes me quite sick."

"I remember when we went to New York." Mimi giggled. Meg had spent almost the entire plane journey with her head on her lap tray, complaining and sobbing that she felt sick.

"We will need to book flights soon. And you'll

need to contact Becky to let her know you are going away."

Becky was Mimi's boss. Throughout her entire bereavement, she had been extremely supportive and told her to take as much time as she needed away from the office. She would hire a temp if necessary.

"I'll call her when we get back. Seriously, that won't be a problem."

"Where will we stay?"

"We will have to get a hotel."

"Austin has a ranch. Can't we stay with him?"

Mimi raised her eyebrows and shook her head.

"No and no. His message basically said he was Joel's brother and he was sorry for my loss. It certainly wasn't an invitation."

"But he made contact." Meg pointed her butter knife at Mimi as she smeared her scone with a thick spread of cream.

"It was the right thing to do."

"Wait…are you not going to tell him that you are going?"

"I don't know." Mimi paused for a second. "Maybe."

Meg crossed her arms in front of her and huffed.

"What?" Mimi cried.

"I don't understand you. My whole idea is for you to get to know more about Joel and already you're blocking things."

"I am not. This is a huge deal, you know. Flying all the way to Texas to find out more about my husband's life is something I thought he and I would one day do together, but I can't because he's just not here anymore." Mimi's words caught in her throat. She hated putting the words "dead" and "Joel" in the same sentence because it affirmed this terrible reality truly existed.

As they left the tea room, a flurry of snow fell like fragile flower petals. Mimi held out her palm and felt the snow land on her hand and turn to water. She thought of Joel. Another wave of sadness came as she realised they had never experienced snow together and they never would.

They bundled into Meg's Mini Cooper. The sound of the engine roared to life as she turned the key. Meg quickly turned the heat up to full, letting the air flow through and clear the windscreen before they drove away.

Mimi and Joel had not yet lived as husband and wife. They hadn't even decided where home was, and she felt so robbed of all those special moments. They would never view houses together; they would never go on another holiday; never buy a dog like they always said they would; never have a baby.

In the last couple of weeks in the wake of Joel's death, Mimi had bought a pregnancy test, praying it would be positive so she would have a part of him left with her on Earth. It was negative and her period had showed up the very next morning—a stark reminder there was nothing of him left except photos, images frozen in time, and a couple of his hoodies, which she wrapped herself in every night. She would hold his sweatshirt close to her face and inhale, desperate to smell him.

There had been a time when Mimi and Larna were just young teenagers. They would explain what their ideal man looked like. Larna had chosen Nick Carter from the Backstreet boys, whilst Mimi had said that GI Joe was her ideal man. Larna had disapproved, saying she couldn't pick him as he wasn't real. Mimi told her sister he was out there, waiting for her. GI Joe was the image, but the man she was going to marry hadn't found her yet. Larna remembered this conversation and whispered to her sister as she dressed in her wedding gown, "So, I guess you got your GI Joe."

The traffic was heavy. Cars built up one after another. Meg was tapping her steering wheel in frustration.

"This A41 does my head in. One thing I'll say about Americans is they are prepared for bad weather and they deal with it. We English get a few bloody drops of snow and traffic is gridlocked."

Mimi was staring out the window, lost in her own thoughts.

"Where do you think he is now?"

"Joel?"

"Yes, Joel."

"I don't know, honey. I'd like to say in heaven. You believe in all those things, don't you?"

"I used to," Mimi said.

"You don't anymore?"

"How can I? If there actually is a God, then why did He take away somebody so special and so young?"

"I wish I knew, I really do. Joel will be at peace, Mimi. I know you don't believe that, but he will be and he will want you to be at peace as well."

"You know we got crazy drunk in LA. We

danced to this very song." The sound drifted out of the speakers. The volume was low.

"What? *Beautiful Dangerous?*"

"Yeah. Seriously, my husband, who never ever danced, got on his feet and he moved…like really moved. It was pretty damn sexy."

"I'm sure. Joel was a sexy guy."

"Hey, that's my husband you're talking about." Mimi playfully punched her friend on the arm. Then that familiar stomach flip grabbed hold of her—he *was* her husband. He *was* sexy, but he *was* no longer.

That was the horrible reality of grief. Just when you felt a little better, you caught yourself in a memory of happiness, but then you always remember the person is gone. The stomach drops, followed by spinning sensations, attack you like a snake pouring venom through your entire body.

Losing Joel was something she knew she would never recover from. There was no escaping these feelings inside her. She wanted to go to Texas and she was so glad Meg suggested it, but she knew changing the scenery would never change the situation. Yet being where he had grown up, walking the same paths he would have, driving down the roads he learned to drive down would somehow make her feel more connected to him than she did in the eternal winter of England. She had never been to Texas. She liked the idea of exploring somewhere totally new to her.

After battling the traffic back to North London, Meg came back to Mimi's flat with her. She walked in the door, picked up the clothes on the floor, and threw them in the washing machine. Then she put the cups in hot soapy water and ran a vacuum around. She spied a man's sweater next to Mimi's pillow. She knew it must have belonged to Joel, so she respectfully folded it and placed it under the covers.

By this time, the snow had turned to icy rain. As soon as it hit the pavement, it dispersed. Mimi stood by her bedroom window, watching the world go by—people returning home after being at work all day; an elderly couple arm in arm walking a small dog. She wondered about others. What was going on in their lives? When she saw people smile, it looked like a foreign gesture to her.

"Right. I think I'm done. All you need to do is take your clothes out when the cycle finishes and hang them up. Don't let them sit in there or they'll smell. Do you want me to stay with you tonight?" Meg placed her hand on Mimi's neck, stroking her gently.

"I would like that."

"Fab. Okay…well, you need to set me up with a night shirt and some clean undies for the morning."

"No problem."

Mimi averted her eyes away from the window and looked at her friend. Just hours ago, she wanted her gone, but here, in this moment, she had never needed her more. She was grateful that Meg was here supporting her through all of this.

Meg was always somewhat headstrong and rarely showed emotion. Mimi often teased her and said she had as much heart as a stone. It wasn't that Meg was unkind or even uncaring. She just dealt with things head on, and she never liked to dwell.

In many ways, she was much like Joel, who never liked to dwell on anything. If something bad happened, he would chalk it up to experience, learn from it, and move on. Mimi was a dweller, always full of emotion and reflection. She kept keepsakes that were years old: cinema tickets, old cassette tapes that could no longer be played, tons of pictures and scrapbooks. She held onto things because maybe, somewhere deep down, she knew how quickly things could be taken away.

After the girls settled in for the evening, Meg took to the kitchen to make chicken stir-fry. She chopped vegetables and seasoned the chicken with some mild spices. The kitchen and the lounge were one big room. She set the smoke alarm off more than once. When she had finished, she set the two plates down on the rounded kitchen table. There were shrivelled up dead roses that looked like they had been sitting there for weeks.

"Just try and get through half of this," Meg said, handing Mimi a fork.

"It smells good."

"It *is* good. I made it!"

Mimi poked the fork into a small chunk of chicken. Flavour exploded in her mouth on the first bite. Suddenly she was salivating, eager for more. She began shovelling food into her mouth like a ravenous dog. Meg smiled and tucked into her own food.

"So, after we finish up here, we can go online and look at some flights and places to stay. Do you have an actual address for the ranch?"

"Yes. I have it from when we sent out our wedding invitations."

"You really do need to reply to Austin and tell him that you are coming over. Personally, I wouldn't be happy if somebody just showed up on my doorstep."

"I guess I can contact him and tell him."

Mimi put her face in her hands, rubbing her temples. Every part of her still ached, but the food had given her a little more strength. She was suddenly thinking clearly, able to make a plan of action.

She sipped a cup of juice and went to get her laptop. She Googled "flights to Texas." American Airlines was the first hit. She searched for two adult tickets flying out to Dallas/ Fort Worth, Texas.

"Departs London Heathrow at 10:45 a.m. Gets into Dallas at 2:45 p.m. What do you think?"

"That's fine by me. May as well book it," Meg said.

"But don't you need to check with work first?"

"Look here, it says refundable. If there is a problem, which I don't think there will be, then we can change them. Mimi, I think if we book this now, you actually might sleep tonight and you might even have a little something to look forward to. I want to be there for you and this is a journey I feel like I need to travel with you. I know it won't bring Joel back, but if you can gather more pieces of him by looking into his history, then I truly think it will give you enough peace to move forward."

CHAPTER 5

Heathrow
London, 2011

Mimi and Meg arrived at Terminal 3 at seven in the morning. It was still dark. They had taken a taxi, and the chill of the winter wind made them shiver as they walked into the entrance of the airport. It was surprisingly busy, with people flocking around from all different directions. After the girls checked in, they moved into the departure lounge.

"Well, we made it this far. How are you feeling?" Meg said.

"I'd be lying if I told you I was okay. The last time I was on a plane was with Joel. Even here, I can't escape the memories. I feel haunted!"

"Hopefully this is the start of your journey to heal." Meg shook her hair out of her ponytail and let her shaggy blonde strands free.

Mimi's gaze went to the floor. It felt like she was living somebody else's life. None of this belonged to her.

"If I forget to tell you later, thank you, Meg. Thank you for being such a good friend to me."

Meg reached out her arms and hugged Mimi. She had that warm, reassuring scent of familiarity, and as usual she smelt delicious and clean.

"I'm so sorry for all you have had to go through. If I could wave a magic wand and bring him back for you, I really would."

"I know. I know you would."

Mimi remembered the first time Joel had told her he'd loved her. They had gone out on a summer evening to have drinks at a bar by St Catherine's Dock. It was one of those perfect nights where you could see all the stars in the sky and there was still a warm airy breeze at midnight. They had met with Meg and her then boyfriend, Darrell. After they left them mid-disagreement, they walked through a darkened alleyway. Mimi clutched Joel's arm tightly, her eyes wide as she looked out for danger.

"What's the matter with you?" He laughed.

"Dark alleys freak me out. You never know who could be lurking around here. Crazy druggies, murderers. Oh, it just gives me the chills thinking about it. I feel so nervous. Let's walk faster."

She had grabbed Joel and pulled him forward, quickening her pace.

He stopped and pulled back.

"C'mon, Joel. Seriously, I don't like it. Let's get out of here."

"Do you really think I would let anything happen to the girl I'm in love with?"

Mimi had stopped. Suddenly she was frozen to

the spot, her heart thudding so loudly she thought her ears would explode.

"You...you're in love with me?"

"Madly." She had felt her stomach somersault. She looked at him and felt a wave of delight.

"I love you," she whispered as he took her in his arms.

"I know," he playfully said. She laughed at him as he took her in his arms and shared a long, open-mouthed kiss.

A passenger announcement brought her back to her present reality. It was calling for them to board. Mimi and Meg grabbed their hand luggage and headed to the gate.

Mimi didn't seem to notice things going on around her. She moved around like a ghost, almost as if she were on autopilot. The only times she felt in any sort of moment was when she was talking about Joel or thinking about him.

Mimi looked at Meg's feet. She noticed for the first time since they had left that morning that she was wearing sky high heeled boots. Mimi had opted for comfort by wearing trainers. She knew Meg would be her usual glamourous self, touting around her Louis Vuitton handbag and her Tom Ford sunglasses even though there was not a smidge of sunlight in the sky.

Mimi was seated by the window. She liked having the view of the outside. After a slight delay, the plane lifted off the ground. She was leaving England behind and breathed a sigh of relief. There had been so much disaster—one dark grey day spilling into another. She needed to be in a new place, closer to Joel's past. She looked out at the white wings of the plane slicing through the fluffy white clouds.

Where are you, baby?

That was a question she had asked herself over and over again.

At night she had talked to Joel out loud, as if he were sitting right beside her. She had begged him to give her a sign, to tell her he was safe…wherever it is he was.

She imagined what it would be like to die. Did you automatically know you were dead? Did you see that bright tunnel of light and walk into it? Surely, you wouldn't just leave your loved ones behind without letting them know you were at peace?

Mimi had been raised Catholic. She had attended church with her family every Sunday. She'd been christened, had her first Holy Communion and her confirmation. When she entered her teen years, she stopped going to Mass, not because she didn't believe, but because she felt there had been a fork in the road where she needed to find herself and religion wasn't a part of that journey. In the deep dark depths of her grief, she wondered if this was God's way of punishing her for all the times she felt it wasn't prayer she needed.

And the irony in all of this was Joel had been killed because of a war regarding religion. She just didn't know why there was so much hatred in the world.

Where had it all come from?

Had people been fighting for so long they had forgotten what they were fighting for?

Mimi never thought she could hate anybody. Of course, she had disliked many people whom she had met in her twenty-eight years on the planet, but hate was never something she had truly felt until now. The person who had so cruelly taken her husband's life away from him, robbed them of a life together—because of that person, whoever they were, she would never ever be held by Joel again.

Did they die with him?

Did Joel's soul go one way and his killer's another?

If there was truly a God, she hoped that was exactly what happened.

She needed to believe there was an afterlife. She needed to know her husband was at peace, and almost as much as that, she needed him to somehow let her know by any sort of a sign that he was all right. Mimi had wondered if that song on the radio was from him.

Joel believed in God. Like Mimi, he didn't follow a religion, not since his father had died.

She sank into her seat and let the plane take her the few thousand miles across the Atlantic Ocean. She surrendered in that moment that this journey would turn out exactly as it needed to be. She knew she had lost control of so many things. She needed to let destiny take its course.

Mimi closed her eyes, and a few moments later, she was sleeping. Sleep allowed her to hear the sweet sound of Joel's voice, if only in her dreams.

CHAPTER 6

Texas, 2011

The taxi driver drove Mimi and Meg to Dallas. When they finally made it to The Omni Hotel, they were both exhausted and in desperate need of a shower and a rest.

What everyone said about the Big D was true. Everything was bigger. It looked like every building sparkled.

"Well, I can totally see what makes Texan men attractive," Meg said as she flopped on the bed, pulled off her boots, and rubbed her sore feet. "That guy at the front desk was gorgeous."

"Was he? I didn't notice," Mimi mumbled. She began unpacking her clothes and putting them in neat piles into the bedside drawer. She looked out at the view. Dallas was spectacular, but it wasn't the place Joel had grown up. He hadn't connected to the big city. He always said that he enjoyed the wide open spaces.

"Have you heard anything from Austin?"

"Nothing. I have checked my emails a thousand times. I guess I find it pretty rude. I mean, his brother is gone, and still he won't make proper contact. I totally understand why Joel gave up…I still want us to go to the ranch, Meg. I told him we will be in town. If he sends us away, he sends us away, but I need to at least see the ranch."

"Fine by me. We need to sort out a rental. By looking at the map, it's quite a drive from here."

"We can do that tomorrow."

"You did bring your driver's licence with you, didn't you? Both parts?"

"Yup. I got everything we need. Good thing you asked me this before we left England," Mimi teased.

"You know what I'm like."

"I do. Right, you are the navigation expert. How about I drive and you co-pilot?"

"That's fine, but you know that you are driving on the other side of the road, don't you?"

"Yes, I know that, Meg. I drove a lot last time I was in the States."

With Joel, when he was alive.

Mimi remembered how nervous she had felt when she set off for the first time on the righthand side of the road. It was after she and Joel had left Yosemite and headed to Monterey Bay.

She was a great driver in the UK, zipping in and out of traffic in her Fiat 500, but the American road was a different beast. Suddenly everything seemed bigger, meaner, and fiercer!

Her fingers felt clammy on the wheel. She remembered wiping her hands on her jeans several times before she pulled away.

"Just drive the same way you do back in London, only remember you are on the opposite side. Breathe and relax," Joel had said.

That was a good day. After she set off, she suddenly became more confident with every mile she drove. She pressed harder on the accelerator, Joel's hand resting on her knee. They were singing along to country songs and enjoying the road. When they had reached the Plaza, she was happy to pull into the valet parking and hand over the keys. Her shoulders felt stiff from how nervous she was, her eyes heavy from concentration. After they checked into the hotel, she took a shower and Joel crept in with her.

She loved how his strong hands felt on hers, the way he was so firm but so gentle. She loved the way he would run his fingers through her long dark hair and pull her in for a passionate kiss. The sound of his Texan accent when he whispered in her ear made her knees buckle.

It was on that trip that Joel had bought Mimi a little shell bracelet. It was tacky and they had laughed about it, but now she wore it as if it were the most precious item. She treasured it and hadn't taken it off since Joel's death.

***

Mimi and Meg drove out of the big city. Suddenly the roads became wider and the air was cleaner. They had picked up their rental and headed off to find the ranch. Mimi loved that Meg was with her on this journey, but she wished it was Joel sitting next to her. As the days since losing Joel went on, she found herself thinking of many different memories. Little things that she had forgotten came back to her. She brushed her fingers over her rings and spoke to him all the time. She wondered if widows ever took their wedding band off.

Three hours into the drive, Mimi was feeling tired and frustrated until Meg shouted, "That's it, right there up on the left."

Mimi looked across at the picturesque mansion sitting among rolling meadows. It was brimming with character and charm. She was instantly taken in by the rustic feel of the area. She saw cattle and horses on the land. This definitely wasn't some rundown shack.

"Mimi…did you expect this?"

"No, no I didn't. It's beautiful. I'm confused as to why Joel would ever want to leave a place like this."

They drove up the driveway. The crackling under the tires sounded like popcorn popping in a microwave. When they came to a stop, Mimi stepped out of the car, lifted her sunglasses, and rested them on her head.

So, this was her husband's childhood home? This was where he learned to walk and talk. It was where he belonged to a family she had not met. A sharp pang of sadness hit her once more. She didn't understand why Joel had never brought her to this place. Anybody would have been proud to call this home.

There was a light breeze. She inhaled the farm-scented air. She was trying to take in every single detail. Her thoughts were running away with her, and she suddenly felt overwhelmed about being in Texas, about trying to find out information about her husband, things she should have known. She wouldn't admit, not even to Meg, how much that bothered her. She decided to keep her feelings on this matter to herself.

"So, do you want me to wait in the car?" Meg asked.

"No, you can come with me." The sunlight bounced off the bonnet, making it difficult for Mimi to look at Meg. She held her hands over her eyes.

"Mimi, I'll go if you really want me to, but I think you need to meet Joel's brother without me, at least for your first introduction. You don't know this guy or how he really feels about Joel. You being here is going to shake things up inside for him, whether he shows you that or not. They may not have been on talking terms, but they were still brothers."

Mimi patted her hand on her back jeans pocket, checking she had her mobile with her. "Keep your phone on you in case I need to call you, please."

Moments later, she began walking up the gravel path, her ballet flats crunching with every step.

She walked up to the front door. It was wide open. She didn't want to go inside, but she couldn't resist taking a peek. She was shocked. The place wasn't basic, like Joel had told her. It was huge and it screamed wealth in a very cowboy Texan style.

"Hello…?" Mimi shouted.

Silence.

She walked around to the back of the property, where several horses were grazing. Suddenly, her heart skipped a beat.

Joel.

He was exactly the same height. He had the same emerald green eyes, but it was when he spoke that she suddenly couldn't catch her breath. He was so like her husband yet so different.

"Are you Austin?" Mimi asked, her voice shaky.

He turned around to face her. He was dressed in a checkered shirt and jeans, wearing a belt with what looked to be a real gold buckle. His Stetson cast a shadow over his face.

"You must be Mimi," he said. His voice was just like Joel's. If she closed her eyes and just listened to that voice, she would think it was him.

"Yes, I'm Mimi. I emailed you to let you know I was coming."

"Yeah, I got that," he answered bluntly.

So why didn't you reply?

He turned his back to her and picked up a rusty pitch fork from the long grass. Mimi felt out of her depth. She wanted to turn back and run, but she was here to find out more about Joel. She hoped that Austin would invite her in, but he didn't even so much as look in her direction.

"I'm here to talk about Joel."

"You came to the wrong place and the wrong person. Joel and I haven't spoken for several years, so you're shit out of luck with me."

"I know you stopped talking, but you shared this home and your childhood together."

"Until he left and left me to deal with everything,

yeah we did. Look, ma'am, I'm sorry for your loss and all, but really, Joel and I…well, there is nothing to tell you. I'm sorry, but you wasted your time coming all this way. Now, enjoy Texas, but I'd like you to leave."

"Firstly, my name is Mimi. Don't call me ma'am. Secondly, your brother is dead. I'm his wife. Don't you think you could just spare a couple of goddam hours to talk to me?"

"No. I contacted you to pass on my condolences, but that's where it stops. I didn't invite you here and I'm certainly not travelling down memory lane to visit my dear brother."

"Joel was right about you. Now I get why he stopped bothering with you," Mimi snapped, tears springing into her eyes. She was trying desperately not to cry, and she didn't want him to get the better of her.

Austin smiled a sarcastic smile. It infuriated Mimi further. She felt humiliated and completely disrespected, and moreover, deeply offended that Austin would act this way when his brother was dead.

The sun was low and it would soon be dusk. She found herself stuck. She didn't want to just turn around and leave even though he had asked her to.

"I know you don't know me. And you owe me nothing, but I am asking you to please talk to me. I feel broken inside. Again, that's not your problem, but Joel was your brother and you shared this place together, a childhood. You are the only person on this planet connected to my husband, so I am begging you to please just give me some of your time."

"Even if I did, it wouldn't bring him back to you. Just leave, Mimi. Take the memories you have of Joel and leave. Trust me; it will be much better for you that way."

"Do you know he was captured? Some son of a bitch captured him and took his life. I don't know who that faceless asshole is. The Corps won't give me any information, not a damn thing, and trust me, I've tried. So I have no idea how my husband actually died and there is no body, so I don't get to say my goodbyes and give him a funeral. Right now, you, his brother, are the only person that can tell me anything and you won't give me that?"

"I can't give you what you want, Mimi."

"You mean you won't." Mimi knew she had lost the battle. She squeezed her eyes shut and listened to his voice. They may have looked alike and sounded alike, but he wasn't even close to Joel, not one bit.

Mimi managed to turn her back and take the hardest few steps in life she had ever taken.

She walked back to the car. Meg had the seat all the way back. She'd obviously drifted into a light slumber but startled upright when Mimi sat in the driver's seat, slamming the door behind her.

"Mimi…are you okay?"

"No, I'm not." She couldn't hold back the tears any longer. She sobbed. Meg put her arms around her and let her friend cry. Her lips quivered. It felt like she was losing Joel all over again.

"It's like I am not allowed to have him. They took him from me, Meg. That coldhearted murderer.

The Marines, he gave his life to them and they won't tell me a thing, and now his own brother is turning me away. What have I done to deserve this?" she howled.

"Mimi, behind you, honey."

She turned her face to see Austin staring at her through the window. She quickly wiped her face with her hands and opened the door.

"Can we talk for a minute?" he said coyly.

"Shoot."

"Alone."

"She's my best friend. Anything you want to say to me you can say in front of her." Mimi leaned her body forward, staring at Austin.

"Look, Joel and I, there is a history. A complicated history. So much happened."

"I know," Mimi sniffled.

"You don't know or else you wouldn't be here. Look, come back here tomorrow, around noon, and we'll talk."

"Thank you."

"Don't thank me, Mimi. You may not like my side of things, but if it will help you move on with your life, then fine."

As Mimi drove away from the ranch, she opened the window, letting the air run through her hair. Her mind raced. The way Austin spoke sounded like he was giving her some sort of warning.

She heard Meg take a deep breath. "How much did Joel tell you about his life? It just sounded like he had something to say. What, I don't know."

"I got that impression too." Mimi was careful not to let her feelings spill out. She wasn't ready to admit that she was worried Joel could have been holding something back from her.

She continued driving and didn't utter another word until they arrived at a small bed and breakfast about thirty minutes away from the ranch.

When Mimi and Meg checked in, they both changed and sat on the two single beds. The room was aglow with sweet oil lanterns, giving it a cosy woodland feel.

The long car journey that day had left them both exhausted. Neither of them wanted to have a deep conversation, and it was evident between them that they both felt this emotional journey needed to take a break for the evening.

Mimi dressed in a white vest and grey PJ bottoms that were at least two sizes too big. She pulled the drawstring in as far as it would go so that she was able to keep them sitting just below her belly button. She turned on the old box TV. It was strange to think that just ten years ago, this television set would have seemed fitting with the times, but now, as technology had rapidly moved on, it looked almost antique.

Meg had fallen asleep almost straight away. Mimi was wide awake. She couldn't remember the last time she had fallen into a restful sleep, even before Joel was killed. At night, her thoughts whirled around her head. She thought of a thousand different things. Had she emailed a client back? Had she paid her credit card bill? Where was Joel and was he all right?

Tonight, she was left with thoughts of Joel and Austin. They were brothers, they had once been close, but something had happened to them, something that split them in half. She thought of Larna. She couldn't ever imagine not speaking to her sister.

Mimi had asked Joel so many questions about his family and how he grew up. He answered her, but suddenly she realised that he didn't stay on the subject for very long. At the time, she put this down to the fact being a Marine was everything he was. She didn't know what it was like to lose a parent like he had, but here, in the darkness of the night, having now met Austin, she was left feeling confused and worried.

Mimi was never the greatest fan of secrets in relationships. She felt they could destroy trust. She had seen many of her friends go through this.

When she finally closed her eyes, for the first time, she didn't see Joel's face. She saw Austin's.

CHAPTER 7

The next day, Mimi and Meg were up early. They wandered through a small town called Willow Creek. It was as quaint as its name suggested, with a selection of adorable shops. They passed a flower shop. The perfumed smell of roses spilled onto the pavement.

A small stationery store caught her eye. Mimi walked in alone while Meg went to grab something to eat. A large woman with thick glasses looked up at her and smiled.

"Let me know if you need anything," she said, and then carried on scribbling some notes into a pretty notebook.

Mimi loved stationary. Over the years, she had collected tons of cute items, from pens to Post-it notes in the shape of hearts. When she had sent care packages to Joel, she always made sure that her letters were written on the finest of paper. She had handwritten everything, feeling it was much more personal. There were times when he had Wi-Fi and they were able to communicate by email, but on the nights that were particularly hard and lonely, she always wrote him a letter and filled her packages with anything she thought he would like.

The last letter she had written him was still sitting back at her flat in Finchley. She couldn't remember what she had even written, and it saddened her to think that he would never open that envelope and would never read her words.

"That there is handmade by me," the lady in the shop said, peeking over the tops of her glasses.

"It's beautiful," Mimi said. She was holding a leather-bound cream journal.

"It's just waiting to be written in."

"How much is it?" Mimi asked, expecting it to be expensive.

"Twenty-five dollars," she replied.

"Wow…okay, well, I'll have to take it." She set the journal on the counter and pulled out her purse to pay.

"What will you write in it?"

"Oh, I don't know." Mimi sighed.

The lady looked down at Mimi's left hand. "Keep it away from your husband. A man can be pretty curious when it comes to his wife's journal."

Mimi almost opened her mouth to tell her that she was a widow, but she stopped herself. She didn't want to stand there and have a pity party. She had enough of that back home. She just wanted to feel normal and at least pretend that all was well with her, even if inside she was a train wreck.

"Well, thank you for stopping by. Whatever you write, make it a good one!"

"I will. Thank you."

Mimi left the shop, clutching the brown paper bag holding the blank journal, looking up and down the road in search for Meg, but she couldn't see her. Just as she headed back to the car, she saw the back of a man that was familiar to her.

The man was loading the back of his truck with supplies of animal feed. She stood in the distance watching him and hoping he wouldn't notice she was there, because if he saw her, she wouldn't know what to say. He was tall and muscular and there was something in his eyes that said he was dark and moody. She hoped to later find out more about her brother-in-law.

***

A couple of hours later, Mimi had showered and was preparing for her meeting with Austin. She dressed casually in a pair of dark jeans and a loose white shirt. She tied her long hair in a ponytail. Meg felt Mimi needed to do this alone and opted not to come. She would, of course, be waiting in the wings for her, ready to wipe any tears should there be some.

"Let him do all the talking. Hear what he has to say, and then ask as many questions as you need to. Remember, I'm right here waiting for you," Meg said.

"What will you do whilst I'm gone?"

"I have myself a little date."

"With who?"

"Oh, a guy I met in town today. He owns the coffee shop where I got my breakfast." She chuckled.

"You don't waste any time, do you? I don't know how you do it," Mimi said as she rolled her eyes.

"I've got my mobile. Make sure you have yours," Mimi said as she headed out the door.

As she drove to the ranch, her stomach was in knots. She had never been the sort of girl that dealt with nerves well. Before exams, she wouldn't eat; before a date, she would constantly second guess herself; and often, before job interviews, she'd arrive early just so she could sit in the toilets in case she got sick.

On her first official date with Joel, she had experienced her usual anxiety. She arrived at the restaurant worried he wouldn't be there. As soon as she walked into the bustling Italian restaurant, she saw him immediately. He stood up and greeted her with a kiss on the cheek and a simple hug. At first she was unsure how to act and she was aware of how positively English she sounded next to his very American accent.

Throughout the evening, he complimented her, made her laugh, and learned she loved books, cats, art, and travel. He told her about his dedication to the military, and although he had been born and raised in Texas, he wanted to see the world. He was grateful to the Corps for giving him that opportunity.

Mimi drove up the sweeping driveway. She checked herself in the mirror and quickly reached for her makeup bag, powdering her nose and applying a quick dollop of pink lip gloss.

She walked to the large oak door, which was closed this time. She rang the bell and waited. A couple of seconds later, she heard the clunk of the door being unlocked. She swallowed hard as she tried to hide her emotion looking at the man that was so like Joel, except he was fair. Joel's hair was dark, but not like Mimi's, which was almost black.

Austin held out his hand to shake Mimi's. She reluctantly gave hers to him. It felt awkward and strained and she felt like an imposter who shouldn't be there. She didn't belong inside these walls. Her heart cracked at the sight of a picture on the wall of a young boy, probably around the age of eight or nine. It was Joel with a toothy grin.

"Would you like a drink?" Austin asked as he walked into the house. Mimi closely followed.

"Just water; thank you."

He took her into the kitchen, which appeared to be the heart of the home. There was a fresh bowl of fruit sitting in the centre island, the cupboards were a light oak, and the granite worktops gleamed in a grey sparkle, like the night sky.

Mimi took a seat at the kitchen table. She loved the smell of real wood. Everything in the house felt beautifully rustic.

Austin brought a pitcher of water and set a tall glass in front of Mimi.

"So, you came," he said. She felt like she was in the room with Joel, only she wasn't.

"Did you think I wouldn't?" Mimi said in a high-pitched tone that was a tad too sarcastic.

When he didn't answer, she moved her gaze away from him.

"So, you want to know more about my brother, do you?"

"I do. I mean, I am a family girl. I have a sister, Larna, and Joel was a part of that. I always wanted to meet you. I was disappointed you didn't come to our wedding."

"I wasn't invited." His voice was deep and moody.

"You were. You said you didn't want to come."

Austin shook his head and smiled. He reached across the table and picked up a bottle of beer. This time his eyes made direct contact with Mimi. He pushed his body into the back of the chair and crossed his legs in front of him.

"He tell you that, did he?"

"I'm confused. Joel told me you didn't want to come. It was then he made the decision to stop trying with you. I mean, he sent you emails, made phone calls, and you kept rejecting him, so he gave up. I'm sure he wanted you in his life."

"You really don't know who you married, do you?"

Mimi felt her heart stop. Her mouth felt dry and suddenly she couldn't find the words she needed. Her hands shook. She gulped some water, but it went down the wrong way and made her cough uncontrollably.

Austin handed Mimi a tissue to wipe her streaming eyes. She cleared her throat and could feel her cheeks flush. She was distracted by the sound of thudding footsteps running into the room.

"Who's she?" The little boy asked.

"This is Mimi. She's visiting us from England."

"Where the Queen lives?" the little boy asked, wide-eyed and impressed.

"Yup. Where the Queen lives."

"Do you know her?" His little face was so handsome.

"No, I've never met the Queen, but I hear she is a very nice lady."

"My name is Jake." He held out his little hand to Mimi.

"Well, it's nice to meet you, Jake."

"Are you and my daddy boyfriend and girlfriend?"

"Jake, go outside now and play with the horses."

"But, Dad, I want to stay here and talk to Mimi."

"Jake, outside. Now."

Jake pouted and stomped out of the room. Mimi was taken by this sweet little boy.

"He's lovely. How old is he?"

"He's eight," Austin answered directly.

"I didn't know you had a child. I didn't even know you were married?"

"I know you didn't. And I'm not married, for the record."

Mimi looked out of the window and saw Jake petting the horses. She had seen his little face before, and then it clicked. He was the little boy in the picture.

She didn't want to ask any more questions because she had a feeling that she was irritating Austin. She wasn't here to find out about his personal life. She was here to find out about the life he had shared with Joel, when they were close.

"So, you and Joel. Was this always your home?"

"Yup. Joel was actually born here."

"In this house?" Mimi gasped.

"Yup. He was born in my parent's bedroom. Our mother didn't have time to get to the hospital. She said he just wanted to be born. I was the late one...but I'm also the one that stayed to pick up the pieces."

Mimi didn't feel entirely comfortable with Austin. She was extremely attracted to him and knew it was because he looked so much like her husband. She was sure if Joel had been alive, there's no way she would have this feeling. Whenever Mimi was in a relationship, she was in it!

There had only been one longterm boyfriend before Joel, a guy named Sean who she met at university. She thought it was serious. They went on a couple of sunny holidays together and shared Saturday nights in with takeaways while watching the X-Factor.

One weekend she had an awful headache and couldn't attend a friend's birthday party, but persuaded Sean to go. Halfway through the night, the pain killers kicked in, so she decided to slip into her little black dress and go to the party. When she arrived, she looked for her boyfriend but couldn't find him. She went up to the bathroom and heard his voice laughing and saying the word "baby." She listened behind the door and eventually pushed it open. She saw Sean passionately kissing another girl, who was pushed up against him in her bra and jeans.

When Sean saw Mimi, he pushed the other girl

off him and called after her as she ran through the crowd of the party. His voice sounded so desperate. Sean had tried for months to get Mimi back, but she refused. After that ordeal, she had a few dates but nothing serious until Joel. She hadn't even looked at another man after she was with him.

Austin allowed Mimi to tour the house. He showed her Jake's room, which was painted in Disney's *Cars.*

"As you probably guessed, this is Jake's room."

"I guessed. Very boyish."

"He sure is." Austin managed an unconvincing smile.

Later, they walked around the grounds of the ranch, exploring the rich green area. There were acres and acres of untouched land. Austin was passionate about the horses.

Mimi actually enjoyed his company. He was so different from Joel. He didn't have that drive for adventure, but there was a wild man in him in that cowboy Texan way.

After they had arrived back at the house, Mimi was desperate to ask more questions about Joel. The words were on the tip of her tongue, but she couldn't seem to get them out. She hoped Austin would broach the subject, but when he didn't, she became frustrated, and her heart felt like it was going to explode out of her chest.

Sunlight fell through the large glass panelled window overlooking the acres of green. Mimi picked up her glass and asked Austin for a drink.

"Something strong," she requested.

The silence between them was extending. The purpose of her being here was to learn more about her husband, but now it seemed like her purpose was to find out why there was a feud between these two brothers. Apparently, Austin's version of their relationship was different from Joel's.

She thought about the wedding invitation. Mimi's parents always told her there were three sides to every story—"Your side, their side, and the truth." She suddenly remembered the day she wanted to post the invites. Joel said that he would take care of the overseas invitations, especially to Austin because he wanted to send him a note to give them another chance of reconnecting again. Mimi hadn't questioned it. She understood how important it was for Joel to hold out an olive branch to his brother.

When Austin told her he hadn't been invited, she didn't think he was lying to her. She assumed one of two things could have happened. Either Joel decided not to send the invitation because he had feared rejection or the post office was responsible. She wanted to believe it was because of an error in the mail, but deep down it just wasn't sitting well with her. She had never questioned Joel's honesty to her…until now.

CHAPTER 8

Mimi arrived back at the B&B later that evening. Meg wasn't back yet. She hoped that her friend was all right. She wasn't entirely comfortable with Meg swanning off in some random man's car.

Mimi removed her shoes, which were caked in mud from the walk around the ranch earlier that day. She stepped into the shower, feeling the water wash over her skin. Mimi wondered how long she needed to stay in Texas. Strangely enough, she could totally envision a life here, and felt connected to the land in a way she couldn't explain. When she touched the horses, she felt something, almost like a calling, that she was exactly where she was meant to be, but surely it was Joel she should have been here with.

As she combed her hair, she noticed that a few clumps had tangled in the bristles of the brush. She knew it was because of stress. An hour or so later, Meg returned and Mimi could tell she had been drinking. Meg was a deliriously happy drunk. She sang silly songs and made ridiculous childish jokes that were so bad they were funny.

"Mimi, my Mimi. How did it go?" she said, holding her arms out to her friend, leaping on her, and pulling her in for a bear hug.

"It was better than I expected. I assume your date went well?"

"Ohh, I can totally see what you see in these cowboys, Mimi. They are such fun!" Her blue eyes were wide and her cheeks slightly pink.

"Are you seeing this guy again?"

"Bo? Yeah, I think so. Maybe another little date is in order before we go home."

They had only been here two days, and the mention of them going home disappointed Mimi. She didn't think she would be able to get all the answers she needed in just ten days. This wasn't a holiday. This was a journey for Mimi, and it was something that was going to define the rest of her life. Yet she knew she had people who loved her back home—her parents and her sister, and she had a job, a flat, and her cat. Meg's life was back in the UK. Her friend had been kind enough to join her, but she knew it would soon come to an end, and in a way, Mimi was prepared to travel this road alone if she had to.

The next day, Meg was still asleep at ten in the morning. Mimi was desperate to get back to the ranch, but she couldn't leave her friend abandoned at the B&B with no means of transport. She wanted to wake her, but didn't feel right doing so.

While waiting for Meg to wake, she looked at the brown bag containing the journal she bought and wondered what words she would use to fill the pages. She thought about using it as a diary, but somehow that didn't seem fitting.

After she dressed in a pair of black leggings and an oversized cream top, she took a stroll outside. She inhaled the warm air, the same air her husband once breathed. She wondered if he had ever driven past this little establishment. Lately she was wondering many things.

She found a small bench hidden in the grounds of the property and took a moment to sit down and take in her surroundings. She had the journal with her and pulled out a pen she had taken from the car rental company. She opened the first page. It was clear, crisp, and tinted cream, almost yellow. Suddenly, as the pen took on a life of its own, it made sense why she had this book.

Dear Joel,

I miss you. I miss you so much. I can't remember what my last words were to you. I have tried so hard to remember, but I can't. I am here in your hometown in Texas, searching for answers and trying to get to know you better...that seems crazy, since I am your wife. Is that what I am? Your wife? We said until death us do part, but that's the problem, Joel. I'm not living up to my vows because I can't let you go. I hate to be called your widow. Every part of me hurts. I can't think straight, and it's like I am having a bad dream.

When I check my emails, there is a part of me that is hoping and praying that your name will be there and you will tell me that you are coming home, wherever home is. So far, I love Texas and the ranch you grew up on. Joel, I wish you would have taken me here! I wish you had shown me this part of you with your fingers entangled in mine. I had such a bad feeling about you leaving and now I wish I had asked you to stay, but if you had, I would have been guilty of keeping you from the man you were. But now I feel guilty because it took you. Somebody took you and I have no idea who that person is!

Not being able to give you the goodbye you deserve is also killing me. I think about your perfect body out there somewhere lost and broken. Every day I remember. It's as if my mind has burst, and every single memory of our time together is spilling out. I feel jealous of all the couples I see, young and especially the old, because they have been given a lifetime to spend together. I only had you for a blink of an eye. How is that fair?

I see that the rift between you and your brother is deep, and I know there is something that you held back from me. I wish you had talked to me about it. I love you so much and I'll go on loving you. Please come to me, Joel, whether it be a feather blowing in my path or a ladybird on my hand. Just give me a sign that you are all right.

My love always,
Mimi Mimi xoxo

Joel had said that Mimi's name was as cute as a button. "So nice, I have to say it twice," a bit like New York, New York. He had come up with her nickname back in London, when they had been having a Sunday lunch with her family. Her mother laid out a typical dinner: roast beef, Yorkshire puddings, roast potatoes, and gravy. They sat around the table sharing stories of all the trouble Mimi used to get into as a child. "Aw, Mimi, Mimi, aren't you cute." From that day forward, her nickname had stuck. At the bottom of her painted canvases, she would sign Mimi Mimi. She grew to love the affectionate name he had given her.

Somehow, writing to Joel gave her a sense of comfort. She felt like the words she wrote would be read by him. It was 11:15 by the time Mimi returned to the room. Meg was only just stirring. She pulled her messy blonde head off her pillow and rubbed her temples. She was visibly hungover.

"Ugh. American shots are not like English ones. The glass is twice as big."

"So why didn't you just have less than what you

would in England?"

"Um, you may have a point." She lifted herself off the bed and headed to the bathroom. A few moments later, Mimi could hear Meg vomiting.

"Can I get you anything?" Mimi shouted through the door.

"I'm okay," she wearily answered. And then she retched once more.

After Meg emerged from the bathroom a while later, she stood in the doorway, not looking at all like she had been sick. She was perfectly made up and as immaculate as always.

"Austin said I'm welcome back to the ranch today. Would you like to come?"

"Oh, I just don't know if this is my place." Meg sighed.

"Well, what will you do if I go?"

"How about you drop me off in town? Bo said I could hang out with him whilst he works today and maybe he'll shut down early so I can explore with him. To tell you the truth, I wouldn't mind heading back into Dallas for a couple of days. Don't get me wrong, it's beautiful out here, but you know me, Mimi. I'm not a country girl. Actually, I can feel my skin itching the longer I'm here."

Mimi sat on the wooden chair, tapping her long fingernails on the arm. She wanted to be alone, she had wished it, but wishing for something and the reality were two different things.

Having the security of Meg so close by made her feel safe. Austin was aloof and moody, and sometimes she didn't know how to deal with that. He was still, in every way, a stranger to her. She came to the conclusion that it was only vanity—his looks and voice—that were so much like Joel.

"Are you sure you feel safe with this guy?"

"Who, Bo? Of course. He's a little kitten. A real sweet guy. I'll be fine. Should I worry about you and Joel's younger, very sexy brother?"

Mimi blushed. She didn't expect to. Meg caught on immediately.

"Oh my God, you like Austin!"

"Jesus, Meg, no, not like that. My husband has only been gone for less than a month. What do you take me for?"

"I take you for a woman with a pulse."

Mimi fell silent.

"Oh shit, Mimi. You know I didn't mean it like that. I'm sorry. Bad choice of words."

"It's okay. I know what you were saying. And yes, Austin is very good looking, but he's not Joel. Please stay in touch with me whilst you are out with this guy."

Mimi got into the car. On the passenger seat beside her was Joel's hoody, which she had taken with her. It made her feel like she was taking a piece of him with her wherever she was going. She cracked open the window to let the breeze sweep in.

Finchley seemed like a lifetime ago. Here, in Texas, Mimi fell in love with the rugged terrain and the wide open spaces.

She had actually travelled quite a bit. She had been to Thailand to visit her mother's family when she was younger, and she'd travelled to Spain, Italy, and France. She had a couple of fun-filled holidays in the land of Micky Mouse and of course her amazing honeymoon with Joel. Yet it was here, in the Lone Star State, that she felt smitten, like she had a deep connection. Perhaps it was because it was where Joel was from, or maybe she loved the horses, or maybe there was something here for her that she hadn't yet found.

When she arrived at the ranch, she saw Jake running around the front of the house with a bed sheet attached to his back. His arms were stretched out in front of him. Mimi stepped out of the car and Jake the superhero ran to her.

"You came back," he excitedly said, bouncing up and down on the spot.

"Hey, Jake. Yes, I've come to see your daddy. Do you know where he is?"

"Yeah, he's inside with my mommy."

Mimi felt her heart sink. She didn't want Jake to see her disappointment, so she quickly focused on him.

"So, Jake, are you Spiderman?"

"No, I'm Superman, silly. Spiderman doesn't have a cape!"

"Oh, yes, of course. You're right."

A woman appeared in the doorway. She had long blonde hair and skin as smooth as buttermilk. She looked across at Mimi and kept her gaze fixed on her. She walked across to Jake and gave him a kiss on his forehead. Mimi gave her a friendly smile, but was met with an emotionless expression.

"Hi, I'm Mimi."

"I know who you are," the woman said.

"Right, and you're Jake's mother?"

She kneeled down to her son and whispered

something in his ear. Jake ran away from Mimi, disappearing into the house.

Mimi rose back to her feet, feeling somewhat uneasy. It wasn't like she came here to steal Austin, as the woman's unfriendly vibes seemed to suggest. Mimi second guessed herself on whether she should walk into the house.

A few seconds later, Austin appeared on the porch. He was far more casual than usual in a pair of jogging bottoms and a white t-shirt that was clean, so crisp and so much more like Joel.

"Are you coming in?" he shouted.

Mimi walked across to greet him and tried to manage a smile. They made their way into the kitchen and he handed her a steaming cup of coffee. She took it to her lips and sipped.

"Thank you," she said.

"Do you want something to eat?" Austin asked.

"I'm fine, thank you." She looked around. "Where's Jake?"

"He's out with the horses and his trainer."

"His trainer?"

"Yeah, he's learning how to ride properly. He's good, but he's still a child and needs proper supervision. He's got a long way to go, but he'll get there."

Mimi paused for a moment. She took a deep breath and then asked, "So, Jake's mum…"

"What about her?" Suddenly, Austin's mood changed. He was distant and started to nervously walk around the room.

"She's pretty," Mimi added.

"She is, yeah."

Mimi ran her fingers through her hair and leaned forward onto the table. "I assume Jake lives with you full-time?"

"You assume correctly."

His eyes were fixed on her. She could tell he wasn't willing to elaborate any further. He made her feel like she was interrogating him when she was asking simple questions. Mimi figured there must still be some tension between Austin and Jake's mom. She thought about changing the subject entirely, but she was drawn in by him. Mimi was here to learn more about Joel. She hadn't expected Austin to pique her interest, but he had.

Austin asked, "Have you ridden before?"

"As in horses?" Mimi said, raising her eyebrows.

"Yup, as in horses."

For the first time, Austin smiled. Mimi's heart stopped. She missed that smile. It was the smile that belonged to Joel. The corner of Austin's eyes squinted the same way the corner of Joel's eyes would squint. Austin had the same dimple on the left side of his cheek. Only he wasn't the same. He wasn't Joel.

Mimi and Austin walked to the stables.

"I got you these." Austin held up a hair of shiny black riding boots.

"Will they fit?"

"You're a size seven, right? UK 5?"

"Yeah, how did you know?"

"Jake looked at the bottom of your shoe when you left them outside yesterday. He thought you would like to go riding."

"Well, I have ridden before, but I was very

young. I'm a little nervous, I guess."

"Oh, you are one of those, are you?"

"One of what?" Mimi stood back, keeping her gaze fixed on Austin.

"Women that are a little scared to try something new."

"You got me all wrong," Mimi tutted. "I'll have you know that this body wasn't earned by sitting around on my butt all day long."

"So, you work out?" Austin said, in a big deal kind of way.

"I work out, sure. I take chances. Joel took me sky diving on our honeymoon, and we climbed a nine thousand foot rock face in Yosemite. I pushed my body harder because I wanted to challenge myself. Admittedly, these past few weeks, I've lapsed, but I'm allowed, right?"

"I'm going to teach you to ride a horse. This here is Kelsa. She's an Arabian."

"She's gorgeous."

"She's also powerful. Now, I want you to know that some accidents are unavoidable. She's great, but if she were to trip, you could be thrown off balance. There is a chance she may depart a bit quicker into the canter than you may expect. What I want you to know is nobody can predict what a horse is going to do no matter how well you know them."

The smell of freshly cut hay stuck in the back of Mimi's throat and she started coughing. She couldn't catch her breath. Austin rubbed her back and gave her a hard pat. His touch made her body tingle. She hadn't expected it. He kept his hand on the small of her back longer than necessary. Suddenly, the stables felt too hot and her loose top was sticking to her.

Austin moved away from her and toward Kelsa. She was pure white. She looked like she could have been in a fairy tale. She was enchanting. She had a finely chiselled bone structure, a concave profile, and an arched neck. She was beautifully graceful.

"So, why Kelsa?"

"She's pretty easygoing. I still want you to gear up. Like I said, you can never predict what may or may not happen."

CHAPTER 9

Mimi and Austin arrived back at the house. There was a cat lurking on the porch. As soon as they approached, it ran off, startled, its tail swaying behind him as it disappeared into the overgrown bushes.

A few droplets of rain started to fall. Mimi inhaled the air, enjoying the smell of the dry earth starting to cool. There was a rustle in the trees, a promise of a storm ahead. A white feather blew in front of Mimi, sticking to the toe of her left boot.

Joel!

She picked up the feather and cupped it into her hand. She held it as if she were holding a fragile bird, careful not to pull it apart.

Austin turned toward her. He didn't say anything. He looked at her. She was caught by a sudden wave of grief. It had come out of nowhere and tears sprung from her eyes. She turned away so that Austin wouldn't see her cry. She didn't know him well enough to start pouring her heart and soul out in front of him. She glanced over her shoulder to see Jake running toward his father:

"Dad…Dad!" he yelled.

"Hey, champ." Austin picked Jake up and swung him over his shoulder.

"I'm hungry. What's for dinner?"

"Ribs."

"Yummy," Jake said.

The sweetness of the child diverted Mimi's attention from her emotions.

"Would you like to stay for dinner?" Jake asked.

"I'm sure Mimi would like to rest. She's had a busy day learning to ride Kelsa. You know how tired you get when you've been out with the horses all day, don't you?"

"Actually, I'd love to. I mean, if that's all right with you, Austin?"

"Sure. There will be plenty of food. Feel free to take a shower if you want to wash up before dinner."

"Yay!" Jake said.

A short while later, Mimi made her way up to the solid oak winding staircase. She imagined Joel and Austin would have slid down the banisters as children. She wished the walls around her could talk and wondered what they would say.

She took a peek into Austin's room. She glanced over her shoulder and let her feet sink into the snow white plush carpet as she took a few steps into the room. It needed a woman's touch. It was quite manly and basic.

In the corner of her eye, she spied a photograph. She picked it up for closer inspection. It was Joel and Austin as young boys with their parents. They were smiling happily in the beaming sunlight in what looked to be a small boat sitting on a body of open blue water. She held the frame, wondering why Austin still had it. Could it have been a memory of such a great day he simply couldn't part with it, despite that he and his brother had parted ways?

She wondered how Austin felt about his brother's death. There could be no more reaching out. Mimi searched Austin's face for emotion every time she had mentioned Joel's name. A woman will wear her heart on her sleeve, her feelings evident and difficult to hide, but for a man, it was often the case that they spent so long suppressing feelings that they lay deeply within. They were masters of deception.

She heard footsteps behind her, so she quickly put the photograph down and crept out of Austin's room, slipping into the guest room next door. Austin gently tapped on the door.

"Come in."

"Towels, fresh ones." He placed them gently on the bed, which was covered in a patchwork throw, and paused for a second, like he was about to say something, but then he just lowered his head and nodded.

Please tell me what you are thinking!

He turned his back to walk out of the room. Mimi sighed loud enough for Austin to hear. He glanced over his shoulder. They must have both had some private grief over Joel.

"Will we ever really talk?" Mimi called after Austin.

"There are so many things you need to know, Mimi. I just can't seem to find the words to tell you."

A flash of lightning lit up the room, closely followed by a distant rumble of thunder. The sound of the rain pelting against the window was the only sound in the room. Silence hung between them.

"Austin, please. I need to know."

"Mimi, sometimes things are best left in the past."

"But you just said there are things I need to know. Which is it, Austin?"

"It was Joel's place to tell you, not mine."

"Tell me what?" she yelled.

"Mimi, don't try and get up inside my head. It's not a place you want to go. Now please, enjoy looking around the ranch. Stay as long as you need to so you can deepen the image of your perfect military boy, but when you're done, you're best off going home and starting over."

He looked at her and she looked at him. Their eyes locked on one another. So many secrets hidden under the surface. Austin walked through the door.

"I'm sorry, Mimi. I just can't go there with you." He disappeared down the stairs.

Mimi sat on the edge of the bed. Her mind was racing. It was clear there was something between the brothers that ran deeper than she ever knew. It couldn't simply be a case of Austin being annoyed Joel left the ranch. Or was it?

Her feelings were tangled in knots. She was grieving, but she felt confused. Frustration flowed through her body like volcanic lava, destroying her and eating her alive.

She reached for her phone and saw she had a text message from Meg. Her friend asked if she was all right and if Mimi would mind if she headed off for two days to Dallas with Bo. For a split second, Mimi was annoyed with her friend, but then she came to the conclusion this is how things were supposed to be. Wherever Meg went in life, she would always find a brand new door open for her and she'd add another awesome experience to her already fun-filled life.

Mimi went downstairs sometime later as Austin was plating the food. The smell of barbeque sauce hung in the air. He quietly set up the table. She noticed how everything around him was in order and everything had its place.

She sunk her body into a chair, her mind regressing to a memory of Joel. She remembered how he hadn't been good in the kitchen. He'd attempted to cook a simple spaghetti bolognaise at Mimi's parents' house, but it had ended in disaster. He burned the mince-meat within an inch of being cremated and then he added too much sugar to the sauce. It could have been mistaken for a dessert. Mimi had twisted Joel's pasta with her fork against the spoon and tried to hide the shocking flavour that sat on her taste buds.

"It's great," she'd said, trying to hide the fact that she wanted to spit it back in the bowl and throw the rest of the offending contents in the bin.

"Its shit." Joel laughed.

Mimi tried to keep her poker face, but failed on

the second bite.

"Go on Mimi Mimi, admit it!"

"Okay, yeah, it's horrendous."

They had both seen the funny side of things and ended their evening by calling the local Chinese restaurant for a takeaway.

The sound of the plates being set on the table jolted Mimi out of her memory.

It was quite clear Austin had mastered his culinary skills. The meat was tender, moist, and fell off the bone with each gentle bite. The glow of a storm lantern flickered on the kitchen table.

Jake munched his way through his meal, smiling at Mimi between bites. Mimi noticed how much he looked like Austin and not so much like his mother. He had a small sprinkle of freckles on the tip of his nose. His eyes were the Marcus emerald green hues, bright and alert.

"My mommy said that you're Chinese," Jake said.

"Jake, stop being rude."

"Why is that rude?"

"Because it just is."

"I'm half English and half Thai," Mimi replied.

"What's Thai?" Jake asked, shovelling another forkful of rice into his tiny mouth.

"It's a country in Southeast Asia. Thailand is beautiful. There are lots of amazing beaches. The sand is white and the water is so clear that you can see the fish swimming."

"Are there sharks?"

Austin smiled at his son. Jake's mind was so full

of imagination and intrigue.

"There are sharks in Thailand, but I've never seen one."

"They eat people, you know. I saw it. There was a movie on cable and the shark was called Jaws. He was mean, really mean. I don't ever want to go to the beach."

Mimi and Austin laughed.

They enjoyed the evening with Jake. They played a couple of games and his innocent laughter filled the room. Mimi wondered why Austin never told Joel he had a nephew. Halfway through the evening, it dawned on her she was Jake's aunt, and it made her feel warm inside.

Mimi and Joel had discussed children. It was Mimi who raised the question when they were snuggled up in the warmth of her bed before they were married. It had been cold outside.

"Do you want kids?"

"With you? Of course."

They never had planned when, but it was always going to be in the cards. Being around Jake, she wondered what it would have been like to have had a son with Joel.

When Jake went to bed, it was just Mimi and Austin. There was a stillness in the room. The storm had finally subsided. Mimi decided she wasn't going to hold back. She was here to find out answers, and she felt that if Austin wanted to keep things that happened between him and Joel a secret, he shouldn't have elaborated on the issue.

"Tell me about your life?" Mimi asked.

"My life? Why do you want to know?"

"Because you're Joel's brother and the father of my nephew," she joked.

"Mimi, I..."

"What, Austin? What is it?" Her voice was desperate, like a radar turned on in full search mode trying to pin point her target, begging for an answer.

He once again fell silent. The soft light of the porch lit the room. They sat on the sofa, locked in a moment of finding out the truth. It had only been a month since Joel had been gone, but Mimi felt like she had aged ten years. She was here on this journey, hoping to find out more about the man she married, but she hadn't expected to be learning more about herself.

"How about we say nothing tonight. I do like you, Mimi, and I can understand why my brother chose you. I get why you are here. I understand your pain. I know it may look to you like I am the difficult younger brother with a problem and I guess that's how I'd look at me too if I were you. Just for tonight, how about you be you and I'll be me. I've been thinking, if your friend is away in Dallas, it would be silly for you to stay in that B&B all by yourself."

"Are you inviting me to stay?"

"Yes I am. If you want to."

"I'd love to."

She had meant it. Mimi hoped that if she stayed with Austin long enough, she would be able to peel away the layers and uncover the cold truth of whatever it was that Austin was concealing. She felt a pang of guilt running through her veins because, if she was honest with herself, as much as she had come here in Joel's name, right now she wanted to stay because she wanted to know more about Austin.

***

Mimi woke before sunrise. She lay in the warmth of the plush duvet shielding her from the slight early morning chill. She studied the room she had slept in for the past two nights. It had come to feel like home, a place that had taken her heart. There was an empty fireplace that looked like it had remained dormant for a considerable amount of time. She imagined how pretty it would be with flames dancing to its own rhythm.

She rubbed her eyes with the back of her hand. It had been another night where her sleep had been disturbed. She pulled out her journal and began to write another letter to Joel:

Dear Joel,

I'm here wishing you were next to me. I awake in a place that feels like home, only you aren't in it. It's like I am waiting for you to walk through the door.

I'm waiting for your brother to talk. He says there are things that I don't know. What are those things, Joel? What are the things that have been hidden from me? I hate being left in the dark like this. There is so much that I don't know. In so many ways, I feel dumb and stupid.

Did you know you have a nephew? His name is Jake and he's adorable. If we'd had a son, he's exactly the child I'd imagine us to have. I have to admit, I'm quite taken by him. I got your feather. Thank you so much. It proved to me that you can hear me. It tells me you are near. God, it hurts living without you. I feel like I don't have a right to smile, although I know you would want me to. I know you would want me to go on, but, Joel, I don't want to move on without you. It doesn't seem right.

Yesterday, I got an email from Jessica, Eric's wife. Is it bad that I actually felt jealous of her? She carries a part of Eric with her, the baby that grows inside her. I am left with doubt and questions. Did you ever want to share your feelings with me? Had we never reached that level of trust, like I thought we had? Austin's lack of information has spoken volumes. Despite all of this, I would give anything to have you here. I miss you!

With love always,

Mimi Mimi xoxo

Mimi placed her pen and journal on the bedside table, and then she heard footsteps. She got out of bed and peeked through the crack of the door. It was Austin. He was fresh out of the shower with nothing but a towel wrapped tightly around his waist. Mimi noticed a large scar slashed across his chest, deep and obvious.

Every scar had its own story to tell, so she wondered where this violent mark could have come from. A short while later, the smell of freshly ground coffee drifted up the stairs. She quickly showered and applied her makeup, enough to make her look fresh and presentable, but not too much so she looked like she was trying to overdo herself and impress Austin. In truth, her perfect tanned face and deep chocolate brown eyes didn't need makeup to enhance her already evident beauty.

Austin was in the kitchen preparing a packed lunch for Jake.

"Morning," he said, his voice low and gruff.

"Morning." Mimi jumped onto a stool and played with a piece of string left on the counter.

"So, I was thinking…I'd love to go riding again"

Austin ran his hand through his dirty blond hair. She watched him move swiftly around the kitchen, cleaning as he went along. Jake flew into the room, grabbed his things, and shouted over his shoulder that his ride to school was there. He gave his father a quick kiss on the cheek, hugged Mimi, and raced out the door. As Jake left, Austin set his hands on the kitchen table.

"I can arrange for that. I can see if Jake's trainer, Uma, is free today. I think she should be."

Mimi felt a rush of disappointment. She tried not to show it by replying in a high-pitched upbeat tone, "Well, that would be great…I mean, if she's free."

"I'll give her a call this morning for you."

"So, what are you doing today?" She kept her gaze down as she tied the piece of string into tiny knots, avoiding looking at him.

"I gotta work."

"What is your work exactly?"

"Running this ranch. I have contractors all over the place. Somebody needs to be in charge."

"Yes, of course. I didn't mean anything by my question."

"No offence taken. This place may have belonged to my parents, but if nobody runs it, then it falls apart."

"Did Joel ever help out?"

The colour drained from Austin's face.

What are you thinking?

"When we were younger, yes. Our mother made him. As you know, Joel enlisted in the Corps a day after his eighteenth birthday. He left immediately. After that, it was on my shoulders. I was only seventeen. I had help from our uncle for a while on the business side of things, but I guess you could say I had to grow up quickly."

"And then you had Jake."

"Yup, and then I had Jake. I took on a lot young, but I don't have any regrets, especially when it comes to that kid. He's my life."

"He's very special."

"Yes, he is. And I'll spend my life protecting him," Austin said with conviction. "If you want, there are some albums of us when we were kids that I have in the attic. You're welcome to look at them."

"Thank you, I'd love that."

"Sure. It will save you from going into my bedroom and having to sneak around, right?"

Mimi felt her cheeks burn red. She thought she had escaped being caught when quite clearly she hadn't.

"I'm so sorry. I shouldn't have gone into your room like that."

"It's fine. Don't worry about it. I get that you are curious and you want to know things, but if you are going to stay here, then we really need to put some boundaries in place."

Mimi nodded in agreement. She knew that she was crossing a line when she went into his room like that. She would have hated for anybody to go into her home and think it was acceptable to walk into her private sanctuary.

He pursed his lips together. "Right. Well, I'll quickly grab those albums for you and then I need to head off for a meeting in the city. I'm going to be gone until Jake gets back from school. You know where everything is, so help yourself to anything you want in the fridge."

"Thank you."

"No problem. I will give Uma a quick call now."

He reached into his pocket and pulled out his mobile.

"Uma…Austin Marcus here." He took his

conversation out into the hallway and returned a minute later.

"Sorry about that. The signal is bad in the kitchen. Well, she can do it. Said she can get here by eleven if that works for you?"

"Sounds great."

"Okay. Enjoy yourself then, and remember what I said."

"Always expect the unexpected!"

"See you later."

In the living room, Austin had placed two small cardboard boxes on the coffee table. She walked barefoot across the hardwood floor and sat on the edge of the sofa. Inside those boxes were important pieces of her husband's childhood.

She drew in a deep breath as she opened the musty flaps of the cardboard box, revealing four large hardback brown photo albums. The sun had flooded the room. She drew the curtains slightly so she could see the pictures clearly.

The first image was of their mother, smiling adoringly at Joel. Next to the photo was a scribble:

Joel aged 3, Aunt Edna's house.

She flicked through hundreds of snaps. This family that once existed was no longer. Austin was the only survivor out of the family of four. She wondered how that affected him. Although he seemed to have his life in order, Mimi knew he had not come out unscathed. He may have buried his feelings deep, but she knew he was carrying a lot of heartache inside. He seemed so serious and

can let him back in the wild. Isn't that right, champ?" Austin said, rubbing the top of Jake's head.

How could you walk out on your own child, Joel? How could you?

"Mimi, Uma said you cancelled today."

"Yeah, I didn't feel too well. I think I'm coming down with something. Actually, if you don't mind, I think I may go lie down for a while."

"Sure," Austin said. "Can I do anything for you?"

Mimi swallowed hard. "I'm fine," she lied as she removed herself from the kitchen. Once again, for the fiftieth time that day, tears washed down her face. She hung her long hair over the front of her shoulders, making sure her sadness could not be seen.

An hour later, Austin tapped on Mimi's door.

"Knock knock," he said.

"Come in."

Austin walked into the dimly lit room. Music was playing, setting the mood to a reflective feel.

"How are you feeling?"

"Just a headache. I'll be all right."

Austin's green eyes looked even deeper into Mimi's. He knelt down beside the bed in front of Mimi. Here they were, two strangers connected by one man and a lie which had changed everything Mimi thought she knew.

She thought about confronting Austin there and then, but she couldn't seem to find the words. He hadn't lied to her, but Joel had. It was clear that Austin was a wonderful father. She wondered if

Jake knew that Austin was his uncle and not his father, but who would tell an eight-year-old that? She knew Austin hadn't told her because he needed to protect his 'son.'

Mimi wasn't ready to be a mother when she and Joel met. She knew she wanted to be some day, but she wasn't ready to raise a child as a single parent whilst Joel was deployed. She wanted to be settled. After Joel died, she felt robbed of the chance to be a mother, but now she felt destroyed.

"I was thinking, Mimi. On Saturday, why don't we spend some time together and go riding?"

"Yeah…sure," she hesitated.

Would this be the moment he would tell her the secret she had already discovered? The moment where at least one of the Marcus brothers would be honest with her?

***

Meg had finally re-emerged. She contacted Mimi by text and told her she was heading back to the B&B without Bo. She sounded edgy during their phone conversation. Mimi suspected things had not gone to plan with this mystery stranger who owned the coffee shop. Meg texted her two days after Mimi had made the shocking discovery. She carried the weight of finding out about Joel and Jake around with her. Mimi had cried herself to sleep into her pillow every night since.

Mimi drove back to the B&B just before lunch. She knocked on the door. It was a different room than the one they had previously stayed in. The door creaked open. There were no lights on and Mimi could see Meg's outline in the darkness.

"Meg, are you all right?" Mimi said, alarmed.

Meg sat on the floor and leaned against the bed. Mimi lowered herself down and sat next to her.

Meg was silent, her expression haunted. Mimi's heart started to race. She placed her hand on Meg's shoulder and whispered, "What's wrong?"

"I should have never come." A single tear ran down Meg's face, and then, through the crack of the curtain, the mid-morning sun caught her left cheek, highlighting the dark grey bruise. Meg quickly lifted her hand to shield her face, but Mimi immediately pulled it away.

"What the hell happened?"

"I didn't want to sleep with him, so he got angry and, well, this is the result," she said, brushing her fingers against the swelling.

"Did he do anything else to you?"

"No…you should see *his* face." She half-heartedly laughed. "We were drunk. We went back to a hotel and he put the moves on me. I guess I led him on, but I decided he wasn't going to get in my pants. Anyway, after I let stupidly him kiss me, he started moving quickly. It felt wrong. I can't explain why, but I told him to stop. He did, but he immediately got angry. He called me a whore. I called him an asshole and that's when he hit me."

"We need to report this to the police."

"Yeah, I already did."

"And?"

"And they filed a report. There were no witnesses, so it's his word against mine."

"That son of a bitch!"

"Yeah. Anyway, lesson learned. I mustn't go off with strange men."

"Are you okay? I mean *really* okay?" Mimi felt responsible since she was the reason Meg was there. Somehow, all this trip seemed to have brought them was additional trouble.

"I'm not going to lie, I'm shaken. I've never been hit before, and I've never been in a situation where I thought the outcome could end in disaster, but yes, I'm fine."

Meg got back onto her feet and walked across the room to the dresser. She pulled out her passport.

"I'm ready to go home. I know we were meant to be here for a couple more nights, but really, I need to get back."

Mimi felt a knot in her stomach. She wasn't ready to return back to the UK. Right now she knew she belonged in Texas, and she needed to gather the last pieces of the puzzle to get a clear picture of how and why Joel kept his love child a secret. And then there was Austin. She felt a pull toward him in a way she hadn't yet admitted to herself.

"Meg, I can't go home with you. I'm so sorry, but I need to be here."

"For how much longer?"

"I don't know. A while."

"I wish you were coming back with me, Mimi. But I understand. Have you started to find out the answers to your questions?"

Mimi felt a lump rise in her throat. She said, "Do you fancy getting out of here for a bit and going for a walk or something?"

***

The girls got in the car and drove randomly for a few miles until they found a bar overlooking an open field that was freshly ploughed. Meg pushed open the heavy door which scraped against the wooden floor. It was instantly obvious that this was a place that was only used to the faces of locals.

Meg turned to Mimi with a smile and said, "Do you want to leave?"

"It will only be more awkward if we leave, don't you think?"

Meg nodded.

They sat in a quiet corner, exposed to the sound of the roadway where large trucks roared past.

A bone thin woman with overly bleached blonde hair walked over to them a short time later, her apron tie twisted round her body three, maybe four, times over.

"What can I get ya?" she asked.

"I'll just have an iced tea," Mimi said.

The waitress rolled her eyes and then moved her gaze to Meg. When the drinks arrived, Mimi took a sip and placed her iced tea on the sticky table. There was a sudden roar of laughter that made Mimi bolt upright.

Meg glanced over her shoulder and saw the man the laughter belonged to. He had his waist pressed up against a pinball machine. It was obvious he had beaten his friends high score, who stood next to him with his eyes closed, shaking his head.

Meg sighed. "So, talk to me."

Mimi told Meg all about Austin and how

guarded he had been. Then she talked about Jake and what a smart, wonderful kid he was. Meg sat and listened, her gaze resting on Mimi. She took in a deep breath and quickly looked around her, surveying the bar as if she was about to share a secret. She leaned her body over the table, took Mimi's hands, and squeezed them tight.

"For the very first time since all this happened, you don't look like a grief-stricken widow when you say Joel's name out loud."

"What do I look like then?"

"You look…how can I say this? Stormy, angry."

Meg was one of the only people that Mimi was happy to let in to the deepest part of her soul. It was the way it had always been ever since they were children. They shared everything. All these years later, nothing had changed.

"Mimi, what is it? Do you know something? Tell me."

Mimi reached into her bag and took out the birth certificate. She unfolded it and smoothed it out with her hand on the table.

Meg picked it up gently, as if it were a fragile sheet of glass that may shatter. She studied it closely, her face full of confusion.

"Mimi…I don't understand?"

"Joel was Jake's father. He had a kid and he never told me about it," Mimi blurted, her anger rising to the surface.

"Holy shit! Joel?" Meg looked at the birth certificate once more. "Could there be a mistake?" she added.

"I wish, but I don't think so."

"Do you know the mother?"

"Yup. Well, I have briefly seen her. She didn't care to give me the time of day. She must have known who I was. She wouldn't even acknowledge me. It kills me. I don't know anything or if Joel was in contact with her during our marriage."

"Do you think Joel even knew?"

"How could he not?" Mimi said, her posture rigid. When she spoke, there was an angry edge to her tone.

Her eyes darkened. "The truth is, I have no idea who I married. I feel like I have lost him all over again because I've been living a lie."

"I'm so sorry, Mimi, but I can't say that you lived a lie. You and Joel were in love, there was no denying that."

"But he lied to me!"

"He just didn't tell you. It's slightly different from a lie, and, like I say, how do you even know he knew? I'm just playing devil's advocate here, but perhaps this was a secret to him as well as to you."

Mimi had never explored this possibility. She knew the only person that would have the answers would be Austin. She vowed to herself, in that very moment, she would find out the truth and would not stop until she got to the bottom of it all.

"Will you be all right here on your own?" Meg asked.

"I made it this far, haven't I? I'll be fine, Meg. Will you?"

"Yes. I just need to get back to London. Truth is, I miss my job, my flat, and mostly my bed. I'm sorry I can't stay, Mimi. Texas just isn't for me, although I can see why it's for you."

Mimi stood up and reached her arms out to Meg with the table wedged between them. The two friends needed to part ways and find their own path. They finished off their drinks and stepped into the car-park, the smell of engine fumes hanging in the air.

They headed to the car and sat in silence for a moment. They had been friends since they were children. Meg was always the troublesome, plotting, scheming little girl that lived next door. Together, they shared every first experience they had, whether it was a test at school or firsts with boys in their teenage years.

They had come a long way together. Their friendship was as solid and true as the day was light.

Mimi turned the key and brought the engine to life. She drove the car along the wide roads back to the B&B. She helped Meg pack her things and waited until she called the airline to confirm an earlier flight.

"I'll take you to the airport," Mimi offered.

"No, I want to get a cab. Go back to Austin as soon as you can and find out what you need to know."

"Are you sure?"

"Certain. I will message you as soon as I land back in Blitey."

The girls stood opposite one another. Mimi suddenly felt empowered and ready to walk this road alone for the first time without using Meg as an emotional crutch. She was grateful to her friend for getting her to this point, but she was now ready to fly solo.

CHAPTER 11

"Mimi, wake up! Mimi!" Austin repeated, his voice rising with panic. He stood over her, trying to pull her out of the nightmare she was having. Finally, she woke, her body sweaty from her night terror, her eyes struggling to focus.

"Joel," she whispered.

Austin took a step back, his face twisted.

"It's Austin, Mimi. And you were having a nightmare."

He was dressed in jeans and a t-shirt, his hair still wet from an early morning shower.

Once she came out of her dream, Mimi pulled herself up and looked at Austin. She stayed still. Her legs felt weak and she tried to steady her breathing.

The room felt warm. Austin walked to the window, pulled back the curtains, and pushed the window open. He looked back at Mimi, her hair in a tangled mess. She watched him from across the room.

When will you tell me what I already know?

His gaze locked on her.

"I can't even remember what the dream was about. I've been having nightmares for months ever since Joel was deployed."

"Did you still want to go riding? It's a beautiful day for it," he said, refusing to acknowledge Joel's name.

"Yeah…I do," she said.

"Okay, well, great. Get ready. I'll meet you in the barn in an hour."

He turned on his heel to leave her bedroom when she called after him.

"Austin, what about Jake? I mean, who will be taking care of him?"

"Sara," he replied.

Sara. Jake's mother and Joel's…What had she been to Joel? United, always, because of the son they created together. A wave of jealously washed over Mimi. She saw her husband touching this beautiful woman. She imagined her pregnant, her stomach swollen with Joel's child.

If Joel had told her about Jake, she wondered if it would have affected their relationship. Although Mimi was a jealous person by nature, knowing about Jake wouldn't have stopped her being with Joel. It saddened her to think her husband was capable of turning his back on his own child.

An hour later, Mimi made her way across to the barn. She had her long hair tied back and opted for a pair of shorts and a long-sleeved t-shirt.

Austin was attaching the saddle when Mimi walked into the barn.

"Hey, Kelsa, how you doing, girl?" She stroked

the horse.

"You have quite a connection with her."

"Do I?" Almost immediately, Mimi regretted how off she sounded.

Austin shrugged his shoulders. Mimi knew she was acting differently, but she didn't know if he would suspect for a single moment as to why. He would probably just assume her level of grief hit a new peak.

"We are going to go off track today through lots of woodlands. It's going to be tiresome, but trust me, it will be worth it."

Mimi managed to smile. She climbed on Kelsa with ease and watched Austin mount his black stallion, Troy. Together, they departed into a gentle canter. They rode down a path that entered a meadow covered in bluebells. The long grass had an array of several shades of green and yellow. It was quiet and peaceful. They hardly spoke, and when they did, it was only about which direction to take.

In the near distance, the sound of running water could be heard. Mimi's mind flashed back to Yosemite, where she and Joel stopped at a waterfall. Her thoughts ran deeper. She remembered his lips on hers, how happy she felt there in that moment.

A bee buzzed close to Mimi's face, disrupting her thoughts and taking her out of her memory. As she swatted the bee away, her grip loosened on the reins. She quickly lost her balance and started to slip backwards off the horse.

"Mimi!" Austin shouted.

A second later, she hit the ground with a thud. She felt an agonising pain in her right wrist. Austin jumped down and ran to her.

"It hurts," she yelped.

"What hurts, Mimi? Look at me. Do you know who I am?"

"Austin, I haven't hit my head. It's my wrist."

He reached out to her and gently took her forearm. He looked at her wrist to examine it further. It was crooked and swollen and most certainly broken.

"It's broken. We need to get you to a hospital."

"I can't ride back."

"We will have to walk. We're not that far out."

A single tear ran down her cheek. He moved his hand toward her face and then quickly snapped back. It was as if he was resisting wiping it away. She couldn't read him, but it looked as if seeing her hurt stirred something inside him. She suddenly wondered if Austin was feeling something more for her.

"Why the hell did you let go, Mimi?"

"The bee—it was buzzing in my face. It freaked me out."

"A bee won't kill you, but falling could. I told you to be careful," he said with emotion.

"Okay, Joel, calm down." She immediately realised her mistake, but it was too late. Austin's expression turned stormy.

"I'm not Joel. I'm nothing like him," he snapped.

For the first time, Mimi burst into tears. "Actually, you're just like him."

He stepped back. His eyes burned into hers. "No. He may be my brother by blood, but he isn't the perfect saint you have created in your head. He's not who you think he is."

"Yeah. I know!" she yelled. She sat on the ground with her knees pulled up to her chest, her white t-shirt caked in dust and dirt. Her wrist felt like it had a heartbeat of its own, thudding and throbbing.

"You don't know shit." Austin swallowed hard.

"I know that he's Jake's biological father. I know he hid it from me, just like you did."

This surprised Austin and his iciness seemed to melt a bit. "How did you know?"

"Does it really matter? I know, and both of you kept secrets from me. So, how I see it, you Marcus brothers are really not that different after all."

Silence hung between them. The midday sun beat down on them. Beads of sweat popped up on Austin's forehead. He sat down on a nearby rock and put his head in his hands.

When he looked up, his face was twisted and strained.

"Mimi, Jake is my son in every definition of what being a dad is. I take care of him. I'm the one who tended to him when he woke up as a baby multiple times in the night—the colic, the colds, the mystery tummy bugs. I'm the one who works my ass off to provide for him to make sure he has the best life possible. I am his dad and nothing or nobody will ever change that."

"But biologically?" she whispered. Mimi prayed there was a mistake and there was a logical explanation, but, as she searched his face, she knew her prayers would not be answered.

"Biologically, he belongs to Joel." Austin

lowered his head.

Mimi nodded and prepared to ask the most difficult question she had ever asked in her life. “Did Joel know about Jake? Did he know he was Jake’s father?”

“Yes.”

The three-letter word held a powerful punch.

Mimi never realized how much it could hurt to love somebody. She believed her relationship was true and pure, but she was living a lie. Her memories, every single one of them, were now forever tarnished. Every kiss they shared. Each time he touched her. Every time they laughed and made love. During all that time, Joel knew he was keeping a secret from Mimi. Did it mean he hadn’t loved her? If he loved her so deeply like he said, then why didn’t he tell her?

And now, here she was, sitting in dirt with a broken wrist and a broken heart.

“We gotta get you to a hospital, Mimi. Let’s go. We can talk more about this later.”

***

When they made it back to the car, they headed into town, taking the quickest route to the emergency room.

A knot of anger sat in Mimi’s stomach as she thought about all the times she and Joel discussed children. He had not once even hinted that he was keeping a secret. It all made sense now as she recalled each time she had suggested wanting to visit Texas with him and he had deterred her.

Why couldn't you just be honest?

That's the problem with a lie. To keep it alive, you have to keep feeding it with more lies until it's so overfed that it becomes fat and out of control. Sooner or later, it will explode.

As they pulled into the hospital car-park, a light drizzle set on the windscreen. Mimi stepped out of the truck. She was careful not to knock her wrist.

The smell of the rain hitting the tarmac hung in the air. Austin walked to Mimi, offering to help her, but she pulled away. She didn't want him to touch her.

Austin glanced at her. He looked like he was desperate to help, as she couldn't conceal the pain she was in. Mimi felt lost and confused. She wondered if he regretted not sending her away when she arrived. If he let her go, she would never have known. She would never have found out the truth. In all those quiet moments, is that when he thought about telling her the truth? Had he even ever searched for the words?

He had raised Jake. To him, that little boy was his. Mimi figured that admitting to anybody else that Jake was not his biological son crushed him.

They walked in silence into the ER. There were a few people in the waiting area and no obvious emergencies. On the surface, it all seemed relatively calm.

"Do you have insurance?" the nurse at the desk asked Mimi.

"I have travel insurance, yes. It's with…"

The nurse cut her short. "I'm afraid we don't accept travel insurance."

Mimi suddenly thought about the UK and how she had complained about the NHS in the past for the long waiting times and the disorganisation, but she was grateful for them. Getting treatment didn't come down to a business transaction. It was about looking after a patient.

"I'll pay for it. Here's my credit card." Austin handed it over.

"There are some forms to fill out while you are waiting." The nurse attempted to hand Mimi a clipboard.

"She's broken her wrist. She can't exactly fill out a form," Austin said as he raised an eyebrow.

The woman glared at Austin over the top of her bright red glasses.

"Then maybe you can fill it out on your wife's behalf?"

Austin took the clipboard, keeping his gaze locked on the not-so-helpful nurse.

They took a seat in the waiting area.

"Thank you. I'll pay you back."

She leaned into her chair and her back touched the cool, concrete wall. Her head hung and she squeezed her eyes shut, grimacing through the short, sharp pains.

***

Austin

Austin sat with his arms crossed in front of him. He wanted to talk and expel the awkwardness, but he was too emotionally drained. When he received the news Joel had died, he was sad, but there was a part of him that felt like a burden had been lifted off his shoulders.

He decided that he would go through Jake's childhood, not telling him that he was not his real father. The lie was like a cancer, eating away at him. Telling Jake at this young age would serve no purpose. He didn't have the emotional understanding to come away from the truth unscathed. Austin wondered what Jake's life would have been like if Joel had taken responsibility for him, if he'd stayed with Sara. Now he wondered how Mimi's life would have been. Joel was gone and he would never be able to explain his actions to Sara or Mimi.

After thirty minutes, Mimi's name was finally called. Austin stood up with her.

"I'm all right. Just wait here for me." She placed her hand on his shoulder, giving him a gentle push.

The doctor took her paperwork and scanned the information.

"Mrs. Marcus, your husband is welcome to come in."

"That's not my husband. He's my brother-in-law." The label *brother-in-law* sounded foreign to her. She felt like an imposter, borrowing somebody else's life.

She allowed the doctor to examine her wrist. He confirmed it was fractured, but was sending her to the x-ray department to assess just how bad the break was.

Austin made a call to Sara, telling her he was going to be late picking Jake up. He hated having to leave him with her any longer than necessary. He was granted full guardianship over Jake. Sara didn't fight. She'd pushed for it. The only reason she saw Jake on the weekends was out of nothing but guilt.

Mimi had been in with the doctor for forty-five minutes. Austin thought about her life with Joel and what their days together would've been like. She painted Joel to be the perfect saint, the perfect husband. He wondered what bullshit he fed her and how he copped out of ever bringing her back to his home. Then he thought of how gullible and naïve Mimi was. He felt pity for her, but he also felt irritated at how stupid she had been to fall for Joel's lies and deceit.

Finally, Mimi emerged from around the white corridor, her wrist in plaster. Her usually tanned face looked pale.

"So, it's broken." Her voice was hoarse.

"Let's get you back to the ranch. Before we do, we need to pick up Jake at Sara's house."

Mimi swallowed. She had hoped that she wouldn't need to see Sara again. She wanted to ask why Jake had come to live with his uncle and not his mother. The whole situation was riddled with craziness.

CHAPTER 12

Mimi

She woke in the middle of the night. Her wrist was throbbing.

Her mind spun back to the day before, when Austin confirmed Joel knew Jake was his child. She wondered if Joel would've ever told her the truth. She had been in Texas longer than the two weeks she had planned. She had placed her entire life on hold to be here. England seemed a lifetime ago.

Back at home, life continued moving forward, as it always had. A temp would have been sitting at her desk at work. Mimi was now a ghost herself; drifting, lonely, and desperate to find closure. She thought about Austin and the way he had paid her medical bill. He hadn't questioned it. He had just done it.

Was that how it was when Jake was born? Did he just assume responsibility?

Something about the story wasn't adding up. What seventeen-year-old voluntarily takes responsibility of a newborn that isn't his own? Alone in the dark, Mimi decided she had to find out the truth. Once she did, she would return back to the UK. Beyond that, she had no idea how to live her life as a widow

At some point during her deep thinking, and after another strong painkiller, she fell back to sleep.

A few hours later, she woke again and pulled back the curtains to blazing sunshine. It was 12.06 p.m. The tablets must have knocked her out cold. She felt embarrassed to be a guest in somebody else's home and have slept for that long. She searched her brain to try and remember what day it was. *Sunday.* Austin would be at home, and so would Jake.

After she got ready, she headed down to the kitchen. Austin was making lunch.

"I'm sorry. I never sleep in this late," Mimi said.

"You needed it. Rest is the best thing to help heal broken bones. I should know; I've had enough of them." He smiled.

"Thank you…for everything"

Austin cleared his throat. His hands rested on the kitchen countertop. "No, I'm sorry, Mimi. You deserve the truth. Are you ready to hear it?"

Mimi froze. Her heart pounded. *Am I ready for the truth?*

She said, "I'm not ready. I doubt I'll ever be, but I need to know."

The water in the pan boiled over, spilling all over the stainless steel stove. Austin quickly turned the knob off and picked up a dish cloth to wipe up the mess.

Despite the worry in her mind, Mimi knew little more could hurt her unless she were to be told that Joel had been in contact with Sara whilst they were married.

Jake was going to a friend's house for the day. Austin decided to give up making lunch. He asked Mimi if she wanted to go for a drive and talk.

"Before I begin," Austin said with seriousness, "you must understand that Jake is not to know a thing about any of this. He's a child. I will not have his world turned upside down." Austin's eyes darkened as he continued, "and if you so much as breathe a word suggesting I am not his father, I won't even let you pack your bags. You will be out of here."

"I understand, and I won't say a word," she said, feeling the threat in his words.

An hour later, Mimi was back in Austin's truck. He pulled out of the gravel driveway and drove away from the ranch. Mimi cracked the window open enough to let her dark hair fly. Austin gave her a sideways look. He pulled up to a dead-end road. The grass was overgrown and wild. There was a beaten pathway that looked like it hadn't had any foot traffic in months.

"We can't go any further. We'll have to walk the rest of the way. Do you feel well enough?" he asked. Mimi nodded and carefully stepped down from the truck. Austin was quickly at her side, offering her his hand to steady her.

After walking for a good ten minutes, the craggily rocky path opened up. A stream flowed into a beautiful body of water. The air was still and calm. Mimi removed her shoes and stepped into the shallow, cool water. She moved her feet in circles and took in the rugged scenery.

"Joel and I used to swim here as kids."

It was the first time Austin had mentioned his brother's name voluntarily. It stopped Mimi in her tracks and Austin seemed nervous. He kept pausing in-between speaking to catch his breath. He reached into a backpack he'd brought from the car and laid out a large picnic blanket.

"So here we are," he said, his eyes blazing.

"The moment of truth."

"Yup." He walked across to her, helping her sit.

"Where do you want me to start?" he asked, looking down at his hands. His confident stance disappeared as he allowed himself to dig deep into his emotions and his feud with his brother.

Mimi felt lightheaded. She'd craved to know the truth for so long, but now her hands felt clammy and her heart felt like it was wedged in her throat.

"As brothers, we were different," he started. "There was only a year between us. Our father was our rock, our hero. He was the head of the family, and he was the one that kept us in line. One day he was here and the next he was gone, just like that. I have gone over it in my head a million times. I've replayed a thousand different scenarios in my head. Joel took our father's death the hardest. We both had our own way of dealing with things. My dad died because of an unavoidable accident. That is the thing that tore my family apart. It should have never happened. After he was gone, my memory gets a little fuzzy. I remember bits, but I was so young, I'm not sure which are real memories or the blanks I have let myself fill in."

Mimi cleared her throat. Austin's version coincided with the story Joel told her. She was grateful that he at least wasn't a total liar. She saw a water bottle sticking out of Austin's bag.

"May I?"

He took the bottle and twisted the lid off for her. She took a sip and fixed her gaze on him. She searched his eyes for emotion, but there was nothing—just a darkened expression.

He recalled how life was difficult after their father died and how they almost had to grow up overnight. They were expected to be responsible from a young age. They had help from other family members, but life had turned a corner and they were thrust into an adult world neither of them were ready for.

"Sara came into my life when I was sixteen, soon to be seventeen."

Mimi's ears pricked up. She turned to her side, ready to hear all about this mystery woman that had carried her husband's baby inside her for nine months.

"So, Sara…she was your girlfriend?"

"She was. Man, I was hooked on that girl. She transferred from out of state. I asked her out on a date and that was that. We spent all our time together—after school, on weekends. I'd sneak her into my room after my mom had gone to bed. She was my first. I was totally in love with her."

Mimi was trying to piece together the picture in

her head.

"One night, Sara was meant to come over. She told me she wasn't feeling well, so she cancelled. I was disappointed, but I understood. I heard a noise coming from the outhouse. We'd already had an intruder before."

"The intruder that Joel caught in your house when he took your father's gun."

"Yeah, that's right. Naturally, after that, we were all pretty nervous. I looked around the house, and everything seemed fine. I grabbed a butcher's knife from the kitchen. I crept into the outhouse. There was somebody in there. I could hear rustling and grunting. I managed to find the light switch after fumbling 'round in the dark, and that's when I found my brother with my girlfriend. I don't need to fill in the blanks, do I?"

Mimi's face was white. She imagined how devastated Austin must have been. She was immediately furious with Joel. She felt sick to her stomach at the image in her head.

"What did you do?"

"We got into a fight. Joel was enraged when I called Sara a bitch."

"Did he love Sara?"

"I doubt that. He was always angry about something. He was out of control. I took the first punch and he got hold of the knife. He slashed it across my chest. He didn't want to kill me—that much I know—but he wanted to hurt me."

"That's where your scar is from? Joel, he did that to you?"

"Yeah. That's not really important."

"What was Sara doing during all of this?"

"She was screaming, crying, and saying how sorry she was. We eventually stopped fighting. I broke up with Sara. She tried to call, and she begged me to go back to her. When I didn't hear from her for a month, I thought she finally got the message. It was during summer break. Joel and I didn't speak. It broke our mother's heart. She didn't want us fighting over a girl, least of all Sara. She couldn't stand her."

"How did you and Joel go on living together and not talking? Was he ever sorry?"

"No. He never apologised, and we didn't talk again. Our mom was the one to tell me he enlisted in the Corps. She'd encouraged it; she felt he was lost. I was happy he was getting the hell out of the house and out of my life."

Mimi's mind flashed back to Valentine night in her flat. She'd burned incense and lit the room in candles. Joel had said that his brother was furious that he'd left to go to the Marines. Her head started to throb as she tried to digest all this information. They say the truth hurts, but this was killing her.

"After he'd enlisted, Sara showed up at the ranch, three months pregnant."

"Well, I am going to have to ask. How did you know you were not the father?"

"I didn't at fist. For the next six months of her pregnancy, I believed I was. Until after Jake was born. He had anemia and needed a blood transfusion. I thought I was the obvious choice, but it turns out the hospital had a policy that close relatives can't donate. I loved Jake, but I had a nagging feeling he wasn't mine. Sara claimed she and Joel had slept together only once and they had used protection. Something inside of me couldn't shake this feeling, so I insisted on DNA testing."

Mimi tried to remember what being seventeen felt like. She hugged her arms around her chest, almost like she were trying to protect herself from the truth that was finally bursting free.

She thought about Sara and how she played these two brothers against each other, how she destroyed a family bond that should have lasted a lifetime. Now it was too late.

"Joel came back on leave. He was tested and that was that. He was gone again. A week later, the lab results confirmed that Joel was the father. The results were 99.9% accurate. Those kind of numbers don't throw you into any more doubt. It simply gives you the cold, hard truth."

Austin continued with the rest of the story. Mimi listened. He told her how Sara's parents disowned her. She couldn't cope with being a teen mother, so Austin and Joel's mother stepped in to raise Jake. Slowly but surely, as the infant cried into the depths of the night, Austin stepped into a fatherly role. He explained that it wasn't a choice as much as it was a calling. With Sara and Joel out of the picture, he wanted to ensure somebody was there for this child, even if his own parents had run scared. After their mother passed away, Austin raised Jake alone.

"Did Joel not want anything to do with Jake?"

"No. Last year he relinquished all of his parental rights and I became Jake's legal adoptive parent."

"Last year?" Mimi said as she thought, *Last year*

is when we got married.

"Yes. I knew he was married. I'd assumed, at one point, you could have been behind it, but the truth always rises to the surface. So that's everything, Mimi. That is why Joel and I didn't have that brotherly love."

CHAPTER 13

Austin

Austin rode his horse hard. He had not been thinking straight since he told Mimi the truth. He rode for miles, off into the peaks and valleys of the ranch. He liked the freedom he felt as he rode as well as hearing nothing but the sound of Troy's neighs and his hooves stomping on the ground.

He took a deep breath and, for the first time, thought about Joel and the fact he was dead.

For so long, Austin had treated his brother like he'd died a long time ago, but he was not prepared to feel the way he did now that he understood it was reality. There was something about Mimi he felt drawn to. Perhaps it was her sincerity, or maybe it was the way her deep brown eyes looked at him as if she understood him.

Twenty-four hours later, Mimi looked like she'd taken several punches to the gut. When he had finally told her the truth, she hadn't said much. She hadn't even cried.

Austin wondered why his brother had lied to his wife. He suspected it was because he wanted to be her perfect man. Austin had no idea if Joel had loved Mimi, but he'd married her and seemingly, for no reason, to serve himself. She had come from a normal working background, so Joel hadn't used her to marry into money.

Austin needed to get away from Mimi for a few hours. He needed distance from her to reflect. Now that she knew the whole story, he suspected it was only a matter of time before she returned to England.

He knew it was best if they parted ways, but there was something about her he couldn't explain. He felt the need to look after her. He *wanted* to look after her. Austin almost laughed out loud at himself when he thought about wanting to make Mimi happy; it was as if he were a guardian angel for the people Joel had touched and damaged.

Now that he processed his thoughts, he decided it was best if Mimi left. If she had not yet made her departing arrangements, he would ask her to do so. Nothing good could come out of Mimi staying longer. Jake already had taken a shining to this mystery British stranger—a woman he mistook for being somebody significant in his father's life.

It was safer to send her away so that he and Jake could go back to a normal life with no complications and nothing to upset or distort their perfect harmony.

***

Mimi

Mimi was back at the ranch, sitting in the guest room that overlooked the green grounds. Out of the corner of her eye, she saw two out buildings. She had never noticed them before.

She knew everything now. There was no need for her to remain in Texas. She knew that she must head back to England and start her life over.

In a way, she was grateful she and Joel didn't have a home picked out together. She would go back to her flat in Finchley that wasn't their marital home. She didn't want to go back to her job. She wanted to find herself, her true self, away from the grief, drama, lies and deceit. She wanted to rediscover herself, and she knew the only way to do that was through art. She needed to paint and keep painting until the picture before her showed her where she needed to go—a path she needed to travel, alone and without Joel.

Mimi sat on the bed and let her body sink into the soft mattress. Her mind was strained and her body exhausted.

You lied to me, Joel. Beyond that, you deceived me. Who are you?

Who did I marry?

Do you know how stupid I feel? How angry and disappointed? Why did you never tell me you had a child?

I've tried to come up with a million different reasons as to why you withheld the truth, but I'm hitting blanks—a big fat zero. I have stayed awake at night, loving you, missing you, but now I stay awake hurt and angry. I still love you, at least I think I do, the you that I said, "I do" too.

What worries me is I have no idea if you really loved me. You had a whole other life, one that was never a reflection of the truth, and I can't wrap my head around that.

And now you're gone. My heart is in a million confused pieces and they can never be put back together without you here to answer the questions I have. You have missed out on your son. Jake is a smart, wonderful little boy. You turned your back on him. How could you?

If we had a child, would you have turned your back on us too?

Who are you?

Mimi wrote furiously, her pen denting the page, the ink dark and angry, and her handwriting scribbled and messy, like her head.

She looked at her wardrobe, at the hanging clothes waiting to be packed and moved back to England. Only she wished she could stay here longer, even though there was nothing keeping her at the ranch. Her entire family and friends were back in the UK, missing her and wanting her back.

She knew that Austin wanted her to move on. He hadn't said it, but her being there was a constant reminder he was to lying to his son.

She set her pen down, crossed the room, and looked out the bedroom window. She watched the sun as it started to set and paint the clouds pink. Austin was on his horse, the jet black stallion that looked just like Black Beauty. He hung his head low, his Stetson covering his face. She watched him, the lone cowboy—a good man keeping his family legacy alive and watching over a young boy with the love of an amazing father. He was worthy of being called *Daddy*.

Mimi quickly straightened herself up. She applied a quick touch-up of makeup and ran her GHD flat iron through her hair to make it shiny and sleek.

A few minutes later, she entered the kitchen, where Austin stood. He was shuffling through some mail.

"Hi," she said with uncertainty.

Austin stared at her. His face looked tired, as if he had been up all night, thinking.

"How are you doing?" he said without conviction.

She handed him Jake's birth certificate.

"I've been keeping hold of this. I had no right to. I'm sorry."

He took the document without reading the content. He knew what it said. He'd read it a thousand times. The truth is the truth, but he didn't need a piece of paper to give him the right to be Jake's dad. The adoption papers mattered to him.

Nobody could take Jake away from him.

"Thank you," she said, tilting her head to the side.

"For what?"

"For your honesty. And for giving me the truth, letting me stay—for everything, Austin. Thank you for everything."

He looked at her lips, soft and full. He wished he could take her in his arms and kiss her.

"You needed to know. I'd say it's no big deal, but, well…it is. Hopefully now you can go home and start your healing process."

Home. He wants me to go home.

She ran her hand through her hair. She was suddenly disappointed. She'd wanted him to ask her to stay for a while longer, not because he reminded her of Joel, but because she liked who Austin was.

Austin started to pull ingredients out of the cupboards and got to work on dinner. He drizzled oil into a large pain and broke up mince-meat in his hands. He added chopped garlic and a dash of chilli. Then he boiled water and put a pack of spaghetti on the counter to put into the water when it finished boiling.

"I'll look at flights tonight. I'll leave as soon as possible."

He nodded and kept his eyes fixed on the chopped tomatoes he carefully scooped up with his hands and tossed into the sizzling pan.

She wanted to say what she was thinking and opened her mouth, but Austin moved away from her and headed to the door, calling Jake to come down from his room.

During dinner, the silence was filled with Jake telling Austin and Mimi all about his day. Mimi attempted to twist the spaghetti with her fork onto the spoon.

"How is your wrist?" Austin asked.

"It's okay. I'm sad I won't be able to ride again before I go home."

"You're leaving?" Jake shrilled.

Austin lifted his gaze, looked at Mimi, and then turned to Jake.

"Mimi needs to go home to her family in England. They miss her and want to see her."

Jake's eyes were wide and filled with tears. "But I like having you here, Mimi."

She cupped his sweet face and held his chin. "I have sure loved visiting, but your daddy's right. My family misses me."

"You'll come back, right?"

She wanted to say yes so badly, but this child didn't deserve any more lies to be woven into his young life.

"No, Jake, I won't be back."

She looked at Austin, hoping that he would cut across her and say that she was welcome to come back to the ranch whenever she wanted, but he avoided her gaze and said nothing. She knew she needed to leave.

Later that evening, Austin gave Mimi the key to his study so she could use his computer to look up flights. He always kept the door locked so Jake wouldn't run in and mess up his paperwork.

She slid the key into the bulky lock and opened the door, revealing a classical and old-fashioned study. There was a bookcase mounted against the far wall with too many books to count. The large polished oak desk dominated the room. The shiny Mac almost looked out of place.

She switched the computer on and carefully typed in the login details Austin scribbled on the back of a magazine. A photo of Jake with Austin appeared. They were next to Troy, the black stallion, on a perfect summer's day.

As she went into the American Airlines website, she felt her breath shorten. She didn't want to go, but she had no reason to stay. She stopped, trying to process the last few weeks, which had been a whirlwind of grief, pain, shock, and now disbelief.

The creak of the door interrupted her thoughts. It was Austin. He looked tired. He was dressed in a pair of ripped, faded blue jeans and a light blue t-shirt. Her heart quickened. He sat on the edge of the desk. She waited for him to speak, but for the second time that night he said nothing.

"What is it?" Mimi asked.

His jaw tightened. "Nothing."

Mimi rested her head on her hand. She wanted to get inside his head and let it all out. She thought back to how Joel used to look faraway in thought, but at the time she had ignored it, thinking it was something to do with memories he would rather not share about the war. She had never pressed him further, but now she wished she had.

When she met Joel, he was ridiculously charming and confident. He made her laugh and he'd interested her with his tales of the Corps, foreign places he travelled to, different cultures he'd experienced, and the friendship of his military brothers. But now she wondered if that had all been true or if he lied about so much more with only threads of the truth. She wondered if Joel had ever thought, *I must tell her the truth. She needs to know.*

Mimi loved Joel. There was never a question or a doubt in her mind he had been anything less than honest with her. He made a stupid teenage mistake that could be forgiven. He betrayed his brother. That was tough to swallow, but she still would have stayed with him. But turning his back on an innocent child was harder to get past and deceiving her was unforgiveable. He wasn't here to tell his side of the story, but even if he was, she didn't know if his words would have any bearing. After all, if you lie before and after you marry somebody, what right do they have to ever win your trust back again?

"What is it you want to say to me, Austin?"

He inhaled and a let out a long, deep sigh. "This is so wrong of me, but…"

He paused once more. Mimi wanted to drag the words out of his mouth.

"I'd like you to stay for a while longer. I mean, you at least should take with you some nice memories rather than coming here to find out you've been deceived and breaking your wrist." He let out an awkward laugh.

Mimi's cheeks suddenly grew from cold to hot. Her stomach flipped. She felt something, although she couldn't quite identify if it was happiness or nervousness.

"For how much longer?" she asked.

"As long as you want to. I know you have a life to go back to—a job, your family—but, well, Jake likes having you around."

"And you? Do you like having me around?" she asked.

She watched his face flush. She had never seen him nervous. He tilted his head and fixed his gaze on her.

"I do."

There was an unspoken attraction between them. It had been born out of the most tragic and unexpected circumstance, but it was there.

CHAPTER 14

The weekend finally came. Austin took Mimi to a bar. It was filled with smiling faces and loud music. A few people curiously looked at the long-haired English girl Austin walked in with. Mimi couldn't remember the last time she went out and had fun. This was exactly the kind of joint she'd expected to find in Texas. The smell of stale beer hung in the air and her feet almost stuck to the worn floor. There was a pool table tucked in the corner and a jukebox playing old country classics. It looked like a big party that everybody was invited to.

"What can I get ya?" The barman yelled over the thumping music.

"Just an orange juice," Mimi shouted. The barman frowned and his forehead creased together like folds of paper.

"Orange juice and what? We like to give our customers a good time here. Now, what else can I get ya?"

Mimi smiled and decided to have something

stronger after all. She ordered a vodka and orange. As she took the first sip, the taste made her remember the night on her honeymoon, when she and Joel had spent the night drinking and dancing.

Just as quickly as her mind flashed back, she knocked back another swig. Tonight she was choosing not to remember. Just for one night, she wanted to be free of all the heavy baggage she had been carrying on her weak shoulders.

They took a seat on a stool and hung out at the edge of the bar. She heard an old Dolly Parton song on the jukebox. She remembered singing "Here You Come Again" in the back of her parents' old Vauxhall Caviller with Larna.

For a fleeting moment, she had an urge to dance and just be in the moment, but she stopped, reminding herself that she was with Austin, not Joel.

Austin bought her several more vodkas and oranges. The barman looked across and raised a glass to her. A large flat screen TV was above their heads. Mimi glanced up, watching heavyset American footballers thrash into each other.

"Do you play sports?" she asked.

"Used to. Back in high school, I played basketball."

"Ah, interesting. To be honest, I can't see you playing. You're not quite tall enough," she teased.

"I like my horses. I'm a cowboy at heart." He winked at her.

A slow song came on and couples moved their bodies to embrace the harmony of the music.

Austin stood up and held his hand out to Mimi.

"Shall we?" he asked.

"I want to, but…"

She left him hanging for a moment longer than he could handle.

"It's fine. I need some air." He turned his back to her and left the bar.

Mimi put her head in her hands and then jumped to her feet to follow him. She pushed herself through the sweaty crowd, trying to find her way to the exit.

When she stepped outside, the cool air hit her in the face and suddenly she realised how drunk she was. She tried to steady her feet. Her eyes frantically searched for Austin, but she couldn't see him among the smokers gathering round, laughing loudly and fooling around.

She walked to the parking lot and stumbled to his truck, but he wasn't there. She leaned against the shiny black exterior and suddenly felt nauseous. She looked up into the night's sky. There were a thousand twinkling stars above her.

Where are you, Joel?

Although she knew he had deceived her, she couldn't help but feel guilty for being here like this with his brother. This journey had all started so she could feel closer to her husband. Maybe it was the booze, or maybe she was finally seeing things clearly for the first time, but she had never felt as sad as she did in that very moment. It dawned on her that Joel was really gone. Finding out about Jake and feeling so angry at her husband had distracted her from accepting that he was gone. Somebody in a foreign land had captured, possibly tortured, her husband and then taken him to his death.

A sound escaped from her mouth that she didn't quite recognise. She turned and let her body fall to the arch of the wheel and sobbed.

A few moments later, the shadow of a man stood over her.

"Ma'am, are you all right?"

Mimi looked up at an older man, his wife standing a few feet away from him, their faces full of concern.

Mimi quickly wiped her face with her sleeve and cleared her throat. "I'm fine," she managed to say.

"You sure don't look okay, miss. Has somebody hurt you?" The man reached his hand out to her and she reluctantly took it.

Austin walked into view. The couple turned to look at him in an accusing way.

"Mimi?" Austin said.

"I'm sorry. I'm all right. Just having a moment," she slurred.

"Let's get you in the car."

"Why is she upset?" the woman demanded.

Austin felt irritated at the couple hanging around. However, he kept calm and turned to face them. "Her husband was killed in Afghanistan."

He left them gobsmacked, steadied Mimi to her feet, and put her in the car, leaning across her and strapping her in safely. He turned the key and the truck roared to life.

"Can you drive?" Mimi asked, her eyes half closed.

"I didn't drink, remember?"

"Ahh, yes…I remember." Her head slumped forward and she fell asleep.

Rain lashed against the windscreen as the truck sped along the road. Austin looked at Mimi. He knew he was wrong for having feelings for her. He knew that nothing good could come of this, but he still found it difficult to let go of her. There was a fire inside of her burning. He wanted to help, but he was jealous of his brother. Even in death, Joel had won the heart of another girl Austin was falling in love with.

They finally pulled up to the ranch. Austin gently tapped Mimi's shoulder. She stirred but she didn't wake. Her body was clammy and intoxicated. Without thinking, he unclipped her seatbelt and slipped his hands underneath her slender body. He carried her up to the guest room and gently lay her on the bed.

He watched her sleep, wishing he could slide in next to her and pull his body into hers. He placed the duvet cover over her. Now she was warm and safe. He began to tiptoe out of the room when he heard her call him.

"Please stay with me. I don't want to be alone tonight."

It took every ounce of his self-control not to give into her. He wanted her so much, but he knew she was drunk and he knew she was grieving, so he pretended he didn't hear her and closed the door behind him.

***

When morning broke, Mimi found Austin sipping a cup of steaming coffee in the kitchen, his eyes fixed on a newspaper. He didn't mention last night. He told her he'd like her to help with some paperwork since his assistant called in sick. She protested, saying she wouldn't be helpful with only one hand to do the job.

"One hand is better than no hands. It would really help me out. Will you?"

She resisted, but he asked again till she couldn't refuse. They went into the office and Austin pulled out a ton of files and threw them out on the floor.

"Thank you for last night," she said, breaking the silence.

"No problem."

"I sort of just landed on your doorstep and piled all my problems on you. Then you have to carry this drunk mess to bed. I'm not usually like that."

"Mimi, I get it. You've been through a lot and it makes sense for you to be here. Stay as long as you need to." He tried to sound cool and laid back, but the words got stuck in his throat.

"Were you tempted?" she asked, her head titled to the side.

"Excuse me?" He was surprised by her directness.

"Last night, when I asked you to stay with me. Were you tempted?"

"I didn't…"

"Cut the bullshit, Austin. I know you heard me. I was drunk, but I'm not stupid."

"Yes," he answered curtly.

"So why didn't you?"

"Because you're my dead brother's wife. Because you were drunk. Because you were desperate."

"Desperate? Excuse me?"

"I mean, you were upset, so you needed comfort," he said, trying to stop the explosion that was about to erupt in the room. "Let's get out of here. This can all wait."

He took her by the hand and pulled her toward the front door, grabbing his keys along the way.

She moved with him, stony faced.

How dare he call me desperate?

Austin walked to the barn. The horses were grazing on hay, looking unfazed as they went in. Troy's ears perked up when they walked toward him.

"I can't ride, if that's what you're thinking."

"I know you can't, but I can."

He opened the door and Troy waltzed out. He had a confident stance and looked like he owned the place, but he still respected Austin as his owner. She ran her hand over his sleek, shiny coat.

"He's a confident chap," she said. His legs were steady and solid and built to run into miles of open land. She was sure that he was capable of going long distances.

"Troy is a left-brainer," Austin said.

"Is this some secret horse whisperer language you're talking about?"

Austin smiled. She liked it when he smiled. His face seemed kind, less uptight, and less responsible.

"Yeah, well…sort of. You see, left-brainers are confident, like you already observed. He's also calm and brave and will not be easily spooked. There was a situation where a herd of cattle had grouped up into the south side of the ranch. They had young, so they can be fiercely protective and aggressive, but Troy walked past them with absolute bravery. The fact he was calm put the cattle at ease. They knew he was no threat. He's my top guy."

"I guess you are hoping I'll ride on the back with you?" She raised her eyebrows.

"You just need to wrap your arms around me. We'll take it slow and only go a couple of miles out. You'll be fine, I promise."

"Don't make promises you can't keep." She fixed her dark eyes on him and, for once, he didn't avoid her gaze.

"I promise."

Mimi had trouble with promises. After all, Joel had *promised* that he was coming home, and yet here she was, a young widow, away from her family and friends, staying with his estranged brother and feeling things that she shouldn't.

The previous night had been a close call. If Austin had climbed into bed with her, she was almost certain that she would have acted upon her desires. In a way, she felt like she was cheating on Joel. He'd not been long dead, and yet here she was, crushing on his brother. Mimi felt angry at herself, but that alone was not enough to resist the pull she had toward Austin.

As they left the barn, the sun burned away the last remaining clouds in the sky. They walked slowly together, Austin holding Troy's rein. Mimi started to feel the effects from her hangover kicking in. Her eyes burned and her body felt like it had been through a vigorous work out. Her mouth was dry and she felt like cognitive fuzziness was taking over her brain.

She thought twice before getting on the back of the horse. The first time had resulted in a broken wrist, but this time her hangover made her feel slightly less enthusiastic about climbing back on.

"Look, if you really don't wanna ride, you can go back to bed and sleep longer, if that's what you feel you need."

Suddenly she thought about going into the guest room, where she would be alone with nothing but her thoughts for company. She knew it would do her no good, mooching around and feeling sorry for herself. She also knew her mind was not a safe companion to be alone with right now. She had too many crazy thoughts that left her questioning too many things in her life.

"I want to come," she said with conviction.

Her heart pounded as she mounted Troy and her breath escaped her. She knew that Austin promised he would look after her, but that didn't stop the nervousness from pulsating through her trembling body.

"Remember what I said. Wrap your arms around me tight and don't let go. I will not let you fall, I promise."

Mimi squeezed Austin tight as Troy started to move. Austin was fully aware of her touch and he liked that there was the excuse of the horse to keep her tanned, slender arms securely around his chest.

When they finally reached the same meadow where Mimi had broken her wrist, Austin carefully dismounted and slowly helped Mimi down to safety.

"Back here again. What could happen to me this time?" she teased.

"Hopefully, you'll just go back with a good memory and no broken bones."

Mimi removed her boots and felt the soft green grass under her feet. She marvelled at the bluebells stretching out into the horizon and the sun tinting the landscape in gold. She heard the flow of the nearby water once more and felt the calmness of the atmosphere. It soaked through her. This was a place where she felt. It gave her mind the quiet it had been begging for.

"Listen, Mimi, I'm sorry for everything. I know you've probably had the worst time in your entire life and, well, I guess I've made things far more complicated than they should be."

"Austin, to be honest, I feel like I am the one who has turned your world upside down."

He held her eye and said, "I have feelings for you, but that's wrong of me. Shit, you are my dead brother's wife."

"I have feelings for you too," she said quietly.

Austin moved toward her so their faces were only inches apart. Her heart felt like it was stuck in her throat. She felt giddy and nervous. She remembered when he took her in his arms the previous night. She kept her eyes closed, pretending she was out of it so she would feel the strength of his arms holding her, touching her. When he put her to bed, her mind was racing. She didn't want to allow herself to feel this, but somehow, she was unable to stop it.

"When you turned up on the ranch, I was completely taken by you." His voice was low and intense as he continued. "I sent you away because I needed to protect Jake and because I was impossibly attracted to you." He suddenly stepped back, putting distance between them once more.

"Austin, all of this…it's crazy, every bit of it. I'm not going to lie to you. I miss Joel so much." Her eyes filled with tears, and she lowered her head. "But you…when I first saw you, I was in complete awe, mostly because you and your brother look like twins. As I have gotten to know you and since I found out about Jake, something has changed. You and Joel even sound so similar, but as people, you are so different."

Austin was anxious and felt desperate to kiss her, but here, in this moment, it was every shade of wrong. He turned away from her. Avoiding her gaze made it easier to resist the temptation.

Mimi bit the bottom of her lip and thought of Joel. She was having flashbacks—the first time they met, the day they got married, their honeymoon, and the moment she learned he'd been killed. And then her mind spun back to finding out her husband had a child, a little boy he had kept hidden from her.

Without thinking any further, she put her hand on Austin's shoulder and turned him back to face her.

"I know this is all insane, every last bit of it, but I can't help what I feel, and I know you can't either."

"Mimi…I can't."

Without allowing him to finish, she pressed her body against him. He knew this shouldn't happen, but when she gently touched his lips with hers, he gave in and held her tight. He lifted her off her feet and pulled her gently to the ground, careful not to knock her broken wrist. He lay on top of her, and she ran her hand under his shirt.

He pulled away for a brief moment and looked at her. "Are you sure this is what you want?" he whispered.

"Yes, I'm sure."

CHAPTER 15

"I miss you, darling."

"I miss you too," Mimi said into the receiver.

Hearing her mother's voice reminded her of home and gave her comfort. She thought of her family sitting in the cosy living room back in North London watching their evening marathon of trashy soaps.

Mimi sat crossed legged on the arm of the sofa in the living area. The room was hardly ever used, although she couldn't understand why, as it had the best view in the entire house, overlooking the green acreage and distant woodland.

"When are you coming home?" her mother asked.

I am home, she thought to herself.

"I'm not sure. I had a little accident."

"An accident! What accident? Are you all right?" her mother shrieked.

"Ma, relax. I'm fine. It is just a broken wrist."

She imagined her mother wide-eyed and worried, thinking the absolute worst, which is why, when minor incidents happen, Mimi had learned not to overshare. If she had so much as a scratch when she was younger, her mother would rush her off to the doctor.

They spoke for over thirty minutes, her mother pressing her for details on her mystery brother-in-law. She gave her enough information not to arouse suspicion, but not too much that she would start prying and asking too many questions.

She didn't tell her about Jake. She didn't know how. Her mother loved Joel, but she never quite trusted him and this would give her the adequate amount of fuel for her to burst into her *I told you so* rants. That was something Mimi fiercely wanted to avoid.

"Do you like it out there?"

"Ma, I love it. And I think you would too."

"Well, we have the same tastes. Your cat is driving your sister crazy. He keeps howling all through the night."

Mimi giggled.

"Cats don't howl, Ma. Dogs do that."

"Well, that's what she calls it. I think he misses you."

"I miss him too."

Just as she rounded off the conversation and clicked the button to end the call, she heard the creak of the door. Jake came in holding a book open on a page about castles.

"Do you live in one of these in England?" he asked, holding the book an inch under her nose.

"Not quite."

"I have to write a paper for my homework about

castles and I thought, since you are from England, maybe you could help me?"

Mimi took a seat and patted the empty space next to her, inviting Jake to sit down. She took the castle book from him and held it open on her lap.

"What exactly do you have to write about?" she asked.

"I just told you. About castles."

She looked at Jake, confused. "Yes, but what about them?"

"I don't know. I wasn't listening."

"Ah, I see."

"Please don't tell my dad. He'll get so mad at me."

"The problem is, Jake, without knowing what your task is, we won't be able to complete it."

He looked down to the floor. Mimi could tell that he was disappointed and felt guilty.

"Don't you have a friend you could call to ask?"

"Brody will know," he said, suddenly looking hopeful.

"Well, all right. Problem solved!"

Jake grabbed the phone out of Mimi's hand and started to run out of the room.

Mimi called after him. "Jake, in the future, you need to start paying attention in class."

"I will!" he promised and then disappeared.

It had been a few hours since their lips touched. Mimi wondered what it all meant. She felt overcome with guilt, and her stomach was twisted up in tight knots. It had been less than eight weeks since she was told that her husband was dead and already she had slept with somebody else. But not just anybody—her brother-in-law.

She wondered how Austin felt about her. Was he just out for revenge? Was she the nail in Joel's coffin? Mimi didn't know how to be patient. When she was younger, she hated waiting for the results of exams. She'd sit at the window waiting for the postman to drop a brown envelope through the letterbox. When valuable documents finally did arrive, she'd spare no time ripping the paper apart to read her fate. Waiting for Austin to come and talk to her felt no different. When he didn't, she knew she had to go to him.

She walked up the stairs and heard the sound of water gushing. She could see the thick steam pouring out from underneath the door. In a moment of madness, she considered sitting at the end of his bed, waiting for him to emerge from the bathroom, but she quickly came to her senses and decided to wait in the guest room.

Mimi took a moment to look out of the window. The sun was setting, symbolizing the end of the day. She opened the door that led out onto the balcony. She took a deep breath and allowed herself to cry.

She thought about Joel and then about Austin. The betrayal happened when they were both so young. They had been teenagers. The past few weeks had been a whirlwind of disaster, and although being with Austin had awoken something inside her, she knew, deep down, that no good could come of it. She was just another layer on an already messed up situation that had pulled the brothers apart.

Mimi tried to dismiss the feelings that kept rising to the surface. Austin felt like home to her as much as the ranch did. There was something about him that gave her a sense of feeling safe.

She started asking herself questions that made her uncomfortable. *If Joel had been alive and she had met Austin, would she still have felt that unexplainable pull toward him?* She had used Joel's deceit as permission to give herself to Austin.

"Mimi, everything okay?" she heard Austin ask, his voice deep and smooth, like bourbon. He moved up behind her, gently putting his hand on the small of her back. She was desperate to turn around and kiss him again, but she kept her gaze fixed on the scenery ahead.

"I'm fine," she firmly answered. Her grip tightened on the balcony ledge.

"Mimi, we need to talk."

Her heart quickened. She knew what he was about to say and she wanted to freeze time so she could stop the crash before the collision.

Of course he wants me to leave, the doubt in her head told her.

She swallowed hard and turned to him, bracing herself for the fall. She fully expected his face to be splashed with regret, but she was surprised to see his lips turned up, giving her a half smile. She had no idea what this meant.

"I think I'm in love with you."

For a brief moment, Mimi couldn't feel her legs. She steadied herself and bit her bottom lip just as she always did when she was nervous. Part of her felt giddy. Her heart swelled with a feeling that was close to happiness, but there was another part of her that was doubtful.

How could he be in love with her? He didn't know her and had no idea what kind of a person she truly was. All he had seen was a grieving widow on a quest to find out answers but instead uncovered unexpected secrets about her dead husband.

She met his gaze, unable to speak. She hadn't expected any of this.

"I thought you should know," he said and turned to leave.

"Don't go," she called after him. She had no idea what she was thinking, no idea what she was feeling, but she was certain she didn't want him to walk away from her.

Tears once again started prickling in her dark eyes.

"I don't know what it is I feel for you, but…"

"Just tell me that what happened today isn't because I am a replica of Joel."

"God no. It's got nothing to do with Joel." She paused. "At least not like you think."

He touched her cheek. She reached for him and kissed him. Her head was telling her to back the hell away, but the intimate warmth of his mouth was too inviting.

Their kiss was slow, not hungry like it was at the meadow. It meant something. For the first time, her mind wasn't with Joel. It was with Austin. The guilt seemed to slide away as she allowed Austin's hands to touch her. Her body trembled as she opened her eyes to find him looking at her intensely.

Just as he took her back into the room and lay

her on the bed, he was startled by the sound of footsteps. He quickly jolted his body backwards and gave Mimi his hand to steady her to her feet. She quickly ran her fingers through her hair and used her palm to straighten out her t-shirt. There was a gentle tap at the door.

"Yup, come in," Austin said, clearing his throat. A guilty grin was across his face. He avoided looking at Mimi so he wouldn't burst into laughter.

"Daddy," Jake said, holding out the phone. "There's a man asking for you. He says it's about somebody called Joel Marcus. Do you have a brother, Daddy?"

Mimi's face drained of colour as she watched Austin take the phone out of Jake's hand. He took it with caution, like it was going to explode.

"Can you go and get me my wallet? It's down in the kitchen."

Jake gave his father a suspicious look, but followed his request and left the room. When Austin heard Jake thudding down the stairs, he took the phone to his ear.

"Austin Marcus speaking."

Mimi stood facing him, straining to hear the muffled sound of the deep official voice at the other end of the phone.

CHAPTER 16

Joel
Afghanistan

It was the first time he had seen light in days. His eyes tried to adjust, but the sweat streaming down his face made it difficult to focus. He felt like his entire body had been crushed. There wasn't a single part of him that didn't hurt. He could hardly move. He'd been offered a cup of water but was reluctant to take it in case it was poison. Somewhere, a voice of reason told him *If they wanted you dead, they would have done it by now.*

He'd lost concept of time. He was a prisoner at the mercy of the faceless people around him. He had heard their voices a thousand times, but he had no idea what they were saying. They kept him alive, but he had no idea why. His troops were dead. He'd seen their bodies lying still and cold.

Does anybody know I'm here? Are they looking for me?

A wave of panic flooded over him. There was an

older man, at least he thought he was older, with only his hands to judge from. His fingers looked like bent crooked branches, twisted and distorted. The old man had tried to wash his wounds and give him what little aid was available. No matter what language barrier stood between people, such an act of humanity was universal and understood.

He tried to remember the last moments before it all went black. There had been an explosion. He had fallen. He had seen his best friend lying dead in front of him, blood pouring out from his head from the fatal bullet that ended his life.

The stench of must and sweat hung in the air. He was huddled onto a small wooden bench with nothing but an old sheet for a pillow.

"You awake?" the old man said in broken English. He studied him as the old man removed the veil covering his face. His beard covered his chin and just a few wisps above his lip, his skin was surprisingly smooth. His dark hair, which was streaked with grey, fell past his ears.

"Where am I?"

"You are somewhere safe. No harm will come to you here."

He looked across to the far corner and saw his jacket strewn on the floor like an old rag, stained with blood. He saw a photograph curled at the edges, sticking out from his inside pocket.

"What is your name?" The old man asked. "Your real name."

"Sergeant Joel Marcus, United States Marine Corps. Now, you mind telling me where the fuck I am?"

"Safe, you are safe."

"That tells me shit. Just tell me what the fuck you want?"

Joel felt completely exposed. The mission had gone seriously wrong. He could feel sweat dripping down his back, soaking through his shirt. He tried to act calm, not to show the fear inside him, but his heart was beating fast and he had to blink the perspiration out of his eyes.

All his years of training had prepared him for moments like this, moments where he would be in the clutches of the enemy. He was a vessel of information, but he knew he could even fool a lie detector test if he needed to. At this very moment, he couldn't allow the nervousness to overtake him. That's how mistakes were made. There was simply no margin for error. He needed to focus, and he needed to find out exactly where he was and work out his escape plan, but without comms and weapons, he knew his chances were slim.

Although his mind was weary, he was processing a thousand thoughts a second.

He tried to ignore the pain. His battered and broken body was failing him. He scanned the shack he was sitting in. It was square, and there was no telling what world existed outside the rough walls around him. As the old man moved toward Joel, he instinctively slid into position to cover himself.

The old man stepped back. "I mean no harm to you," he said, his voice gentle, but Joel didn't trust it. *How could he mean no harm*?

The first thought he had was that he had been captured, that he was a hostage. If that were the case, he knew he was screwed. The American Government never negotiated with terrorists.

His second thought was Mimi. He had made her a promise that he would come back to her. He thought of her anxiously waiting for news, no doubt sitting in the comfort of her childhood home with her parents reassuring her that he was alive. He had never ever intended to break a single promise to her. She was his every motivation to keep going, to get out alive.

The old man reached into Joel's jacket pocket. He looked at the photograph of Mimi.

For a second, Joel felt his anger rise to the surface. It was only a photo, but he didn't want his enemy looking at his wife. Dread washed over him as he suddenly thought that somehow they had gotten to her. He could feel his breath quicken, his shoulders tense. He wanted to get up and rip the picture out of the old man's hand.

"This is your wife?"

Through gritted teeth, Joel nodded. He was surprised when the old man respectfully handed Joel the photo.

Ever since September 11, Joel had pictured himself out in Afghanistan. He'd imagined targeting Al Qaeda and Taliban commanders. He wanted to be the hero who took out the enemies that declared an unexpected war on America that day.

Throughout his warfare training, his only focus was to catch the enemy and kill. Never did he imagine he would be at the mercy of the enemy, fearing for his life. It was him and him alone. None of his other troops were here to have his back.

Unlike his target, he hadn't gone in sacrificing himself to die by blowing himself up into a million pieces. He knew death was probable but wanted to get out of this war alive. The Marines had opened themselves up. Nothing else mattered but success. However, when they had families, wives waiting at home, the stakes were so much higher. It mattered to get out alive and not to end up as another name engraved on a tombstone with stars and stripes waving in the wind above it.

"If I set you free now, you are in grave danger. Your people have killed our leader." The old man had his back to Joel, and then he turned to him. "You are on a list and they will want your head. They will stop at nothing. To them, you are not a person. You are an American, and so they will stop at nothing to get you. The pain you feel in your body now is nothing compared to what you will feel if they get you. Understand…leaving now will kill you."

Joel knew that Washington had approved the mission to assault the compound where Bin Laden was believed to be.

Did they succeed? Did they do it? Joel thought.

"Bin Laden?"

"Yes. He's dead."

Joel swallowed hard. For the past ten years, thousands of man hours, intelligence, and bloodshed had been spent gearing up to take out the mastermind behind the 9/11 attacks, and now that day in history had finally been marked.

"What do you want with me?" Joel asked, his head in his hands.

"Nothing. I want to bring you to safety."

"And what is it that you want in return?"

"Nothing…I want nothing from you."

"Bullshit. You all want something. What's the price on my head?"

"You believe that we are all bad. It is not so. Some of us are not the radical extremists that you think we are. Some of us want peace. There has been so much death. It has killed so many men, ruined so many lives. If I can spare you, then I have played my part in making peace happen."

"What is your name?" Joel asked.

"Abdul." He paused for a moment. "Please ask nothing more about me, for I cannot tell you. It is best you know very little about me. And from now on, I will ask nothing more about you."

"Just tell me. Are you one of them?" Joel asked.

"One of who?"

"Taliban."

"No, I am not," Abdul responded. "Now please, I can tell you no more."

Abdul handed Joel a cup of water, but this time, Joel put the cup to his lips and allowed the lukewarm liquid to slide down his throat.

After a few moments, Joel removed his trousers, writhing in pain. The fabric stuck to the blood congealing on his inner thigh. He could tell by the smell that his wound was infected. He was in desperate need of antibiotics. If a terrorist wasn't going to kill him, he knew there was a high probability that septicemia would.

He lay his head down and felt his breathing become rapid. Time was not something that he had much of. Abdul sat over Joel's body, filled a bowl with water, and used a cloth to wipe the infected area clean. Joel bit into his fist and tried to pace himself, mind over matter, thrashing through the barrier of pain.

Without warning, he felt a sharp blow of a fist connect with his face. It was the last thing he felt before passing out.

***

When Joel opened his eyes, the orange glow of light coming from the oil burner in the corner of the room was the first thing he saw. His head pulsed as if it had a heartbeat of its own. He tried to understand why Abdul knocked him out, and then he realized he did it to block out the pain while treating his wound.

He thought of Mimi and wondered where she was. He wanted to be with her, holding her. He thought of the time they spent an entire weekend in bed, back in rainy England. They'd eaten junk food and watched DVDs. As he lay down in this foreign place, everything felt like a lifetime ago. He thought of the rest of his platoon and asked himself why he was the only survivor. Did it mean something?

The military had been Joel's life and he had dedicated himself to it in ways that led him to believe he would be nothing without it, but all of a sudden he was left with a nagging feeling that his country had left him for dead without looking for him. If that were true, he wondered why he had spent his blood, sweat, and tears serving the Corps without them ensuring he was brought home to safety. Then he tried to think of the other possibility—they were searching for him but they had to act with extreme caution and vigilance when operating a rescue mission.

His mind was a mess, and for the first time, he was emotional. When a man's life is in jeopardy, he is forced to think about the things that truly matter to him. For Joel, it was to keep his promise to his wife and return home to her. He thought about the fact he hadn't been totally honest with her, but he swore if he could just get back, he would fix everything. He would be a better man. He would be the best husband he could be.

Joel examined his leg. The wound was clean and wrapped in an off-white cloth. Fresh blood had soaked through, which was a good sign. At least the earlier signs of infection appeared to have subsided.

He looked down at his feet, blistered and battered. One of his toenails had completely blackened. He gently bent over and touched it, surprised he could bend his body that far. His left arm had swollen to the size of a balloon that looked like it was going to pop any second. Abdul had taken care of that too, as it was tightly wrapped to keep it in a cast-like form.

If Abdul really was the enemy, Joel was sure that he would have taken some sort of action by now, dropped some hint, some clue that he was not the Good Samaritan he claimed to be.

Joel had no choice but to trust Abdul because right now, Abdul was the only person on the planet who could keep him alive. Even if the Corps had issued a rescue operation, his body needed aid.

Joel could hear the sound of footsteps. His body tensed.

When Abdul appeared, he almost cried with relief.

"I bring you food. You must be starving."

Abdul handed Joel a bowl of rice, which Joel snatched. He devoured the food like a ravenous dog. With every bite, he was filling his hand with more.

Abdul respectfully averted his gaze from Joel. The mouthfuls of food took off the edge of his starvation. Joel began to slow down his food intake, taking the time to chew his food.

"How long have I been here?"

"A few days. After your men invaded and you were left for dead, I brought you here. If I am honest, I didn't think you would survive, but God must have a plan for you. I thought the fever was going to take your life, but you pulled through the worst of it."

"Are they looking for me?"

"I have no knowledge of your country. It's possible, and if they come, I'll hand you to them, of course, and you will be free."

"And if they don't? How the hell am I getting out of here?"

Joel was met with silence. He searched Abdul's face for answers, hoping he had a plan.

"For now, my focus is to keep you alive. Beyond that, I cannot give you the answers you seek right now."

Maybe Abdul wasn't keeping him a prisoner, but the harsh reality showed that he still was a prisoner in a foreign land.

"Can you at least tell me where I am?" Joel asked.

"You are in the mountains approximately forty miles east of where you invaded. If your people are looking for you, they will find you."

"Are you going to give them some sort of fucking clue? With all due respect, if they don't know you took me, how the hell are they going to think to look here?"

"You ask too many questions."

"So you have a plan? I mean, please tell me you have some sort of fucking plan."

Abdul turned away and began pouring a steaming cup of hot water into a cup. He handed it to Joel and didn't utter another word.

CHAPTER 17

Kanchana
London

In the weeks since Mimi had been away, and with the news of her son-in-law's death, Kanchana held herself together by keeping busy. That, and secretly harassing the American Embassy for information. This was all done without her daughter having any knowledge Kanchana was working relentlessly behind the scenes to provide answers that might bring Mimi peace.

Kanchana knew unless her daughter was given closure, Mimi would forever be chasing shadows in Texas, trying to feel close to Joel's ghost in a place that was splattered with his memories, even if she had not shared these memories with him.

Kanchana wanted her daughter back home. Mimi was a grown woman, but she still felt the urgent motherly responsibility to make everything right in her life for her.

So she kept trying. She kept doing.

Simon warned her she was meddling again. He told her she should let their daughter find her own path. Mimi had always been a feisty, independent, free-spirited girl. Whilst Kanchana thought this was the best quality in her daughter, she also thought it was her worst.

She'd been surprised when her eldest, Larna, had moved to Yorkshire in pursuit of her career. Larna had always been Kanchana's dependent sidekick, the daughter in need of her mother's approval and support. Out of both of her daughters, she never expected Mimi would be the one living minutes from her, just two roads and one left turn apart. Now that she was thousands of miles away, Kanchana felt her heart breaking with every day Mimi was gone. It was as if Joel's death had taken Mimi too.

Night after night, Kanchana had stayed up with her daughter as she cried herself to sleep. She'd wiped her wet cheeks, thinking she could make it all better for her, just as she had always done, but none of her old tricks had worked one bit. In fact, the opposite was true.

Kanchana couldn't cut through the layers of grief that Mimi was suffering. So, when Meg came to her and said that she was taking Mimi to Texas, Kanchana had smiled brightly and told her what a good idea it was, but inside she felt she hadn't been the mother she wanted to be by not being able to put Mimi back together.

On the morning that Mimi left for the airport, Kanchana told herself that she'd be back soon, but when the days turned into a couple of weeks, and then those weeks turned into over a month without so much as a hint of coming home, she started to worry.

Deep down, she had a hunch something wasn't right. The morning she sat opposite the two officials at the Embassy, she didn't believe they had been completely transparent. After Mimi was thirty thousand feet off the ground, travelling through the air across the Atlantic Ocean, Kanchana started making calls, and then emails, and then more calls.

Kanchana confided in Simon, saying, "Something about Joel's death just isn't quite right."

"War is never right," her husband responded. "People die. Families get torn apart."

They sat in the safety of their living room, Kanchana cradling a cup of peppermint tea in her hand. Simon sat in his armchair, the one he had dubbed his reading chair, but he never actually did any reading in it. It was his nodding-off-in-front-of-the-TV chair.

It saddened Kanchana to think her daughter would never be a mother to Joel's child. She had dreams for both of her daughters, but somewhere along the line, those dreams had become tangled.

"Without a body, how do they know he's dead, Simon?" she asked, leaning toward her husband. When she was on to something, her dark eyes turned almost black, her cheeks would redden, and her bottom lip would pout.

"They know. My God, Kanchana, they know so much more than they tell us. These guys are the crème de la crème at what they do!"

"Exactly, which is why I don't believe that Joel is dead."

Simon looked at her with an expression that asked for an explanation.

"Well, anybody who avoids telling me an entire account of what happened, or at least what they believed happened, must be hiding something," Kanchana said.

"Have you mentioned this to Mimi?"

"No. I don't want to give her false hope."

"So, love, you're not convinced either way?"

Kanchana frowned at that. She hated it when her husband challenged her beliefs. Out of all the years they had been married, Kanchana had lived her life by following her hunches, and on the rare occasion she hadn't, something had gone wrong and she'd scolded herself for not trusting her instincts.

"Something is not sitting well with me, Simon. I feel it!"

She saw how easy it was to get her husband on her side, and she felt a rush of love for him. She wanted to kiss him. No matter what reservations he had, at the end of the day, Simon was always playing on her team.

"We will start making calls. Just don't get upset if we hit a wall with it."

Deep down, Kanchana knew she would find something. She had always been a determined woman, especially when it came to her children.

"Thank you," she said.

Tears pooled in her eyes. She promised herself she would find out the truth because Mimi deserved to know. Even if the truth hurt, at least she could heal.

Kanchana remembered the day that Mimi brought the tall, dark, handsome American to her door. He looked like one of those models who should be standing at the doors at Abercrombie & Fitch, but she also knew he was trouble. She didn't know how and she didn't know when, but she knew her daughter was going to be crying many tears over this man. Kanchana had let him in anyway because she had never seen Mimi's eyes light up like fire, at least not until Joel had come into her life.

***

Mimi

Mimi woke to the hazy morning sunshine. She hadn't slept very long, perhaps only three hours. She wondered how she'd fallen asleep at all.

For a moment, she lay still. Her stomach was in knots. As soon as she tried to remember why, it all came flooding back to her, making her heart drop. This is the news she had been dying to hear. She had prayed for it. She had willed it. But now, everything had changed. She no longer belonged to just him—at least her heart didn't. She wanted to cry, but didn't have the tears. Guilt caught in her throat and she couldn't find the words to speak. When she got out of bed, the tension in her muscles sent tremors through her body.

There had been so many times when she had reached into the darkest depths of her mind and asked herself how Joel had been killed. Was it quick, or was it a slow painful death?

Her vivid dreams had shown Joel face down in dirt with blood pouring from an open wound. Whenever she reached for him, he had suddenly lifted his head, only when his face turned to her, it wasn't Joel. It was a face she'd never seen before. Now, she had received confirmation that Joel was alive, but too many things had changed. She had discovered Joel was dishonest to her, she had slept with his estranged brother, and she had fallen in love with another man.

After the call the previous night, Austin had left the room.

He didn't say anything. She stood, paralyzed by shock, and then she let out a cry that sounded inhuman. She threw herself onto the already creased duvet. She could smell Austin's aftershave clinging onto the fabric, a stark reminder that she had already given half of her heart away and now the man she promised it to was coming back to her, expecting it to be untouched by another.

As she lay on the bed, staring into space, she felt the vibration of the phone persistently shaking. She fumbled around, looking for it. When she took it into her hand, she saw that she had seventeen missed calls from her parents and one text message.

Kanchana: Mimi, call us immediately. God has answered your prayers.

Kanchana: They found Joel…He's alive, Mimi, he's alive!

The American Embassy had tried to contact Mimi back at her flat in England, but when they failed, they reached her parents. Her mother had been the one to receive the information. She'd obviously told the embassy that Mimi was in Texas with Joel's brother and they'd called.

Mimi still loved Joel, despite his hidden secret.

She felt a mix of emotions—lost but no longer empty, relieved but incredibly fearful.

CHAPTER 18

Austin

When Austin stepped outside into the warm sunshine, a bird soared above in the perfectly blue sky, the feathers on its wings struck by the mid-morning sun.

He found Mimi standing by the fence, looking out to the land where the horses grazed peacefully. It was a contrast to the storm raging in Mimi.

Austin approached her with caution, careful not to get too close. She looked so fragile and beaten down by emotion he thought the touch of his hand would be enough to make her shatter into a million tiny pieces.

"Are you okay?" His face was twisted. His green eyes were full of despair.

She nodded quickly, but as she took a breath, tears streamed down her face.

He wanted to take her in his arms, to tell her everything would be all right. But instead he said, "I want you to leave."

She took the palm of her hand and wiped her face. "You don't mean that." She paused and looked at him. "Do you?"

"Yes. This is so fucked up, Mimi. You don't belong to me. You belong to him."

"But…God, Austin, I don't know what the hell I'm thinking or feeling."

"I don't care. The truth is I got caught up in everything with you. I felt sorry for you. I pitied you."

"Austin, stop!" she cried. "You don't mean that."

"Mimi, I do. The truth is you were my final up-yours to my dear brother."

"You're lying."

He took his hands out of his jean pockets, placed them on her sunken shoulders, and looked firmly into her eyes. "No, I'm not. Everything I told you about loving you was a lie. And this, what we had, was nothing but revenge. Joel played it well, the son of a bitch. He even cheated death. Now get your goddamn bags packed and get the hell out of my life."

She jolted back, falling out of his grip.

Austin stood in silence after the hard slap connected across his left check. It caught his lip, making it bleed. She turned on her heel and ran away, her long hair flowing in the breeze behind her.

He stood there for a second, but it seemed like an hour. He walked a little, and then for the first time in his adult life, he cried.

When Mimi reached the house, she was panting and out of breath. Her head and her heart were at war with one another. She dashed up the winding staircase, taking two steps at a time. When she reached the guest room, she opened the drawer next to the bed and pulled out her journal filled with her letters to Joel. She tore out the pages and slammed the book against the wall. She got her phone and furiously typed a message to her mother:

Mimi: Where is he?

Wherever he was, she knew she needed to be there. Her life as she knew it was in pieces. She didn't even recognise who she was anymore. The Mimi she knew herself to be would have never rushed into another relationship, let alone with her husband's brother. Maybe, just maybe, Austin was telling the truth. She had been nothing but *revenge,* the last hurrah.

She tried to pull her heavy suitcase out of the fitted wardrobe. It was wedged in, so she had to keep pulling it back and forth 'till it eventually came free. She grabbed her clothes off the rail, throwing them into the empty case. She had no idea where she was going. She'd figure that out when she was behind the wheel of the car.

When she finally cleared out the room, she checked everything twice to make sure there would be no trace of her ever being there.

She dragged the suitcase down the steps. It made a loud clunk with every movement. When she finally opened the front door, she made a promise to herself that she wouldn't look back.

A droplet of rain landed on her forehead,

followed by another and then another. By the time she reached the rental car, she was soaked to the bone.

She sat in the car and let out an angry scream, thumping the steering wheel. She reversed over the stones, leaving that already familiar crackle behind, but for the last time.

As she drove and built up speed, the lashing of the rain fell hard across the windscreen, the tires crashing through the puddles, sounding like waves in the ocean.

Her phone vibrated on her lap. She looked down to see a text message from her mother:

> ***Kanchana: Call me, Mimi. We need to talk. I love you!***

When she averted her eyes back to the road, the headlights of a truck blinded her vision. She heard a loud monstrous honk, followed by screeching tires, and then the sound of metal crunching. It was only when the car started to roll that she realised she was the one who had been hit.

CHAPTER 19

Austin

The doorbell rang several times followed by a hard knock at the door. Through the small pane of glass, he could see the flashing of blue and red lights. His mouth turned dry, making it difficult to swallow. When cops show up at the front door, it's never a good thing.

"Austin Marcus?" The sheriff asked.

"Yes."

Jake came into the room and asked, "Dad, what's wrong?"

The sheriff removed his hat, revealing his receding hair line.

"Can you confirm that a Mimi Marcus has been staying at your property?"

"Yes, why?"

"How are you related?"

"She's my…" Austin lowered his voice, gently pushing Jake back with his hand so he was directly out of ear shot. "She's my sister-in-law. What is this all about? Is she all right?"

"I'm afraid she's been in an accident, sir. Can you locate her husband?"

Austin felt bile rise at the back of his throat. He found it hard to keep his balance and to act normal around Jake.

"He's de—" he began to say, but then quickly retracted. "He's deployed. Is she alive?"

"Yes, she is. She's lucky to be alive. The wreck was pretty bad."

"Where is she?"

"At St. Joseph's Memorial."

"I'll just make a few calls for somebody to look after my son and I'll be there," Austin said.

***

Mimi

Mimi dipped in and out of sleep. When she finally woke, she tried to move her body, but it ached from head to toe. She tried to sit up, pushing her long, tangled strands of hair away from her face. It took a moment for her to process where she was and what happened.

She lay in the hospital bed, the persistent sound of the heart monitor beeping. Her mind was muddied with thoughts of the vivid dreams she'd had. At first she thought of Joel. She thought about being at the American Embassy when she was told he had been killed. Then she saw herself kissing a man, but when she pulled her lips away from his, she didn't see a face.

Her memory may have been cloudy, but she knew who she was and what led her here. So much had happened, and it was hard to believe that this life belonged to her. Most of the time she felt like she was watching somebody else, like an outsider looking in.

Before her eyes started to focus clearly, she saw a dark figure move into the arch of the doorway.

Austin. His face was full of concern. He wearily walked toward her. He knelt next to the bed and took her delicate hand in his.

"I'm so sorry," he whispered.

A sudden surge of emotion rose in her throat. "What are you doing here?"

"The cops came to my door and told me about the accident."

"Why did they call you?"

"I guess they connected your ID to me since we share the same last name."

She blinked her eyes in understanding.

"Any news about Joel?" Mimi asked.

The mere mention of his name reminded Austin that Mimi was not his, and now that his brother was alive, he knew he must let her go, which is why he'd sent her away from the ranch.

He swallowed. "He's coming to Texas."

Before they could continue, the female doctor entered the room.

"Well, Mimi, it's good to see you sitting up. I'm Dr. Parker and I have to say, Mimi, somebody was looking after you. In my experience, victims don't usually survive the extent of the accident you had, let alone escape from it without any life-threatening injuries." The doctor was a small framed woman, her southern accent soft and cool, just as her blonde hair was.

"Your wife is a strong woman," Dr. Parker said, smiling. Neither Mimi nor Austin corrected her.

The doctor spent a few moments checking Mimi over. After she finished examining her, she took the clipboard hanging off the end of the bed and scribbled her observations in a messy scroll. Mid-morning sun spilled into the hospital room. A thought popped into Mimi's mind.

He survived against the odds, and so did I!

"I'm pretty happy with what I see, but since you were unconscious, I want to keep an eye on you for a few days. Then I think you'll be good to go home," Dr Parker said with enthusiasm.

"So I can fly?" Mimi asked, trying to prop herself up further against the pillow.

The doctor looked confused, shot Austin a look, and then fixed her gaze back on Mimi.

Austin said, "We're not married. She's my sister-in-law. My brother is coming back from Afghanistan. Mimi lives in London."

"Right, I see. Okay. Well, Mimi, I don't recommend you fly for a good five to six weeks. You are doing wonderfully, but you need complete rest."

Dr. Parker politely told them that her other patients were waiting for her and left.

Austin looked at Mimi and said, "You can come back to the ranch and wait for Joel."

After a moment, she looked at Austin and asked, "What about Jake?"

From the way she was looking at him, he could tell she was thinking not only about Jake, but the three of them being in the same room with nothing but secrets and lies between them like a bomb waiting to explode.

"I have some business to do in Dallas. Jake will be on school break. You and Joel…" he quickly cleared his throat to catch himself from displaying any emotion that could give away his feelings. "You can reunite at the ranch, but I need you to be gone before Jake and I get back."

Mimi looked at Austin, confused. "I don't get it. You would leave the ranch and let your brother, whom you have not spoken to in years, and me stay. Why?"

"Because I don't want Jake to be exposed to any of this." He stood and looked out of the window. "I just want you to be happy, Mimi."

Suddenly, Mimi felt her anger rise to the surface, and instead of feeling grateful, she was irritated. Before she could second guess herself, her words were already spilling fast out of her mouth.

"Why are you such a martyr to Joel? I don't get it. First, he steals your girlfriend, then you take on his kid, and now you are prepared to let him into your home so he and I can be reunited. What gives?"

She heard a sarcastic low gruff of a laugh. "I'm not doing this for him. None of this has ever been for him, Mimi. Jake was in the care of my mother and I so happened to fall in love with that child. I am his father no matter what, and you, well…I'm letting him in because it will make you happy. None of this is about my brother. It just looks like I pick up his bullshit. I'll never let him have Jake. Not even over my fucking dead body will he ever be able to be a part of my son's life, but you and him? You belong to each other."

Mimi couldn't hold back the tears any longer. "I don't know where I belong or who I belong to!"

"You belong with your husband."

"And not with you?"

She couldn't believe she just said that out loud. She wasn't even sure why she said it. Despite Joel lying to her about Jake, he had treated her with nothing but love and affection. Somewhere, in all of this emotional mess, she had cast that aside.

When she drove away from the ranch, she had contemplated turning her back on both Joel and Austin since being with either of them would leave her with nothing but doubt and heartbreak. She had equally dishonoured Joel by sleeping with his brother, but worse than that, by actually allowing herself to have feelings for him.

Austin rubbed his hand over his unshaven jaw. She could see the weight of the stress splashed across his face, and she knew she was fully responsible for it.

They sat in silence for a little while. Mimi asked a few questions about Jake, but then Austin could tell Mimi needed her rest. She had to keep catching her breath, and she couldn't seem to find any comfort.

"I just don't feel good," she said through gritted teeth.

Austin pushed the call button next to her bed. A

short while later, a nurse came in and administered pain relief.

Soon after, Mimi fell into a deep slumber. He watched her chest rise and fall with every breath she took. He thought about how she must have felt when she was told Joel had been killed. When the cops had showed up to the ranch earlier that day, he thought the worst.

He felt caught up in a world that his brother had created, and he was angry. He fixed his gaze on the fullness of her lips and thought how he would never again kiss them.

Why didn't you just die, Joel? Why didn't you just fucking die?

Mimi winced a few times, but didn't wake. He sat uncomfortably on the cold, leather chair and glanced at his watch—three p.m. He needed to leave and get home for Jake. He knelt over her and gently kissed Mimi's clammy forehead. Just as he walked to the door, a shrill noise deafened him.

Austin quickly spun on his heel and saw the peaks on the heart monitor screen suddenly start to even out until it straightened to a flat line. The room started to whirl. He tried to call for help but before he even opened his mouth, several medics pushed past him. It was like he wasn't even there and somehow they just walked through him.

He tumbled backwards, unsteady on his feet, watching as they pulled open Mimi's gown to reveal her bare chest. The paddles of a defibrillator were placed on her, and he heard a man shouting orders. He watched her body convulse as she sprung inches from the mattress beneath her.

***

Simon

When the phone rings in the middle of the night, it is never good news.

Simon, Mimi's father, had been in a restless sleep the entire night as the rain pelted against the Velux window. Their old dog snored in the corner of the darkened room. Simon felt hot, so he kicked the covers off. After the hundredth time of tossing and turning, he had finally fallen into a light sleep. When the phone rang, he wasn't sure if he was dreaming until Kanchana leaned across him, blindly reaching for the receiver.

Simon bolted upright as he heard his wife shriek, "Is she alive?"

His first and only thought was Mimi.

Suddenly, he had a flash back: he was holding Mimi in the park and she was three years old. He turned away just for a second and she wandered toward the road. A speeding car roared round the corner. He ran and grabbed hold of her, pulling her so hard backwards that she sobbed with shock. If he'd gotten there just a couple of seconds later, she would have been killed.

When he saw Kanchana's tears run silently down her face, he feared the worst.

"Kanchana…what is it?"

"It's Mimi. She's been in a car accident," she answered, her voice full of despair.

"Please tell us everything you know," Kanchana said to the person on the phone.

When she finally finished the phone call, Simon stared silently at his wife, waiting to hear the verdict. Kanchana pulled her shoulder-length hair away from her face and took a deep breath. "She's alive. Her car had a collision with a truck and it flipped."

"But she's okay?" Simon asked. "I mean, no life-threatening injuries?"

"She has been in the hospital for two days. She was stable."

"Two days and we are just getting this call now? What the hell is all that about?" Simon blurted. "This is outrageous. I want to find out who is in charge over there and when I find out, somebody's head is going to…"

"Simon, Simon!" she yelled. "Something is wrong with Mimi's heart. We need to get to her. Call Larna now. I'm going to pack. We need to get to Texas immediately."

When life throws you devastating news, it can seem like you are not inside your own body. That's how Simon felt as he sat on the edge of their bed in the middle of the night. He called his eldest daughter, knowing that he was about to turn her world upside down too.

***

Austin

Austin sat in the waiting room with his head in

his hands. He was anxiously waiting to hear news from the doctor. He wanted to hear Mimi was fine, but when the seconds turned into minutes, and the minutes turned into over an hour, he feared the worst.

An older woman with overpowering perfume came and went several times, her face expressionless. There was an overweight man coughing and spluttering sitting nearby. The smell of his stale sweat lingered in the air. With every cough the man made, Austin became more and more agitated. There were posters plastered on the walls giving warnings, things to look out for, but they didn't have the answers to Mimi's condition.

There was tension between a younger couple who sat nearby. Austin heard the odd snipe and insult, followed by stony faces and silence. An attractive blonde clearly mentally distressed sat near the opposite wall, clutching her rosary beads as she muttered Hail Marys.

Everybody in the room had a story to tell, and even in the midst of their personal tragedies, not so much as a compassionate smile was shared among the strangers.

Austin thought of Jake. He was a bright kid; he would know something was going on, no matter how hard Austin tried to dress it up and pretend everything was all sunshine and rainbows. Jake would know all was not well, especially when Austin sent his assistant to step in and look after him with no notice at all.

After sipping the remainder of his black sweetened coffee from the vending machine, he scratched the rim of the polystyrene cup ‘till it started to crumble, bits falling to the floor.

As Austin began gathering the littered pieces up, familiar pointy red shoes were in his view. He looked up to see Dr. Parker, her expression serious. He tried to search her eyes for clues before he was able to ask the question he dreaded the answer to.

“Is Mimi okay?”

When he’d met the doctor before, she seemed confident and happy, but now it felt like he was looking at another person who was direct and almost cold.

“Mr. Marcus, is Mimi’s husband going to be here any time soon?”

“I have no idea. Look, please, I need to know, is she all right?”

“Mimi is in a very serious condition right now.”

“But you said…you said she was doing well. I didn’t imagine that—you said it,” he stuttered.

“It all appeared that way, Mr. Marcus.”

“Austin. My name is Austin.”

Dr. Parker made direct eye contact with him. “Mimi didn’t show any lasting injuries. She suffered a traumatic aortic rupture that occurred because of the car accident.”

“What the hell does that mean?” Austin said, pulling his hands out of his pockets and running his hands through his hair.

“It’s a condition of the aorta, which branches directly from the heart to supply blood to the rest of the body. Now, the pressure of this injury is very great and the blood can pump out very rapidly. In many cases, this can be fatal due to the profuse bleeding that can result from the rupture. In Mimi's case, we have managed to keep it under control because we were able to give her immediate treatment. She's not out of the woods yet, Austin, but like I said before, she is a very lucky woman and it seems she's a fighter."

"Can I see her?"

"You can."

As he made his way through the white corridor, Dr. Parker called after him.

"It may not be my place to say, but does your brother know how you feel about his wife?"

He stood silent for a moment and then pursed his lips together.

"Not yet, but he will."

Austin slowly crept back in the room. Mimi's usually tanned skin looked pale, almost grey. He stepped closer to her but was afraid to touch her in case something else happened to her. Since arriving in Texas, Mimi suffered a broken wrist and now a car crash. Austin almost felt he was responsible for her bad luck.

He sat quietly, listening to the electronic beeps on the monitor. Out of the corner of his eye, he saw a nurse walking down the corridor. She made her way into Mimi's room.

"Hi. I'm the duty nurse this evening."

She was a short, plump woman with black curly hair that looked like it hadn't been washed in a week. Her patchy dry skin looked taut, but she was friendly enough. She carried out some checks on Mimi, wrote down a few notes, and turned to leave. Austin nodded and turned his attention back to

Mimi. He thought back to a couple of months ago, before he got the call about Joel, when life was far simpler.

He almost wished that he had never contacted Mimi. That way she would have never seen him as a gateway to enter his world. It had all started because of her grief over Joel, but now things were far more complicated. Even though he tried to deny it, there was now a "them." It seemed ironic, that somehow his brother had been the one to steal his first love, and now here he wanted his brother's forever love.

CHAPTER 20

Mimi

Mimi eyes fluttered open. For a second, she couldn't seem to move her body, and it unnerved her. The amount of wires plugged on and around her body alarmed her; the life monitoring machinery around her told her she had suffered from the accident far greater than she thought.

She was alone in the room, and in that moment a wave of dread fell over her. She was so weak and vulnerable. She had a distant look in her eye as she stared out into space. She had always been into signs, and as she lay here in this hospital bed, she saw it as justice that her heart had failed her. She gave it to two brothers and now this was her punishment.

Whatever it was that she felt for Austin, she knew it was born out of her grief and no good could come from it. The truth was, she had never really let Joel go, and Austin was so like his brother and the similarity had allured her into a false feeling. She had confused everything. Austin had seemed to be the cure for her pain, but their relationship needed to end.

Running her hands over her bruised arm, she noticed that her wrist had been rewrapped.

There was a button to call for assistance, so she pressed it. A few moments later, a cheerful nurse with brilliant white teeth came in smiling, almost like she was a friend.

"Ah, you are awake. How are you feeling?"

"What happened to me?" When Mimi spoke, her voice was strained and hoarse because of the tube that had been inserted at the back of her throat.

"I think it's better that the doctor explains everything. You suffered an aortic rupture. You are very lucky, ma'am. From what I know, people usually don't come back from this sort of thing."

Tears pricked Mimi's eyes. She had no idea what to feel. Her body felt broken. She gently lifted her hand and put it to her chest. She felt the warmth of her skin and the beating of her heart. She was alive.

"Your husband left you a note. He said he will be back later this afternoon," said the nurse, who she learned was called Kelly, whilst she gently lifted Mimi's head and puffed out her pillows.

Her husband. Joel came back. She had longed for this moment, but somehow she was so deeply unprepared. Suddenly she wondered if Kelly was confused.

Was it Austin that came to see me?

"My husband, did he leave his name?" Mimi asked. The nurse looked at her like a deer in headlights, her expression almost twisted.

"Don't you know your husband's name? I better call the doctor in."

"No. I know I sound crazy, but my brother-in-law came to see me, at least as far as I can remember. My husband is deployed, so I just wanted to know who you meant. They look so much alike," she tried to joke.

"Oh, right. Okay, I see. You had me worried there. Let me check. I'll be back in two ticks."

Nurse Kelly disappeared out of the room. Mimi rested her eyes for a brief moment. When she opened her eyes, she saw Austin poised in the doorway. It was as if he was waiting for her permission to enter the room.

He crossed the room and pulled his body over the steel safety bed rail. He put his hand on her cheek and held his gaze on her. Without waiting a second longer, he placed his lips on hers. Mimi started to pull her head back, but she did not give into her hesitation as his tongue slid into her mouth. He was gentle and tender, just like the kiss they had shared before the phone call.

Her head was telling her to stop but her heart refused to. She wished she could pull off all the wires and pull him closer to her. She longed to feel the warmth of his skin on hers, to feel the strength of his hands over her body. Suddenly, Joel was pushed to the back of her mind. In this moment, and in hundreds before, she realised that Austin was who she wanted.

They heard footsteps come into the room. Nurse Kelly stood in the doorway.

"I guess I don't need to tell you." She gave a

polite but suspicious smile and left the room. It was clear she knew Austin was not her husband, but she remained professional and left.

Mimi let her shoulders sink back into the bed. She remembered waking up next to Joel. And yet here she was with his brother, the man she had wondered about, who she pictured to be the bad guy. The two brothers were like Cain and Abel—so similar and yet so different.

In the moments that Austin had his lips on hers, it was easy for Joel to drift out of her mind. Yet the second he pulled away from her, guilt crept in and punched her in the stomach.

"I'm so sorry. This is all my fault," he whispered. She reached out and touched the stubble on his chin. His eyes were full of regret but alive with passion.

"I know everything I said, Mimi. Even what I said to you yesterday before I left and saying I'll go away so you and Joel can be together. And I know that is what I should do. Fuck. I can't believe I am about to say this." He swallowed hard and turned his back to her.

Mimi studied the broadness of his shoulders. Her fingers clenched as she braced herself for what he was going to say. She wanted him to say it, but she knew it was going to confuse everything. The sting of his words when he sent her away still haunted her. She was at war with her own heart. Part of her wished that she had died because then she wouldn't have to make this choice.

"Stay with me. Don't go back to him. Choose me."

The words were out and they hung in the air. She wanted to shout yes, but she knew she couldn't.

"Why?"

"Because I'm in love with you, Mimi."

"This has nothing to do with the feud with Joel?"

He turned to her and she saw how his face had darkened.

"For once in my life, Mimi, this has nothing to do with my brother. I almost lost you. You are so lucky to be alive. I have always done the right thing, but I can't do it now, not when it means losing you. I want you to stay with me."

She took a deep breath. "Austin, there is so much. Give me time. I need to see Joel. I need to find out his reasons for not telling me the truth. I thought he was dead, and then I meet you and you tell me the truth and the truth is it was all a lie…my marriage. But the problem is, I still married him and we still…"

"You're choosing him, aren't you?"

"He's my husband."

He rubbed his fingers on his tired eyes. He knew he took a risk by telling her how he really felt, and he knew the odds were against him, but somewhere in the darkness of the night before, he decided he needed to tell Mimi how he felt. He said nothing as he started to walk out of the room.

"Austin, please don't leave." Her voice was desperate.

"What do you want, Mimi?" The longer he stayed in the room with her, the longer he was holding onto false hope.

"I want you to give me time. Please. I need

time."

"For what?"

"To decide if my marriage is worth saving. And to understand my feelings for you."

"So you admit you have feelings for me?" He hated how pathetic he sounded.

"Yes. Too many," she whispered.

Relief washed through him. "How many?" he asked.

"Enough for me to question if I should end things with Joel and be with you."

His heart started to pound, and his head felt like it was going to explode. He was not used to all this emotion and he didn't know what to do with it.

"I'll give you as much time as you need. You know where to find me."

"Austin," she called once more. She held her hand out to him. He took it and pulled it up to the warmth of his mouth and gently kissed it.

There were no further words between them. He turned to leave her once more but this time he didn't say goodbye. He gave her a weary smile, an unspoken assurance, she perceived, that he would give her the space and time on her own to decide. After he left the room, she closed her eyes, taking a deep breath.

Behind her eyelids, the hidden truth emerged. There was only one man she saw.

CHAPTER 21

Joel
Afghanistan: The Rescue

Standing at the tip of a ditch, Joel was weak and tired but driven by determination to survive. He had made it this far and there was one reason: *Mimi.*

He could hear the whine of the helicopter engines. It was the sound of freedom.

In the distance, he could hear the steady hammering of a machine gun. He knew he was on borrowed time. The extent of his injuries didn't seem as bad in that very moment. He had a surge of adrenaline pumping through his body, giving him a life force he had never known.

Over the steep mountains, he could hear the roar of more helicopters—fierce, dark, and ready to fight if necessary. As they drew nearer, the CH-47 engines were deafening. The sand and mud whirled like small tornadoes.

He waved his arms up into the air. In his mind, he feared he would die, but somewhere deep within he knew he would get out of this alive. There were too many times in his life where he had come close, but he knew this cat had nine lives and he sure as hell hadn't spent them all.

One of the helicopters settled into a hover and started to descend. This was his ticket home. His boys had come to rescue him.

Soon after, all the helicopters landed. Darkness swept over the area. It was almost as if somebody had turned the lights off. A team of medics ran toward him, immediately working on his wounds. They brought out a stretcher and hoisted him up on their shoulders, moving swiftly into the back of the CH-47.

Joel searched for Abdul, but he was nowhere to be seen. His job was done, and Joel knew that he had disappeared into the shadows and he'd never see him again. Through his weary breathing, he mouthed thank you and went in and out of a light slumber.

Once he was safely secured, the roar of the engine came to life again. He knew he was on his way to a hospital to receive treatment and then he would be making his way back to his wife. As he closed his eyes, his thoughts were of nothing but her. When one of the medics pulled open his jacket, the photo of Mimi flew across the floor.

"Looks like she kept you safe, man," one of the medics said.

"She sure did."

Joel kissed the photo with tenderness. He couldn't wait to run his fingers through her long, dark hair and kiss her full, red lips. He would hold her close, make love to her, and never ever let her go again. He imagined seeing her again. His heart swelled inside him.

***

It seemed like hours before he arrived at the hospital. He was immediately treated for severe dehydration and given antibiotics through an intravenous tube.

He was allowed to rest for a while. He knew there would be questions, he knew he would be asked about the raid and any information that would be useful, and he knew he would be asked about the man who kept him alive.

After what seemed like endless tests and treatments, Joel fell asleep. He woke to a gnawing pain in his leg. He winced as he pushed himself up on the pillow. He had never been in so much pain. It felt like he had been beaten to a pulp. There wasn't a single part of him that didn't hurt.

All he wanted to do was get back to Mimi. When Captain Mills came to see Joel, he first thanked him for his heroic efforts during the raid. Then he sat beside his bed and began asking about the events before the attack.

"I remember some things, but not everything." Joel said. He didn't want to revisit the moment when he had seen his best friend's life drain from his cheeks.

"Tell us whatever you can. Anything that you think will help us move in on our target."

He talked, recalling all of the earlier moments

from when they were briefed right up until they were attacked. And then there was Abdul, the kind stranger that had saved his life.

"I have no idea what his name is. He didn't tell me. And I have no idea what he looked like because his face was always covered. I'm sorry I can't help you there."

Joel knew his dishonesty could cause him to be court-marshalled if they found out the truth, but it was a chance he was willing to take.

"I guess you want to get home to your wife. We've contacted her."

"You've spoken to Mimi?" he said, bolting upright, ignoring the pain shooting through him.

"Actually, we spoke to your brother. Austin, is it?"

"Why?" he asked sharply. The mention of Austin's name was like poison sitting in his mouth, and he dare not swallow.

"Your wife is with him. I guess they must have been supporting each other during this very difficult time, but I bet they are elated now that you are safe and coming home."

She'll know everything!

Fear washed over him. And there, in that very moment, if there was anybody he should have been honest to, it was his wife.

"She's in Texas," Joel said.

"That's right. As we understand it, she's at the ranch where you grew up. Eastleigh?"

The last time Joel had walked away from the ranch, he had left his mother crying behind him with nothing but a rucksack on his back. And for the last time, he had left his brother behind, he had hoped forever. But forever had come too soon!

***

Mimi

Mimi had only been in the hospital for two days, but she could already tell you how many cracks were in the ceiling, what times the nurses changed shifts, and how many cabinet doors were in her room.

She had no idea, however, what was happening in the world outside the sterile walls.

It was a Friday morning when her parents arrived. She had been pushed back into her room on a wheelchair after the nurse had sponged her body clean. She sensed they were there before the wheels glided around the curve of the corridor.

At first she thought she heard her mother's sweet voice, high-pitched and as tangy as a lemon. Her father's signature Brut cologne that he'd been wearing for years hung in the air. When she entered the room, there they were, waiting for her with eyes full of tears and a twisted smile of sadness and relief all in one.

Simon and Kanchana jumped to their feet. The chairs legs scraped loudly against the newly bleached floor.

It was her mother who was the first to break. She was unable to control the tears that fell freely down her face, her small frame rising and falling with every sob as she held her daughter tight. Simon stood a distance behind. He was in shock. It took several moments before he reached his hand out to hers.

When he moved forward, Mimi looked into her father's eyes. They had once been so bright and blue, but as the years had passed and she had grown, she had never noticed her parents change. Since she saw them every day, they simply looked like her parents, but now she noticed her father's salt and pepper stubble, the deep hollows under his eyes. Her mother's hands were no longer slender and smooth. She now had bulging veins, and her fingers had started to twist.

She wondered how she must look to them. Even thinner than when she had stepped into the black cab taking her and Meg in the chill of the early morning mist to Heathrow. It was that very journey that led her to this very moment, a journey to discover truths that had not been told. Her heart was broken not only in the physical sense but in a way that she knew was now changed.

After the storm of the emotional reunion, Mimi settled back into her hospital bed.

Her father made his usual jokes to make light of a difficult situation. It was just his way. Her mother, on the other hand, was dying to extract as much information from her daughter as possible. Mimi had always thought her mother would make a brilliant detective.

Every so often, Mimi would check her phone, waiting for a message, but this time she was unsure of who she wanted the message to be from. She was frustrated with herself for feeling this way. She hadn't yet decided if she was going to reveal to her parents what she had learned about Joel and Jake. In a way, she thought she needed permission from Austin to do so, although the communication between them had frozen solidly since he had left.

She knew it was her decision to put the distance between them, but with every moment that he was gone, she missed him. She imagined him deep in thought, riding Troy off into the dazzling sunset that felt like a golden sheet over the ranch. He would be sitting at the dinner table with Jake, laughing at his son's jokes. At night, she could see him sitting in the leather chair working, and she hoped that when he went to bed at night, he would hold his pillow close and wish it was her.

When she had first met him, he had come across as cold and distant. She had never imagined that the hard shell could be broken, but as she peeled away the layers, beyond that moody, hard exterior was a man with a heart so pure and true. Her attraction to him had been instant. He had the same features as Joel—emerald green eyes and a classic, strong jaw line.

As much as they looked alike, Austin was different. It wasn't something physical—it was in the way his body moved, how his voice was deeper. Then it was the way he held her; it was something not even a thousand words could explain.

In ways, it was like Joel had been a writer, deciding the script of their marriage. By not telling her the truth, it changed how she saw him. If somebody had asked her if her love for him would ever be questioned, she would have sworn blind that nothing would ever cut through the ties that bound them together, until now.

Her time with Austin had been short, but there was a powerful connection. So much of it was in the way he was a father to Jake, supporting him, protecting him, and although he was moody, he made up for that in kindness. Sometimes, when his temper was short, he made up for that with tenderness, and when he had no words to say, he made up for that by the touch of his lips.

And then there was her GI Joe, the man she had promised her life to. He was the man who made her laugh when she wanted to cry, the man she believed she would have children with. He had always been the cure to her pain, until now.

***

After Mimi spoke to her parents about everything from the English weather to what mischief her cat had been causing, her mother cut to the chase to ask the question that was the elephant in the room.

"You haven't asked about Joel," she said, her lips pursed together.

"I know," Mimi whispered.

Her father rose from his chair and let out a loud yawn, stretching his arms out wide.

"Oooh…jetlag is catching up with me. Think I need to get some caffeine in my system. You want anything, love?" He gestured to Kanchana by placing his hand loosely on her shoulder. He knew when the girls talked, it was his time to leave the room.

"I'm fine," she answered curtly.

Without saying another word, he disappeared out of the room.

"Are you going to tell me what is going on, Mimi? I know you so well, and I know you are hiding something. How do I know?"

"Because I can't look you in the eye," Mimi whispered.

"Exactly. Now, I don't care if you're five or fifty-five. It's my job to fix you. Mimi, I can't tell you how your father and I felt when we got that call. It felt like our whole world was about to end. You and your sister mean everything to us."

"I know that, Mama," Mimi said, lowering her head and avoiding her mother's gaze once more.

"I know, my darling. Oh, do I know, love. I've loved your stupid father for over two decades." She gave a playful laugh, but then her face turned serious again. "I know the love I have for him and the love that I have for you and Larna. And that love wouldn't suddenly fade after weeks if, God forbid, I should lose one of you. You are so much like me. There is so much love in your heart. I saw how crushed you were the day that we were told Joel had been killed. It's a day that I'll never forget."

She took a deep breath and tightly held her daughter's hand. She lifted her chin into the curve of her fingertips. "So, Mimi, why is your heart not with Joel?"

"Because I found out things," Mimi said, her voice beginning to tremble, "that he has a son."

Kanchana covered her mouth in an effort to hide her displeasure and shock.

"And there's something else," Mimi continued.

"Go on…"

"I think I've fallen in love with his brother."

Saying the words out loud sounded so different to how they sounded locked up in her head and in her heart.

"I don't understand. You've only known him for five minutes, and Joel is your husband."

"Mama, I know."

"Are you even thinking straight? You've had such a shock. Maybe you are just confused."

"I'm confused, I know, in every sense of the word, but, Mum, as much as my head is spinning, I can't deny what I am feeling. I mean, is it even possible to love two people?"

"I don't know." Kanchana shook her head. "I've only loved your father."

There was a short silence and then the sound of a chirpy whistle belonging to Simon. He was holding two steaming cups of coffee in plastic cups. He lifted the cup up to his lips and blew the steam that gently rose. He raised his eyes, stopping suddenly before he entered the room as he caught Mimi's gaze.

She looked at him with wide eyes, a warning to her father he had walked in at a bad moment. There had been hundreds of awkward moments over the years. Being a father of two daughters, Simon had always joked that he was used to girl talk and the sudden silences. The fact that Mimi was no longer a little girl but a woman didn't mean any of the family dynamics had changed. There were just some things Mimi could only share with her mother. This was one of those things.

"I'm hungry. You hungry?"

"No," both women said together.

"Right then. I'll just go and make myself scarce." He left the room once again and started wandering down the maze of corridors.

After a moment, Mimi continued. "I can't believe he's alive. I can't believe I'm alive. That has to mean something. It must mean that we are destined to be together, right?"

"Are you asking me?" Kanchana said gently.

"Yes. I need your guidance because every decision I seem to make is the wrong one. I'm so lost, Mum. I'm so torn." She began to cry.

Kanchana learned forward and put her arms around her daughter. They had a bond so strong. Over the years, they had gone from being mother and daughter to the best of friends. Mimi regretted not calling her mother sooner and confiding in her. Since she didn't understand what she was going through, she hadn't expected anybody else to understand the tangled mess going on in her own head either.

There were thoughts that made no sense. Nor could she see clearly. Mimi had always been the rock amongst her friends, the one they called when a relationship was in trouble, the one who didn't just mop tears away, but gave good, sound advice. Over the years, those close to her said she should become a psychiatrist and now here she was, living in her own drama, unable to calm the storm inside her.

She needed a saving grace from all of this, a hiding place to think things over. Kanchana had been liaising with the Embassy regarding Joel's current medical condition, which she had candidly shared with Mimi. She needed to know the truth. He was due to be in Texas in two weeks, maybe less.

The doctors said that Mimi could be out of the hospital in ten days if she continued to steadily progress, but on strict orders that she was not allowed to fly. She could either stay in a hotel with her parents, now that they were here, or stick to the original plan and go back to the ranch. There she would reunite with her husband, and there she would be grateful to be back in his arms again.

She told her mother the whole story, right from the very start. The fears that she had when Joel left for Afghanistan, right to the moment she found Jake's birth certificate and when she tried to drown her sorrows at the bar. She admitted her feelings for Austin could have been born from somewhere inside her that had been devastated by Joel. Yet, out of a dark place, she had seen the light that existed through Austin and most certainly around Jake.

Kanchana said very little; she just listened. Simon eventually crept back into the room. He pulled out a chair and took a seat next to his wife. He rubbed his eyes and smothered a yawn. The jetlag was slowly creeping up on both of her parent's faces. From the time they had got the early morning call about Mimi's accident, they had been awake for a solid forty-eight hours. Neither of them had slept on the plane. They had been too consumed by worry. They had powered through fatigue by pure adrenaline alone.

They watched Mimi's eyes begin to grow heavy. She took a deep breath before her eyelids gave way and closed, the thin white bed sheet sitting gently across her protruding collarbone.

"I spoke to the doctor. She said Mimi is doing well, but she will need to be closely monitored. Even when she gets back to the UK. I've given them our GP details," Simon whispered.

Kanchana nodded. "Did you give them all her insurance details? I know that she has coverage through her bank. At least she used to."

"Her bills to date have all been paid for."

"How?" she said, her voice rising.

"Austin. Sounds like a good bloke, considering he and Joel haven't spoken in years."

Kanchana took a deep breath. "I think there is a lot this family doesn't know."

wasn't a victim.

He hesitated on whether to visit her again in the hospital. As he lay in bed in the stillness of the moonlight, he came up with ten good reasons why he shouldn't. Yet, there was one reason that overrode them all. He couldn't let her go.

She'd asked for distance. He knew she had every right to ask that of him. And then there was Joel. The distance between them over the years had grown wider and stronger until they had become nothing but strangers, yet they would always be connected through blood and now the love of one woman.

She would make her choice, and when she did, the bad blood would thicken. His mind was array with different possibilities. All this thinking gave him a headache, and finally, at almost two in the morning, he got under the covers and forced himself to fall into a dreamless sleep.

***

Mimi was sitting up in the hospital chair, feeling physically better. When she caught sight of herself in the bathroom mirror earlier that morning, she had turned away in horror. Her face was puffy and swollen. The bruises had faded, but makeup wouldn't be able to hide the ordeal she had been though. The injuries on her face, however, were nothing to what her soul had been through.

She wondered if emotions had a colour. If they did, what colour would she be? *Grey,* she thought, the colour of uncertainty; *a grey area*, a colour of neither here, nor there. *A grey day, bleak, unsure.*

She thought about Joel. When she closed her eyes, she remembered his smile, and she could almost hear his laugh. It all seemed so long ago, but what was months in a timespan of a long marriage?

On their wedding night, they had spoken of the future, his strong arms wrapped around her, two people so intertwined that they felt like one. They had discussed faraway lands where they would travel, how they would document every place with a photo, how they would keep every ticket, every tacky souvenir. Yet their dreams were always tarnished by Joel's deployment hanging over them like a thick fog, threatening to destroy all their dreams.

Mimi was always afraid of the war he would be fighting, but she had understood it. Many of her well-meaning colleagues shared their points of view on the war in the Middle East. It was as if they were voicing their opinions through her, as if she could change it.

She'd listened. She respected their opinions. In the end, the military would still fight, people would still die, and families would be torn apart, and for the lucky few, their loved ones would come home to them. They'd get normal jobs, live normal lives, and share war stories with their friends over beers on a Friday night.

Mimi should be one of those lucky few. And then Austin happened. She hadn't planned it, and she certainly had not meant it, but her feelings had overtaken her in ways that she couldn't understand. The thing that had perhaps shocked her the most was how easy it was to have feelings for him when she was grieving her husband and still coming to grips with her new title as a widow.

Her mother's words had echoed in her mind: *I know the love I have for him and the love that I have for you and Larna. And that love wouldn't suddenly fade after weeks if, God forbid, I should lose one of you.* So, why had she let herself give into her feelings? Why did she have these feelings at all?

"I know you asked me to give you space, Mimi," Austin said.

Mimi pulled herself out of her chair. She smiled and began to lean forward when she realised she was too weak to do so.

There was a beat of silence.

"I'm glad you are here," she said, and she meant it.

"Actually, I'm here because I have some news for you."

He paused for a second and cleared his throat. She noticed he had recently shaved but still left some stubble so his face wasn't baby smooth. She inhaled his scent, which now felt like home to her. As he dragged another chair across the floor, she quickly tried to straighten out her hair with her fingers.

Austin cleared his throat, but he kept his eyes fixed on hers. "I got a call this morning. Joel is going to be on a flight to Texas on Sunday. He still needs a little more rest time before he is allowed to fly, but they are pretty confident that Sunday will be the day."

Her heart skipped a beat. This was real. Joel was coming home.

"Does he know?" she asked.

"About us?" Austin answered, a little too high-pitched.

"About my accident, and that I'm in the hospital."

Austin suddenly felt foolish for his stupid assumption.

"Yes. He was told this morning. I think he wasn't told straight away because of his condition. They wanted to make sure he could take the news that you'd been hurt."

"My parents are here," Mimi said, swiftly changing the subject.

"I bet you were glad to see them?"

"Yes. I didn't realise how much I missed them. I was so swept up by everything."

"I think anybody could forgive you for that."

"How's Jake?"

"He's good. He misses you. Keeps asking where you are and stuff."

"What have you told him?"

"I told him that…" Austin was interrupted by a nurse who walked into the room.

"Mimi, there is a phone call for you." She handed her the handset.

Mimi held the phone up to her ear, fully expecting to hear her sister's voice. She'd wanted to come out too but in the dead of the night, things had been too rushed for her to make the trip from Yorkshire to London.

"Baby," the voice said.

Joel.

His voice was as smooth as butter, like a song she had known and could recite all the words to but had not heard for a long time.

By the look on her face, Austin knew who was on the other end of that phone. He respectfully stroked Mimi's hand and drifted out into the hallway. This time he wasn't going to leave. He decided he needed to face things head on. He decided he needed to finally face his brother. The time had come.

Mimi's bottom lip began to tremble. She was overcome with emotion.

"Mimi, are you there?" he asked

She started crying. A lump got caught in her throat that was making it hard for her to speak.

A sharp feeling of guilt stabbed her.

She imagined him in a land faraway, expecting her to be there waiting for him.

"Joel," she finally managed to say. Her head was spinning and suddenly she couldn't see the room clearly because of the tears filling her eyes and spilling down her face. "I thought you were dead."

"I told you I was coming back. Remember on our honeymoon? I made you a promise."

How could I forget?

"Are you all right?" he asked. "I mean, I was the one fighting a war and it seems you are worse off than me," he half joked.

"I'm fine. Joel, what happened to you? They told me you were dead."

"I can't say over the phone. I'll tell you everything when we are together."

“This is real?” She thought of how Joel had been a ghost to her. She was haunted by memories, dreams so dark and vivid. A series of events had led her to this moment where his voice was real and he was keeping his promise; he really was coming home to her.

She cradled the phone tightly, hanging onto his every word. She wondered if he could hear the guilt in her voice. What if he knew she had slept with his brother? And what reasons would he give her about not telling her about his son? There were so many questions unanswered. A lie hanging between all of them, making her loyalties constantly sway.

“You kept me alive. It was all about you, getting back to you. Keeping my promise. I promise you, Mimi, from now on, I’m staying with you.”

She took a deep breath, her heart pounding, her voice trembling. “There is so much to talk about,” she managed to say.

“Mimi…I’ll tell you everything, I promise.”

They knew the secret was out. Neither of them addressed it, not over the phone. It was something that needed to happen in person, when they were together, a time she thought would never come again.

***

Later, when Austin sat sipping his fifth cup of coffee in the hospital cafeteria, he caught sight of a woman bearing a striking resemblance to Mimi, only much older. There was no doubt the woman was her mother. She’d caught him staring at her. It was as if there was a magnetic pull between the two of them. He knew who she was, and she knew who he was.

When she headed toward the table, he stood up. There was a moment of silence between them.

"You must be Mimi's mom?"

"And you must be Austin?" He was relieved that she didn't label him as Joel's brother. It told him that Mimi had confided in her. She knew.

"I'd thank you for looking after my daughter, but it's not as if she is in the best shape."

"I'm sorry…I know this is all my fault. The accident, the..."

"I don't blame you. This is just how things were meant to happen. The most important thing is that she is alive and she will recover. Nothing else after that really matters."

"I think it matters," he answered, his eyes fixed on hers.

Kanchana slid into a seat and invited Austin to sit next to her.

"I was with my daughter when we had been told your brother had been killed. I saw the way it destroyed her. I was with her in the nights that followed. I wish I could rescue her from the pain. No matter what I said or what I did, it could not offer her any comfort. When she decided to come here to Texas, I was upset because I was the one that wanted to fix her. However, I put my feelings aside and put hers first. Deep down, we both knew that this was a journey that she had to take. It was you that seemed to put her back together. You gave her hope in her life, in her heart."

She remembered how unneeded she had felt. She had shared her feelings with Simon, and as usual, he had told her she was being too harsh on herself, too sensitive. She knew that Mimi was a strong girl, but she had never truly known how strong until now.

"Do you have feelings for my daughter?" The question came out of the blue. Asked so boldly and directly, it had taken him off guard.

He didn't have time to think about how to answer the question when suddenly he blurted the words out. "I'm in love with her."

He almost felt embarrassed by how he let his feelings so out in the open.

"You hardly know her."

"I know her enough."

"How so?" she asked. He could feel her eyes burning into him. Suddenly, he felt hot. It was as almost as if this were some kind of test.

"Does anybody have the actual words to explain? It was the moment I met her. She's got such a way about her, a way that I wouldn't be able to describe to you. I guess I feel like she feels familiar, like I have always known her."

Kanchana nodded. She knew how people have always spoken about her daughter. She loved both of her daughters equally. She knew Mimi was a people magnet, never short of friends and never short of people who wanted to be with her, and yet, she only ever allowed a select few in.

The smell of hospital food began to filter through the air, burnt toast and the fumes of overcooked meals. Slowly, people started to drift in, visitors with heavy, tired eyes and doctors floating like zombies from the graveyard shift, taking in a hot meal before they clocked off.

"This should all be a miracle. Your brother is alive and he is coming home to his wife. Yet it isn't because something has changed in my daughter since she met you. I'll always support her choices. I'm her mother, and I'll always be there for her."

"I know I can give her a good life," Austin said with conviction.

"Perhaps you will," she continued. "I know she can't come home for a while. Back to England, I mean. So it will be up to you to prove that." She raised her eyebrows.

"I'll do that. And if she wants to leave with Joel, it will break my heart, but I will still make sure her needs are taken care of."

It was in that moment that Kanchana knew Austin really did love her daughter. He was willing to let her go, if that's what she wanted.

"I need to get back to Mimi. I trust you know about Joel's arrival back to the States?"

Austin lowered his eyes and nodded. "I know."

"Thank you for talking to me, Austin. Maybe we will meet again." She extended her hand out to his and they shook.

"Maybe," he said.

CHAPTER 23

Joel
Coming Home

Joel crossed the gravel driveway, his boots crunching over the stones. Everything looked the same. It was just as he had remembered it. He felt the warm breeze blow over his skin. The smell of his childhood hung in the air, and it was no longer welcoming. He yanked at his jacket and pulled it off because of the sudden wave of heat flushing over him.

He stopped midway up the path. There, in front of him, was the ranch, the sunlight filtering through the trees, the horses and cattle grazing the fields that surround the house. This had once been his territory, the place he called home, but in the years since he left, he had never found home in a place, only in his wife.

Whenever he thought of Mimi, his heart grew, and it gave him the determination to fight any battle, any emotion, so long as it meant she was there waiting for him at the end of it. It had been ten days since he was last able to speak to her. When he found out she had been in a car accident, he was desperate to get back to her, even if that meant he would put his own life at risk.

She had sounded different on the phone. Her voice belonged to her, but her pitch sounded cool, not like the warm, loving Mimi he was used to. His heart had sunk, but he tried to reassure himself that it was just the shock. Then, there was the nagging doubt at the back of his mind that his brother had poisoned her thoughts against him. He was unsure if she knew about Jake.

He knew it was selfish, keeping this information hidden from her for all this time. With Mimi, he felt like he had made a brand new life. He didn't want the tragic events from his feud with his brother and a child he was too young to have to be woven into their future.

She had never pressed too hard for the details. He was able to pacify her curiosity by blaming his younger brother for not wanting any contact. He had lied to her by saying he tried to reach out to him, but it was clear the door would never be able to be re-opened again. He never imagined that fate would have brought him back to the beginning. Never did he think, in Mimi's grief, this is where she would have turned.

He glanced up at the porch and saw her. She was as beautiful as the day he left her, but for the first time he felt afraid, petrified of the strength of emotion he felt. She slowly moved down the steps.

They said nothing. They were caught up in a

moment of disbelief. It was as if this was another one of Mimi's vivid dreams and she fully expected to wake up, only it wasn't not a dream. It was real. Joel kept his promise and he really had come back to her.

He reached out his arms and she slowly moved toward him. She fell into his arms, unsure of what she should be thinking or feeling. She couldn't control the tears that fell.

He said nothing. Instead, he wrapped his arms tighter and tighter around her slender frame. She was so fragile, like a bird that lost her way. Her head spun as he gently kissed her forehead.

***

Mimi

She looked deeply into his eyes, the eyes she believed to once be so true and sincere. Her heart beat fast, and all of her doubt fell away for a few seconds. She didn't want to believe he was capable of keeping such a secret. When she thought he was dead, it was easy for her grief to push him aside, but now, as she was cradled in his arms, she just wanted him to be the man she said *I do* to.

She had felt in the days after he'd first gone missing that part of her had died every day she waited for him. There was a connection between them that was so powerful. Today she was a step closer to finding out the truth. There was a chance she could get past this. They could work through the web of lies together, finally exorcising the demons of his past.

But then there was Austin. He had been the one to pick up the tiny pieces of her broken heart. She tried to learn to live without Joel, but it only ever seemed to be possible if she had Austin's arms to fall back into.

She had no idea what she felt or who she was the day her heart failed her. That day it felt as if it had been torn apart and she'd given a piece to Joel and a piece to Austin. It left her with no direction to follow. And as she inhaled the familiar scent of her husband and felt drunk on emotion, she knew everything in her life was riding on Joel's version of the truth.

Later that afternoon, after the tears had finally dried up and the shock of seeing each other had mellowed, they went for a walk through the land surrounding the ranch. Mimi stopped halfway through, her breath becoming short. The heavy weight of the accident's wrath reminded her that she was not in the fighting shape that she was just a few short weeks before.

They sat among the overgrown shards of grass. She felt the coolness of the damp soil on the palms of her hands as she gently lowered her body to sit. The sunlight was beginning to disappear, marking the end of a long day, the warmth giving way to the gentle chill of the dusk setting in.

There were so many questions that she wanted to ask, each thought aching for the truth.

As she glanced at Joel, he had a faraway look in his eyes. Both of them knew the words that should be spoken, but neither of them broke the strained silence between them.

"What happened out there? They told me you were dead," Mimi whispered.

"In truth, I should be. Mimi, that day will never leave me. It was as if I was alive and then I was dead…only I wasn't. I know that makes no sense."

"It sort of does," she said, her head resting on her knee.

His hand lay flat on the grass. She longed to reach out for it. Before, it would have been the most natural thing in the world. Now, the distance between them and the truth that had risen to the surface had made the simplest gesture tangled with doubt. Only the sound of chirping crickets filled the brief silence.

Mimi's voice was quiet and low when she said, "I know Jake is your son."

"He told you," Joel said in a tone that could have easily been mistaken for anger.

"I've tried to think of a thousand different reasons why you never told me. I have given myself a million more excuses, but the truth is…you lied to me."

She heard Joel inhale deeply. She felt her anxiety rise to the surface once more.

"I thought about telling you so many times," he finally said.

"Then why didn't you?"

"I don't know. I was selfish, I guess. I wanted to leave all of this behind," he said, throwing his hand backwards.

"You have a son. A smart, wonderful, little boy called Jake."

"I know his name," he said quickly, almost trying to defend himself.

"We talked about children of our own, so would you have just up and left them and me?"

"God no, of course not. I would never, ever leave you."

"But you could leave behind a little boy and never give him a chance of knowing his real father?"

"Sara was sleeping with both of us. He could have been either of ours."

Blood rushed to her ears. She twisted her body and faced Joel, looking squarely at him.

"You knew he was yours. DNA results don't lie, do they?" He gave her no answer to her question. "How could you?" she said. Tears started to sting her eyes.

"I was so young. I had no idea what I was doing, no idea what I was thinking. It has nothing to do with us."

Mimi felt her grip tighten. The surge of emotion felt too much to handle.

"Did you ever really love me?" she asked.

"What? I loved you and I still love you. Mimi, you are my wife. It was you that gave me the fight to survive."

"Is that so?" she said, the knot in her stomach pulling tighter.

He reached his hand out to hers. Their fingers intertwined. There was so much doubt between them. Mimi wished she could just push all of her hurt away, but she couldn't.

No matter what direction she took, it would still

leave her with a hole in her heart. There would be no happily ever after in any of this, mainly because of a boy named Jake. The people he should have trusted most in the world lied to him. Whether it was for the greater good, he'll never be given the chance to grow up knowing who his real father is.

"There is so much to talk about," Joel said.

"I can't imagine what you must have seen out there."

He stayed silent. The house of cards that was their life had all come tumbling down. Mimi tried to push deeper, but his expression was haunted. By what, she was not sure—the war he had just returned from, or the past that was threatening to ruin their future.

When Joel had left for his second deployment, she knew he would come back to her a changed man. She knew what he would see and experience would alter the psychological and emotional mind of any human. She had spent many nights wide awake thinking about her husband in combat. She tried to give him comfort and security in the handwritten letters and the thoughtful care packages.

The extended absence between them was survived by the promise he was coming home to her. He had kept that promise. Now, there were so many other layers.

Joel no longer had to deal with the fear of car bombs, roadside bombs, suicide bombers, and mortars. Not only was he taking the psychological beating of the war, it was now about a battle that remained with his brother. The price was bigger, because if he lost Mimi to this, he would rather have taken a bullet to end his life.

If somehow Mimi could get past everything, she had no idea if Joel could get past her sleeping with Austin. She also wondered if she could get past the feelings she had for two men, two men that were brothers.

"When I was a kid, my dad took me out hunting."

"You killed an innocent animal?" Mimi gasped.

"Yeah. It's the Texas way, Mimi. I know how you feel about animals, but it's just the way things are around here. It was the first time. I knew what it was like to watch the life drain out of something."

"What was it you killed?"

"A deer. Actually, hunting is considered to be a bonding session between father and son. My father never offered to take Austin. I don't know why. He had my mother's love. I didn't. It was as if both of us belonged only to one parent. Austin belonged to my mother and I belonged to my father. I just went with it. Austin hated that my dad and I were close. On that hunting trip, I actually asked my father why Austin wasn't invited. He told me it was because he wouldn't be able to take it. At the time, I looked at that like I had one up on him, I was the braver one."

"And yet he is the one raising your son. I don't really see how you are the braver one." She realised how defensive of Austin she sounded and she hoped that it would not giveaway the truth about her feelings for Austin. It was too soon for that.

"Austin was with my father the day he died. Not me. I was supposed to be with him." A lump rose in

Joel's throat. "If I had been there, I would have never have let my father die. It's because of my brother that I lost the man that was my hero."

"Joel, accidents happen," Mimi said softly.

"If he had run to get help, he would have saved my father's life. Instead, he just left him there to die."

She'd never seen Joel cry before. As the tears pinged up into his eyes, she wanted to reach out for him, but she didn't.

"Did you tell him how you felt?"

"No. I waited for him to tell me. Every day I waited. The bond between him and my mother only grew stronger. Without my father, I was lost, I was angry. And then Sara happened."

"So it was revenge?"

"Yes," he answered directly. "I had no idea it was ever going to result in a child."

"Why did you leave?"

"Because without my father, I had no place at the ranch. I left to find a new home, a new family. In the Corps, I found that. Those boys were my brothers, more than my own blood. And then there was you."

"I still don't understand how you signed your child over to your brother. If you hated him that much, then why let him, of all people, raise him?"

"I couldn't come back here. I know it was selfish, but I'm just being honest."

"Did you ever love your brother?"

Joel was taken aback by the question. As boys, they had always been competitive. There was always a race to be won, whether it was swimming in the lake at the meadow or just who could finish dinner the fastest.

Love, perhaps, hadn't ever been a feeling or emotion that either of them had explored. It was a given they would protect one another, but neither of them could protect themselves against one another.

Mimi still wondered where Austin's feelings for her were born out of. Was it revenge? Was she just another cog in the wheel of the never-ending battle between them both?

Yet Austin had been the honest one. So far, Joel hadn't told her a version much different from what Austin had. If she had not come to Texas, would Joel ever have told her that he had a son? She wanted to believe that he would have, but deep down, she just didn't.

CHAPTER 24

Austin

In Dallas, Austin took Jake out to lunch at a burger bar. They talked about ordinary things.

Behind his smile, Austin felt broken inside. His mind kept wandering to Mimi and Joel. He imagined her being so overwhelmed by emotion she would easily fall back into Joel's spell. He hadn't known what sort of couple they were. He didn't know their likes and dislikes, what they had experienced with one another.

What he did know was that he felt beyond jealous. Love is like an endless tapestry of truths. Austin always tried to be honest, but somehow, it never paved the way for an easier life. If anything, he would always end up the loser.

After Jake sucked the last of his strawberry milkshake with a straw, he gave his dad a toothy grin.

"That was good."

"I'm glad. Want another?" Austin asked.

"Nah, I'm good. Dad, I need to ask you something."

"Shoot."

"Is Mimi your girlfriend? I know you said she wasn't, but…well, since she's been gone, you've been really sad."

Austin leaned back in the chair and let out a loud sigh. Jake was a very bright kid, and he had insight into what people felt. Even when he tried to hide things from his son, Jake always had some kind of way of finding out. This worried him.

Amid all the chatter of others around them, and the booming juke-box playing Rascal Flatts, it was strangely silent where Austin and Jake sat. His wide eyes burned into Austin, waiting for an answer.

For the eight years of Jake's life, he knew there would come a day when he would need to tell him the truth. The thought almost crippled him. Although Jake was wise, he was also still a child. He had no idea how telling him he was not his father but his uncle would affect him. It could not only shatter their relationship, but it could also do untold damage in the years to follow.

Then there was the other side of the spectrum—he worried what the weight of a lie would do. Austin had never been tempted to tell Jake the truth. He always told himself he was too young, and when the time was right, he'd tell him, only he could never truly imagine there being a right time.

Back at the ranch, he asked Uma to stay. She knew the truth. He wanted her to be his eyes and ears, he wanted to ensure that Joel did not start wandering through his home. It was too dangerous.

There had been several times he was tempted to call her and find out if Mimi's lips had touched Joel's, or if their hands were joined, but each time he'd reached for his phone, he managed to stop himself.

"I've told you before, Jake. Mimi is not my girlfriend."

"But you love her, right?"

"You ask a lot of questions."

"Well, do you?"

Austin was caught off guard, but he didn't want to keep lying to him. "Yes, I do."

"Then why don't you tell her. She can come live with us. "

"Because Mimi is already married."

"To whom?" The question felt like a kick in his gut. *To whom*. The man who was his real father; a man he has never met. A man who means so little, but so much.

"Do you know him, Daddy?"

"I used to. Remember when you asked me if I had a brother?"

Jake looked at him, confused. He tilted his head to the side "Yes, and you never answered me."

"Well, I do have a brother. And he is the man that is married to Mimi."

A waitress came over and asked if they wanted anything else. Austin was grateful for the interruption. He knew there would be more questions, but at least he would have a few moments to collect his thoughts and work out what he should say next.

The blazing sunlight hit them as soon as they left the coolness of the air conditioned restaurant. Cars and motorcycles were gathering in the street—honking, starting, stopping…it was a far cry from the wide-open spaces and the quiet of the ranch. Tall, angular skyscrapers towered above them.

Jake looked up in amazement. He had never been to Dallas before. The awe on his face was worth a thousand words. He was dazzled by the buzz of the city and watched the sea of people move with a fast pace.

Austin took Jake's small sweaty palm in his. They walked in silence. A beggar sat in the doorway of a store with white-washed windows and a handwritten sign that it was for lease. Austin reached into his back pocket and pulled out a five-dollar bill and dropped it into the beggar's lap. He could smell cheap liquor.

"Buy yourself a decent meal and lay off the booze," he said and continued ahead.

"So, if Mimi's husband is your brother, then that makes him my uncle. Right?"

"Yeah, that's right." He paused for a moment and placed his hands on Jake's shoulders.

"You know what, Jake. I don't think it's a good idea that we talk about my brother for now. He's not a very nice guy."

"Why? What did he do?"

"He left something behind that was very important was his responsibility to take care of. It's a good thing that he did, because that something is now in a very safe place where no harm will ever come to it."

"What was it, Daddy?"

"I can't tell you that. Not yet, but maybe when

you are a little older."

Jake squeezed Austin's hand. "All right, Daddy."

Jake's trust in him made his heart swell and then break. Austin hailed a taxi. They climbed in, instantly feeling cooler as they sat back on the cool leather.

"The Avery," Austin told the driver.

After a short ride, the taxi pulled up outside a stylish hotel, the tinted windows gleaming gold.

Austin paid the driver and pulled Jake out. They walked into the marbled reception and rode several floors in the scenic glass lift.

When they reached their room, Jake said, "Let me do it, Daddy."

He took the key card and swiped it. The green light flicked on and Jake opened the door to a breathtaking suite. Jake headed straight to the fridge and grabbed a bottle of orange juice. Austin reached for a beer. He let the cool liquid slide down his throat, taking off the edge of the day. He threw Jake his phone to play with.

"Batteries are dead, Dad."

"The charger is in the blue bag there on the chair," Austin said, pointing as he disappeared into the main bedroom. On the bedstand, the red message light flashed. He lifted the receiver, fully expecting it to be a courtesy message from the hotel.

After he heard the computer-generated voice tell him that he had one message, nothing prepared him next for the voice at the other end of the phone, a voice that he had not heard for several years, and yet it was a voice so well-known to him it was if he heard it yesterday.

The past was catching up to him in ways that he had not planned for. If it wasn't for Jake, there would be nothing for him to fear. But now so much was at stake.

He sat at the edge of the bed with beads of sweat on his forehead. Somehow, it all felt like a dream, and he wished it only was.

Jake skipped into the room and threw himself onto the bed.

"I'm bored," he complained.

"Jake, I need to talk to you about something," Austin said. He stood for a moment and then knelt by the bed. He put his head in his hands and let out a loud sigh. This was a moment that he had thought about but never planned. If he had a choice, it would never have to happen this way.

His mind flashed back to the day Sara had arrived at the ranch. There was a heavy rain storm that evening. It was late. His mother had stood at the door as Sara cradled Jake in her arms using her denim jacket to shield him from the lashing rain.

"I can't do this," she had sobbed.

That was the night she left the baby in his mother's arms. Just a teenager herself and totally unprepared for the demands of a newborn, she relinquished her responsibility and left.

Joel had already left for the Marines. Her own parents had disowned her. This was the only place she knew she could turn. Austin was just a boy himself. He had no duty or obligation to the child that was his brother's. In a twist of fate, there was a connection that ran far deeper than DNA.

In the weeks and months that passed, Austin had fallen in love with Jake. He assumed all fatherly responsibility. It came so naturally to him. When his mother was diagnosed with cancer, he knew that soon his whole family was going to be his nephew.

One evening, in the wake of his mother's death, he had asked Sara to come to the ranch to discuss Jake. She'd come to the house just past seven, when Jake was down for the night.

The last bit of the coppered coloured evening light glowed. They sat in the kitchen. Austin had offered Sara a drink, but she refused. Austin had thought long and hard about his decision, and it seemed like the most natural one to take. That was the evening that he had asked Sara if he could legally adopt Jake. At first, she had acted outraged. Throughout, Austin had remained calm and explained why he thought it was best.

It took less than thirty minutes for her to agree to a formal adoption. In ways, Austin had thought she would put up a little more of a fight, but when she hadn't, he knew he was making the right choice. Jake would be with somebody who truly wanted him.

The legal process hadn't been straightforward, but eventually, after just under four years, the adoption had become final.

By then, Jake had been calling Austin daddy and he had no intention of ever making him think otherwise, but here, in this moment, when the threat was impending for him to find out, he felt he owed it to his son to tell him the truth.

"You know how much I love you, don't you?" Austin began.

"Yeah." His dark hair was wavy around his face, his cheeks slightly flushed.

"And you know that nothing will ever change just how much?"

"I think so," Jake answered nervously.

"Jake, do you know what DNA is?"

"Yeah, yeah, I do. It's that stuff in your blood. I learned about it from Jurassic Park."

Austin managed a smile. "That's right. Well, the reason that I want to talk to you about this is about something biological. Do you know what that means?"

"I think so. Doesn't it have to do with washing powder?"

"No. I guess I am going about this all in the wrong way. Remember how I told you that I have a brother and he is married to Mimi?"

"Yeah, I remember."

"Jake, I love you so much. You know that, right?"

"Daddy, what is it?" Jake asked. He watched his father with his head in his hands, his shoulders rising and falling. "Daddy, are you crying?"

CHAPTER 25

Joel

Joel found Mimi in the kitchen drinking a hot drink, lost in thought. She wore a light blue cotton dress, her hair hanging in loose curls down her back.

"Morning," he said.

She turned and looked at him. She didn't take her gaze away from him. They had slept separately. There was too much between them, too many lies, but not just on his part.

"What is it like being back here?" Mimi asked, setting her cup gently on the table in front of her. Joel pulled out a chair and sat down. He paused for a moment. All he wanted to do was make his past disappear. He wished he was back in London, curled up with Mimi on the sofa, making love, being grateful that he had survived.

He'd hardly slept the night before. The slightest noise startled him and he'd immediately pounce up, ready to fight, but he was back in the States now, living a new nightmare. He was constantly on edge. Many Marines had spoken of this, but he didn't want to admit that he was suffering from post-traumatic stress syndrome even though the signs were there.

"I'm happy to be alive. And I am happy you made it through that car wreck. Jesus, Mimi, when I heard that you were hurt, all I wanted to do was get to you."

He noticed a small red blotch on the bottom of her neck. She caught him staring.

"Bruises are everywhere," she quickly said. He pressed his lips together and nodded.

"What made you come here?" Joel asked.

"After they told me you were dead, I was a mess. Actually, it was Meg's idea to come to Texas. She came with me."

"Meg is here?"

"She only came out for a couple of weeks. You know Meg, she had her life to get back to. But she was really there for me. After she left, your brother invited me to stay."

"How did you find out about Jake?" He swallowed hard, imagining the glory that his little brother would have taken in telling her that he was a deadbeat father who had run out on his only son.

"Austin didn't tell me. I was looking through some old photos, trying to find out about you as a child when I came across Jake's birth certificate. That is how I learned you were his father."

"I wanted to tell you, Mimi. There were so many times that I wanted to."

"Then why the hell didn't you, Joel?" Tears

sprung in her eyes. “When they told me you were dead, I seriously wanted to go to sleep and never wake up again. I came here to feel close to you and then I find out everything you told me was a lie. I have no idea who the fuck I married.”

“You know me, Mimi. I never lied about loving you. I’m so sorry you found out this way. If I could change everything, I would.”

“Do I know you? Everything you told me was a lie.”

“Not everything.” He stood up and walked toward her. He knelt on the floor, cupping his hand under her chin, catching the tears that fell.

“I love you. I never lied about that. I made so many mistakes, but I will do everything I can to fix it. When I was out there, my life was hanging in the balance, but I promised myself that I would do everything that I could to fix everything.”

“Did you ever think about Jake?” she asked.

“Every day. I’m not the asshole Austin has probably told you that I am. I had a kid with a girl I didn’t love, but that’s not Jake’s fault. I know that now. I was young, I was angry, and I felt guilty for not being with my father the day he died. I blamed Austin for my father’s death, and I wanted nothing to do with this ranch or my brother. I wanted out. Nothing was going to keep me here, not even Jake. Now I see that I was wrong.”

“I want to believe you.”

“Believe me, Mimi Mimi.”

She raised her head and locked eyes with his emerald green eyes. He ran his index finger in circular motions around her cheek. He moved in even closer to her and gently kissed her lips. At first, she pulled away, but he kissed her again, this time harder.

She allowed his tongue to slip into her mouth. His arms gripped her tight.

"I'll make it right," he said in a breathy voice.

***

Mimi

Later that morning, Mimi went into the guest room. She sat at the end of the bed, her mind drifting back to when she was here with Austin. Her heart felt torn. She wondered how she allowed herself to fall for two men, two brothers.

She had a choice to make. She thought about going back to London and letting go of both of them because no good could ever come of this, yet the thought of leaving Texas left her with an overbearing weight of sadness. She knew she had to follow her heart, but in this very moment, she wasn't sure which man her heart belonged to.

Her head filled with images of both of them—of Joel back in California, under the glass bus stop with the rain pouring, promising her he was coming back to her; of Austin in the meadow, kissing her tenderly; and watching the way he was with Jake, a beautiful child that Joel had left far behind.

She wished she knew what to do. She wished none of this had ever happened.

When she thought about her journey that had led her to this, she was overwhelmed with emotion. She had no idea who she was anymore. If she didn't know who she was, how could she ever decide what was best?

She took in a deep breath. Austin felt like home, like safety and belonging. Thoughts of Joel made her stomach knot. It was like being at the top of a roller coaster and waiting for the fall.

Her body was tired and stiff, like it had been wrung out. She thought about how she almost died, how Joel almost died, and yet here they were, back together again, as if fate had tested them.

The last time she saw Austin was two days before. He had driven her back to the ranch after she had given a tearful goodbye to her parents, who had begged to stay with her to make sure she was well looked after, but they hadn't the money or resources. Mimi had appreciated their love and promised to call them every day. She promised them that as soon as she was given the all-clear to fly, she would go back to London.

The smell of coffee wafted up the stairs. It suddenly reminded her of the mornings she spent watching Austin prepare Jake's lunch for the day. The days she had spent drifting through the house like a ghost, wallowing in pity and grief over losing Joel were not that long ago, but now he was back, and she had a new kind of grief that she shouldn't have and it made her feel sick with guilt.

She crossed the room and curled her fingers around the door knob. She suddenly sensed something. When she stood at the top of the staircase, her blood ran cold and her palms started to sweat. At first, she thought that she must be imagining things, but when she ran into the front bedroom and saw Austin's black truck with mud splattered up the doors, she knew he was home and he was about to face Joel for the first time in years.

She ran back to the stairs. She was not ready to have her own dishonesty to Joel burst out into the open. She had no idea what to think or feel. As she took the first step down the stairs, she felt rooted to the spot. She held the banister rail to keep herself steady.

She tugged at the hem of her blue dress and locked eyes on Austin standing in the hallway. He was unshaven, and, by the creases in his clothes, it looked like he had gotten dressed in a crazy hurry. There was darkness in his eyes. His jaw remained tight and fists clenched.

"It's been a long time," she heard Joel say. Neither of them noticed her on the stairs. She tried to move closer to the wall, as if that would somehow shield her from being seen altogether.

It had been seven years since they were last in a room together, only this time the open casket of their mother wasn't there to keep them from finally coming to blows with one another.

Seeing them together for the first time, Mimi felt a wave of sickness come over her. These two men were so similar in appearance, but so different in heart. Things had never been that way for Mimi and Larna. As the years had lengthened, so had the love that she had for her sister.

Joel was the man she had promised her life to. To this day, she had still, even after she had found out that he had fathered another child, kept her wedding ring on as if it was a symbol of hope. When she had made love to Austin, the glint of the shiny diamonds had reflected as if they were blades passing through her body, reminding her she was married; only she believed Joel was dead. Mimi had told herself that, time and time again.

She thought about the ranch and how this once was a family home. She wondered many times, *If these walls could talk, what would they say?*

Over the past few weeks, she had been faced with so many emotions. What most people would go through in an entire lifetime had unravelled itself to her in the most dramatic of explosions. She had lived through her husband going off to war and then being told his life had ended in bloodshed. Then she had met his estranged brother keeping her husband's love child and raising him as his own. Her own life hung in the balance, and now it had come to this very moment of truth.

Yet it was not just a truth between Austin and Joel. It was a truth about a child and Mimi's heart. There had been so many thoughts rushing through her head the day she had found Jake's birth certificate. The feeling of betrayal had burned into her and it was laced with so many other doubts. She questioned what else Joel had lied about. Up until then, she had considered Joel to be a man that lived in the moment, but what she hadn't known was the truth, and the truth was, he was trying to hide a past.

"Stay the fuck away. You've been gone all this time. You are nothing but a stranger to him." Austin's voice was eerily calm, but it carried the weight of threat.

"I've made mistakes. I know that, but he has a right to know about me."

"You signed him away. Mom begged you. Why now? I don't care what epiphany you may have had out there. You were already dead to me, Joel, and to Jake, you don't exist."

The words hung in the air. Joel may have come back from a war alive, but right now, he wasn't sure he would come away from the war of his past and be rescued from it all.

Mimi was confused. She could only assume that Austin was talking about Jake.

Without thinking for a second longer, she moved down the steps. They both turned to her.

Joel moved toward her and put a protective hand on her shoulder.

"Don't," she said, and pushed his hand away. "What the hell is going on here?"

"Why don't you ask your brave military boy?" Austin said.

"Fuck you," Joel spat.

Austin lunged forward, but Mimi quickly stood between them.

"Stop it…stop it!" she screamed. Her voice cracked like glass shattering. Every last emotion spilled out of her, bursting free out of her body.

She looked at Joel, his face twisted. She had never seen him like this before.

"Mimi, I want to see Jake. I called Austin when he was in Dallas."

"Ah well, look at that. Is your mouth on fire? You just told the truth for once in your sorry ass life. You think you are some big goddam hero, fighting in a war with your big guns, your ooh-rah buddies, but you're not a man. What real man runs out on their kid?"

"I need to get some air," Joel said. He pushed past Austin and pulled the front door open.

The air was humid and thick. Sunlight drenched the fields in a golden light. The echo of a voice came from behind him. Joel felt as though he were surrounded by a cyclone of memories. In the distance, he saw the place where his father took his final breath.

The day their father's life had ended was the day that their war had started. Or so Joel believed, but for Austin, it had been way before then.

Mimi stood in the doorway, watching Joel walk away in the distance, and for the first time, she didn't think of him as the brave super hero she had painted in her mind. She saw a coward, a deadbeat father who turned away from a beautiful child.

She felt a wave of sadness wash over her.

"I can't let him take him," Austin whispered. She turned and saw his eyes spring with tears.

"I'll talk to him," Mimi said.

"Like he's going to tell you the truth."

His words stung her. She wanted to yell at him, but she had no fight left in her. And as much as she wanted to disagree with him, she knew he was right, and it killed her.

***

The rest of the day moved forward in a blur. It had been a few hours since Joel left out the front door.

Mimi ran after him, but he told her he knew how badly he had messed things up. He said he would make it all right again, especially with her, but for now he needed a few hours alone.

She had no idea where he went. Without a car, she assumed he couldn't go too far.

Back at the house, Mimi walked into a wall of silence except for the ticking of a clock on the wall. She moved through the house, searching for Austin. She finally found him sitting in his office, holding a glass of whisky. The room was in darkness, the heavy curtains drawn, shutting out the final glow of the orange sun.

Mimi thought of the days she had soaked her pillows with tears back in her tiny flat in London, trying to piece together how her husband spent his final moments on earth. She'd had no idea he'd been rescued. The past swept in, no longer willing to wait to come forward.

"Tell me why you love him." The slur of Austin's voice was drenched in pity and anger, maybe even jealousy.

"Where's Jake?"

"Safe. I can't let him see him. He can't know. I almost told Jake, but I couldn't shatter his whole world. I can't let him get dragged into all this shit. I will be honest with him one day, but right now, he's too young. He wouldn't understand why his real father never wanted him and why I lied to him. So you told him where I was, then?" His gaze met hers, waiting for an answer.

"I told him you were in Dallas. That's all I said,"

Mimi answered in a defensive tone.

"Amazing. Out of all of the hotels, he happens to find me at The Avery."

Mimi rubbed her finger along her temple.

"I must've mentioned it," she confessed.

"This is out of control. All of it. I cannot allow Jake to find out, not like this."

Mimi wrapped her arms around her body and took a seat. There seemed to be too much at risk with her being there. She finally realized what she must do.

"I'm going to talk to Joel. And I'll get him away from the ranch. That way you can protect Jake from all of this and then you and Joel can decide what is best, but I think the distance needs to be put between you both again. It will never work like this."

"And you, Mimi? What is it that you want?"

"It doesn't matter what I want. The most important person in this is Jake. He needs to be kept away from all this drama. Where is he now?"

"With Sara."

"Does she know?"

"Yes. She is going to keep Jake with her until I deal with things. I can't believe all of this. I mean, shit, how did we get here?" Austin said, pouring more whiskey into the glass. Glancing up at her, he gave her a sorry smile. "Look at what you got yourself tied up into."

"You know, my wish when I was told that Joel had been killed was to go to sleep and be told, when I woke up, that it was all a bad dream. When I came here and found you and then Jake, I almost believed that somehow it was all meant to be. And then, finding out that Joel was alive and surviving my car accident…I don't know what anything means anymore. When I saw Joel again, I thought it would all make sense, that all my old feelings for him would come flooding back, but he feels different to me, like a stranger. I feel like I don't even know my own husband. And then there is you. I don't really know you, but somehow you feel like home."

Austin got up and moved across the room. He sat by Mimi. His breath was hot and heavy from the whiskey. "I wish I'd found you first," he whispered.

"I feel so confused." Mimi looked into his eyes.

"None of this is going to be straightforward. My feelings for you, they haven't changed, but I need to protect my son. He's my son, Mimi. I raised him."

"I know he is. I know I shouldn't say this, but I've fallen in love with you, and now I understand why you let me go that day of the accident. So now I know I need to let you go to keep your life safe. Where Joel and I go from here, I don't know, but it's because I love you that I need to keep you safe and keep Jake safe."

Austin tilted his head back, breathing in deep. "It was never going to happen for us. I'll never forget you."

"And I'll never forget you."

She took Austin's head in her hands and kissed him tenderly on his lips. He gripped her tighter, but she pulled away. If she didn't resist him now, she would hold onto him and never let go. In that moment, she knew where her heart was. If Jake were not at risk, she'd choose Austin.

Too much had happened with Joel. She didn't know the man she married. Their relationship was laced with too many secrets and too many lies for her to ever feel the way she once did.

Her heart chose Austin, but her head kept her with Joel.

Our brain makes millions of unconscious choices everyday—to turn left or to turn right, what food we eat—but it's matters of the heart that have our undivided attention because those choices determine the rest of our lives and map out our future.

"I sort of wonder why you are letting Joel stay here. I mean, this is your home."

"Yeah, it is, but technically my parents left it to both of us, so I can't tell him he can't be here. Under the circumstances with your accident and all, it was easier for him to be here and me be gone, but after he called me in Dallas and said that he wanted to see Jake, I had to get back here, even if that meant facing him after all this time."

"This is all so fucked up," Mimi said and shook her head.

"Yeah, yeah, it is."

Many times Austin had wondered about Joel's life. He was living as a Marine, and Austin had stayed true to his roots as a cowboy. They were worlds apart, but they would forever be connected.

Even as children, there was a distance between them. Austin could never remember feeling close to his older brother, not in the way he thought that most siblings should. They had spent time together, that was a given, but a brotherly bond had never been formed.

Neither of them had ever tried to understand what had gone wrong, nor had they tried to fix it. Instead, they competed against one another. The older they became, the more serious the competition.

It had never really been about Sara. She was just something else they could fight over. With Mimi and Jake, everything was different. It wasn't about winning or losing. It was about doing the right thing.

There would be no kiss and makeup between the two brothers. It had gone way beyond that. There could be no reconciling and beers on a Friday night as they watched the game. They needed to be apart because if they were together, the friction between them could ruin their lives forever.

***

Joel

Joel walked for several miles, thinking and feeling unsettled with the way Mimi had seemed to almost protect Austin. He took himself to the meadow. His mind flashed back to when he used to come here with his father. He could almost hear his voice in the whisper of the wind. He was certain that if his dad had never died, things would have never turned out the way they had.

He settled onto a rock jutting out by the lake and started skipping stones into the flattened surface of the water. He counted the bounces before the rock sunk into the lake's depths, never to resurface. That is how he had always thought his secret would be kept from Mimi, *sunken beneath the surface*.

He realised he had spent so long running away from the truth that he was tired. He thought about everything he had been through in the last few months and realised that his demons were not only in the war that almost took his life, but deeply rooted into his history, and it all stemmed from the relationship with his brother.

He never really knew where it had all gone wrong. The memories he had were now a blur. Being back at the ranch brought back so many unwanted memories. The Marines had carved out a new life for him, had given him a new purpose. It was as if his childhood belonged to somebody else.

The day that Joel joined the Corps was the day he thought he was becoming a man. Nothing could have prepared him for the vigorous training he received. The decisions he had made were the ones that change lives. There was a drive inside him. When he had wanted to give in, something deeper had pushed him forward.

On the first day of boot camp, he stepped out of the stifling bus and onto the yellow footprints on the sticky tarmac. He locked eyes with his drill instructor, a burly hulk of a man. His voice boomed like a stereophonic surround sound system, and he had a growl that sounded like it had come from the belly of a beast.

Joel, along with the other recruits, moved into the receiving phase. His body was no longer his own; it was the property of the Corps. As the buzz of the clippers pushed on his head like the mowing of grass, he felt as if the clumps of hair that had fallen to the floor was shedding the skin of who he used to be.

In the weeks and months that followed, his body and mind were pushed to places he never thought were possible. There were times he had almost given up, particularly one night in the depths of darkness with the lashing rain soaking through his tired and weak body and his drill instructor yelling in his ears.

Then he remembered how his father had always told him to never give up on a dream. His dad always said anything worth anything in life was worth fighting for; the road ahead may not be smooth, but it's the bumps, bruises, and scars that build character. It's what makes a man a man, so he stayed.

He pushed harder because he had something to prove, and he made it through the thirteen weeks of being knocked down to nothing to become something—the man that made him tough enough to fight a war.

He dismissed his history, his life at the ranch the day that he shed his old skin. He had buried it deep. The Marines allowed him to travel to places in the world that he probably would have never discovered if he had chosen to stay in Texas.

In the drizzle of an early London morning, the fog just starting to burn away from the sun burning through, he had been running when Mimi crashed into him. His attraction for her had been instant. Moments like that one don't just happen. He believed it was fate.

When he heard her well-spoken voice, he thought her tone had a golden ring of class and sophistication. He just wanted her to keep talking and never stop. Her laugh was girlish, but her eyes had a fierceness about them.

He couldn't let her go. It was a moment in time that he knew was a once-in-a-lifetime thing. If he had let his raven-haired girl walk away, he knew that he would spend the rest of his life thinking about her and what if? He was a risk taker by nature, but this was the one time that he wasn't prepared to risk letting go of a woman he knew was about to change his life.

A warm breeze blew over him. His legs still had cuts and bruises, marking the journey that he had just survived. He thought about Abdul and where he was now. He was the enemy who had spared his life and restored his faith in human nature.

Then he thought about his real enemy. His kid brother, his blood. He could feel emotion rising through him. Austin had taken Joel's place as Jake's father, a job that Joel should have taken responsibility for, even if he had never loved the woman he created the life of a child with.

When the DNA results were in, he had hoped, prayed, and begged God to not be Jake's father because then walking away would have been easy.

He thought about going back, about meeting the little boy that was his son, but he could never summon enough heart to do it. Keeping his head in battle somehow kept him in a place he felt he belonged, and so he let Jake go without ever holding the infant in his arms or feeling his warm, sweet breath on his cheek.

Once he gathered more of his thoughts, he stood up and realised he had been reflecting on his life for hours. His belly growled for food and his body was tired and weak. The sun was sinking in the horizon, its rays of light glimmering in the darkness, the clouds starting to shadow as the day transitioned into night, just like he and his brother—day and night.

He didn't know where he belonged now. Mimi looked at him in a different way than the way she had before. He deeply regretted not telling her the truth.

On the day of his rescue, he never imagined that he would be back at the ranch, and he never thought that he would have to fight again, only this time for his wife.

On the day he married her, he never imagined anything would break them, but he knew he only had himself to blame. The warrior inside him was determined to win her back. He would fix the wrongs he had done in his life and make things right between them.

He walked back to the ranch. The air was starting to cool after the long, hot day. When he pushed open the front door, the house was quiet. He moved into the living area, careful as he did so. He felt like an imposter in a home that was once his kingdom.

Surrounding him were photos of a life that did not belong to him even though the boy in the pictures did. He was not sure how he felt looking at this young child who bared such an undeniable resemblance to him, and yet he did not know the sound of his voice, the touch of his hand, or who his favourite band was.

For the first time since Jake was born, Joel felt truly ashamed that he had not been in his life. He carefully sat down on the sofa, wiping away the beads of sweat on his forehead with the back of his hand.

He could hear the sound of footsteps outside of the room becoming louder as they passed through the corridor. He quickly and carefully placed the silver photo frame of Jake on a fishing trip back on the glass table, next to a small crystal lamp that had belonged to his mother. He did not want to get caught touching anything in the house. It was his brother's house now. No longer was it the family home.

He wondered if Austin had any regrets. He couldn't imagine that he did. When he had spoken to his brother for the first time in years, he was met with a stone cold silence. When he had said that he wanted to see Jake, he was met with rage.

Joel had lots of regrets and secrets that had kept him awake at night whilst Mimi had slept peacefully in his arms, blissfully unaware of the life he had turned his back on. He thought there would be a moment in time when he would be able to tell her, to let his secret out of the hidden depths he had buried within himself, but that time had never come. He had gone to war, fought the enemy, and moved like a cat in the jungle searching for prey. He had been brave, but facing the mistakes of the past and saying those mistakes aloud to his wife had become too tall of a task.

Later that night, Joel crept into the bedroom where Mimi lay. Her dark hair flowed freely over the white, crisp sheets. Her bare arm was draped gently across her stomach.

Back in London, he would never have hesitated to slip in next to her and tenderly pull her body close to his. Now, everything was different. This wasn't just a simple argument that could be settled with a wise crack and a kiss.

"Are you awake?" he whispered.

Mimi stayed silent. She was unsure what to say to her husband. She turned and looked at him. In a way, it was as if he was a ghost. She was sure that if she rubbed her eyes, he would disappear.

Joel's gaze moved to Mimi's eyes.

"I'm so sorry," he said quietly.

Mimi sat up in bed, pulled her knees into her chest, and sighed.

Joel took a small step toward her, and then stopped, staying rooted as he waited for her permission to move closer. Mimi felt awkward and uneasy. She was in the same room where she had made love to Austin. She was afraid that Austin would hear them talking.

"Are you all right?" Mimi asked.

"Truthfully, no. I am every inch of fucked up right now."

"Where did you go today?"

"I just walked for miles. I needed to think. There is a place I used to go to as a kid, a meadow where my dad used to take us to fish and swim."

Mimi tried not to show any recognition about the fact that she knew the meadow well. It was a memory that now belonged to her and Austin. She felt sick knowing that there were so many secrets between them both. She thought about telling him the truth about her and Austin. She tried to justify things by telling herself that it wasn't cheating if she thought she was a widow.

Mimi knew that wasn't reason enough in her own head to do the things that she had done, so she decided to keep it inside. She also had no idea what Joel had just been though, where his mind was, or how far the psychological damage of a war had affected him.

"So this is what happens to us when we are apart," Joel said, pointing at Mimi's cast. He ran his finger gently along the fading bruises on her cheek.

"Seems like it." She managed a smile.

He noticed that Mimi was still wearing her wedding ring. It gave him some small reassurance that she had not given up on him entirely.

"What was it like out there?"

"Another world. Another planet. You are constantly looking over your shoulder, waiting for somebody to jump you or waiting for a bomb to explode in your face. There were a few moments when I really thought I was going to die. And the whole time I was thinking of you."

He gently moved himself further onto the bed, but he was careful not to touch her.

Mimi propped the pillows up behind her and sank her shoulders into them.

"Were you scared?"

"I was scared of not keeping my promise to you. I promised you I was coming back. After Eric died in front of me, I thought I was next."

Mimi nodded thoughtfully. "I'm so sorry about Eric."

"Thank you, but that's what we all signed up for. We know that when we go in, there is a good chance we are not coming back out."

"You are here," she said with a smile that was both sad and happy.

"Did Austin take care of you?"

Mimi froze. His question caught her off guard, and she felt her cheeks flush. She was certain that Joel could see their story written all over her face. She'd never been good at keeping secrets. She was always lousy holding her cards close to her chest.

"Yeah. Well, I mean, he took care of all the medical stuff."

"Is that all he took care of?"

Mimi was unsure how to read Joel's tone. She felt her mouth go dry and wished that she could somehow disappear.

"He's been accommodating," she said flatly.

"Good," Joel said with a weak smile. She tried not to breathe too hard, to indicate her relief that he was not pressing her about Austin any further.

"Can I stay with you tonight?" Joel asked.

"I'm not ready. Joel, there is nothing more I wanted than for you to come back to me, but I can't move past you not telling me the truth. Did you think I wouldn't have understood?"

"If I told you that I had a kid, I know that you and I would have still been together. Sure, it would have complicated things, but we would have gotten through it."

"So why didn't you tell me?"

"Because I ran away from my kid, and I don't think you would have gotten past that."

"How do you know?"

"By the way you are looking at me right now, it's like I've already lost you."

"Don't you dare put this on me, Joel. The mistakes that you have made are…well, I don't even know what to say, but it's the secrets that you kept from me, that's the part I can't seem to get past. I have no idea who the hell I married."

"You do know me, Mimi Mimi."

"Don't call me that," she said, shaking her head. "Just don't call me that."

***

Mimi

In the early hours of the morning, a storm rolled in. Mimi had fallen asleep, but the wind rustling in the falling leaves stirred her. Thunder rumbled, followed by jagged lightning bolts. The rain lashed hard against the windows.

When she opened her eyes, she saw Joel still next to her, staring at the inclement weather.

She thought back to the morning when she had awoken from a nightmare, the day before she was told Joel had been killed. Back then, she would have given anything for him to be right back next to her. She had been so in love with him, the Joel that he made her believe he was.

Her feelings for Austin snuck up on her. She certainly hadn't planned it. When she learned the truth about Joel, the prism through which she saw him distorted and blurred the parts of him that were familiar to her.

She also realised that she never shared a real life with Joel—the daily things, like paying bills, going food shopping, or reading next to each other in bed. She had been wrapped up in an adventure with him, exploring places with each other and sharing their hopes and dreams for the future.

They lived in the moment together because they always knew they were on borrowed time, awaiting news of his next deployment, so they had used their time together as a bucket list, loving passionately without condition. Now Mimi thought she had deluded herself. She hadn't pushed for the truth hard enough, and as much as she hated to admit it, there were signs, but she had chosen to ignore them.

Meg had her reservations about Joel. Mimi had chosen to ignore her and tell herself that as much as she loved her friend, she had no idea what being in love felt like. Meg always had a new exciting man on the go. Even her short time in Texas had proved that.

She remembered Meg's warnings. "Don't forget that old saying, honey. They have a girl in every port." Mimi had laughed off her friend's playful but meaningful jibe.

"What else have you lied to me about?" Mimi whispered.

"Nothing, I swear it."

"Have you ever cheated on me?"

"What? No, of course not," he answered quickly.

In the past, when she asked him a question, she had taken his answer as the gospel truth. Now she was searching for clues. Did his gaze meet hers? Did he answer too quickly, too slowly? Was his voice even and cool, or was it anxious? She knew her trust been broken with him, and she wasn't sure that she would be able to find a way back to that trust.

Joel turned away from the window. Her question was to be expected. He had prepared himself for it; he'd even gone over what he was going to say in his mind, over and over.

Have you ever cheated on me?

Her words echoed in his head long after she said them.

CHAPTER 26

London: The Third Date

It was just past 10:30 p.m. The last orders were put in at The Mad Hatter, a nineteenth-century pub located off Portland Place. It had been a gloriously sunny, hot day in London.

Joel met Mimi after work. They went out for dinner and prepared for a night where they would meet friends for drinks. This was the night that Joel met Meg for the first time. When she had pulled him in for a kiss on his cheek, she had seductively brushed her hand across his chest. Mimi was smiling and hugging another friend, Fiona, who she hadn't seen in weeks. She hadn't noticed. The night was fuelled with too much red wine and fun-filled laughter. The crowds of office workers had come in droves, ready to shake off the pressures of a long, hard week and let a beer or two take off the edge.

After the evening drew to an end, a feisty bunch of men gathered in the archway of the pub door. Mimi had hailed a black cab, unaware of the commotion going on behind her.

When she turned back, she saw Joel with his arm around Meg, leading her away from the jeers. "Those guys are trouble," Meg slurred, unsteady on her sky high black heels.

"I could talk to them, tell them to shut the hell up, but I'm afraid I'd kill them. And if a Marine gets into a fight with a civilian...well, let's just say that I'd get in some serious shit."

Mimi looked back at the men, feeling a knot in her stomach. "Meg, you need to get in the cab. Come back with us."

"I can't. Have to get back to my flat. My mother is coming for the weekend. You know what she's bloody like. She'll be at my door at the crack of dawn, so I need to get back."

"Joel, go with her, please," Mimi pleaded.

"Oh, don't be daft. I can handle myself," Meg said.

"Seriously, Meg. I don't trust those guys. I have a really bad feeling. Just let Joel go with you."

Meg gave Joel a sideways glance. He paused for a moment. "Yeah, okay. I'll see you in the morning." He gave Mimi a firm kiss on the lips.

"Oh, and Joel? Be a gentleman and give my bestie your jacket."

Mimi got into the cab with Fiona. Joel and Meg watched the taxi roar down the London street. The indicator flashed left and disappeared out of sight, then Meg turned to face him. "So, back to my place, soldier boy?"

He hadn't planned it, but he didn't resist it either.

When Joel walked Meg to her door, the security light flipped on. A voice in his head was telling him to leave it there, but he was drawn in by her mouth—her full, pouty, and lustrous lips were too inviting.

"So, are you coming in?" Meg said, propping herself up against the door frame and removing her heels, gently rubbing her tired feet. Meg locked her gaze directly onto Joel, speaking in a husky tone.

"You're drunk, Meg."

"So are you." She giggled.

Joel stood with his hands by his sides. He was attracted to Meg, but he knew that it could only lead to something bad if he were to accept her invite. If he walked through that door, whether or not something happened, it would only scream out what his intentions were.

He craned his neck. Looking past Meg, he could hear the sound of music in the background.

"Do you live with somebody?"

"No, I'm all alone. I just set the TV so people think I'm in. As you can see, I'm not in the best neighbourhood. So many break-in's and drug deals around here. Actually, I feel a little uneasy tonight, so a big, strong Marine staying with me would make me feel, shall we say...safe."

Joel shook his head. "I don't know. This isn't right. I'm seeing Mimi. You're her best friend, remember?"

Colour rose to Meg's cheeks. She stumbled backwards, looking slightly embarrassed. Joel grabbed her by the arm, stopping her from falling.

"Easy there, girl."

She glared at his hand gripped around her and then looked up at him. She slowly moved her lips towards his.

Suddenly, he stepped back. "What are you doing?"

"I...I thought this is what you wanted. Jesus, Joel, you were flirting with me all night at the pub. I'm not an idiot, I know the signs."

"You read them all wrong. I'm with Mimi."

"Right, Mimi. And you've known her, what, all of five fucking minutes?"

"Watch yourself, girl," he said, leaning into her, whispering in her ear. "I've known her for a short time, but you've known her for your whole life. She's your friend. As I see it, you are nothing but a whore hitting on your best friend's boyfriend. Now, take yourself to bed and sleep off your stupidity. I'll never mention this to Mimi. It would break her heart. Hopefully in the morning, you'll wake up and thank your lucky stars I'm not there next to you. Once you deceive somebody, it can never be undone."

Meg looked at him like a deer in headlights. She couldn't find the words to say, so she nodded and sank her body into the darkness of the flat with nothing but the light from the TV highlighting the shame on her face.

When she closed the door, Joel reached into his pocket and called Mimi. It went straight to her answer phone.

"Hey babe, it's me. Just wanted to let you know that Meg is safe and sound back at her place. I'm missing you already. I'll see you tomorrow."

He stared at the bright red door and at the corner of his eye he saw the flicker of the curtain.

Meg was watching. He raised his hand and waved her goodbye, then he started walking away.

"Joel…you forgot your jacket," Meg said, standing in a t-shirt, her bare legs tanned and long.

He eyed her up and down. Without saying another word, he walked back up the path and took his jacket. Meg planted her mouth on his. He ran his hand up her shirt and then grabbed her bottom.

"Do you want to see just how much of a whore I can be, soldier boy?"

Without thinking further, he walked through the front door.

When Mimi got home that evening, she threw her keys onto the kitchen table. She was exhausted, but happy. She was so pleased that her friends seemed to really like Joel. It meant so much to her. Winston, her cat, jumped off the sofa, arching his back and stretching. He then circled around Mimi's legs, purring like a car motor, clearly seducing her for food.

Bending forward, she stroked the cat and let her hand glide across his silky black fur. She felt her phone vibrate and saw that she had a voicemail from Joel. She listened to his deep Texan accent and smiled.

"Winston, I've met somebody really special. I think you'll love him too."

The next morning, back at Meg's flat, Joel lay next to Meg, his breath steady, his body sweaty. Meg was on her back, gazing up to the ceiling, not uttering a single word. The reality of what had just happened suddenly hit her.

"She can't ever know," Joel said.

"Hardly a match made in heaven. Cheating on your girlfriend already," Meg responded.

"And I don't see you getting the best friend in the world award any time soon."

"Touché."

"Seriously, she can't find out about this," Joel said.

Meg turned on her side, holding the bed sheet close to her body.

"It will be our little secret."

Meg knew what she did was wrong, but her determination to get what she wanted in life was always her first priority, no matter who it hurt.

When Mimi and Meg were children, Meg had envied her life. She came from a family who loved her and wanted her around. Unlike her own parents, who were divorced and argued over who would have her, not because they wanted her, but because they didn't. They wanted to be free of her, so she had spent most of her time at Mimi's house.

Not only did Mimi have the perfect parents who actually gave a damn about one another, but she had an older sister who always had her back. Was she jealous of her friend? Absolutely. Life was good to Mimi and it just wasn't fair. Meg resented it, so if she could have a slice of Mimi's good fortune, she was going to take it. They lived only a door away from another, a fence apart, but they may as well have been worlds apart.

Meg rolled out of bed. She looked out of the window, which faced a small garden area. The sign saying no ball games had recently been vandalized, a spray of red graffiti freshly smeared on it. It was seven in the morning, but the sun was already shining. It was going to be another beautiful day. The dew was still visible on the blades of grass nearby.

Joel got out of bed, covering his naked body with a towel draped across a wicker chair, a gift from Mimi when Meg had moved into her new flat just six months before.

He looked at Meg, his jaw rigid.

"This was a mistake."

"There are no mistakes in life. I won't tell her. You are off the hook. Now please get dressed and leave. My mother's going to be here soon and it's best if you're gone before she gets here."

Joel reached for his jeans and took his scrunched up t-shirt into his hand, pulling it over his head as he left. In his pocket, as he shut the front door behind him, his phone rang.

Mimi.

"Morning, babes." Her voice was so bright and breezy, and he instantly felt a stab of guilt.

"Hey."

"Sounds like you're out."

"Yeah, I went for a run. It's going to be a nice day," he said, looking up into the perfect deep blue sky.

"Ready for the big day?"

"Sure, yeah, I can't wait to meet your folks. Look, Mimi, I..."

"Everything all right?"

"Yup, great, sweetheart. I'm just really sweaty. I

need to go home and shower. I'll meet you at Finchley Central at two p.m."

"Joel," she said before he ended the conversation, "you were a hit with the girls last night. I know my parents will love you too."

He swallowed the lump that had risen in his throat. "I'll see you at two."

And then he hung up. He could still smell Meg's perfume clinging to his skin. He couldn't wait to shower her scent off him and wash away the guilt that had hit him hard in the light of day.

***

"Are you nervous?" Mimi said when Joel slipped into her Fiat 500. She had her Gucci sunglasses on, which framed her pretty face. Her hair was loose and free.

He gripped the door handle and managed a smile, which he hoped looked convincing enough. "Really looking forward to it."

His mind flashed back to the night before. He walked away. He actually didn't give into temptation until Meg came out once more, standing there, inviting him back. Her allure became too overwhelming for him to resist.

Mimi drove out of the station car-park, humming along carefree to a song on the radio. She had no idea.

As they pulled into the paved driveway, a high-pitched bark filled the air. Arf arf arf.

"Don't mind Stanley. He's old and pretty blind," Mimi said, clicking her key fob to lock the car.

A woman came to the door. She looked just like Mimi, and there was no doubt that she was her mother. Joel had been looking forward to meeting Mimi's family, but now, with one deep hidden secret and a fresh one to his list, he was afraid a mother would be able to read between the lines and somehow sense the things that were hidden.

Kanchana pushed the door open and opened her arms to hug Mimi. She kissed her daughter on her forehead and brushed her hand through her hair. "So, this is your young man?" Her gaze turned to Joel.

"Nice to meet you, ma'am."

Kanchana turned and smiled at Mimi and gave her a wink.

"Call me Kanchana, please. Ma'am makes me feel like I should be living on Southfork." She giggled.

"Ma," Mimi said, playfully prodding her mother in the ribs.

Joel lowered his head and chuckled. "Actually, I'm a Dallas boy, born and bred."

"I look forward to learning all about you. Now come. Dinner is ready and I know my husband wants to meet you."

The dog, a small white terrier, started sniffing around Joel's shoes. Once he was satisfied, he toddled down the hallway, his little claws clicking on the hardwood floor. The smell of home cooking filtered through the air. Joel saw photos cascading up the stairway—family photos, marking happy moments in time.

As time crawled forward well into the late

afternoon, Joel sat next to Simon, telling him about life in the Marine Corps.

"I can't imagine it. I mean, not knowing if I'm going into something and not going to come out alive. I mean, bloody hell, don't that scare you, mate?" Simon asked, resting his head on his hands.

"Yes, sir, of course it does, but I guess you could say that every time you step out of the house in the morning. I'm serving my country, and if that means my life is the price I have to pay for it, then so be it."

"What about family? Don't they worry? I know I bloody would if Larna or Mimi were out fighting a war."

"My parents are both dead," Joel said and took a gulp of Coke.

"Sorry to hear that, mate. You got any brothers, sisters, both?" Simon pressed.

"One brother, but um, we no longer speak."

"Bloody families, eh? Can't pick 'em. This lot here, these are my people, but outside these walls, nah. My brother is a right prick and my sister, well..."

"Dad!" Mimi said, and shot her father a look.

"Well, it's true, ain't it, love?"

Joel looked up. He was sitting among a real family, people that truly cared about one another. The house was relatively small and there were areas that needed updating with paint peeling away from the wall, but this was a real home.

Joel looked at Mimi, so beautiful and so unaware. His mind flashed back to the night before, when he was with Meg. He wished to God he hadn't given in.

If Mimi was just a girl, somebody he would date and move on from, none of it would matter; but watching her with her family, he felt something deeper for her, and he knew that if she ever found out, he may have just ruined it all. He decided that somehow he would do everything he could to make sure she never found out the truth.

What was one more secret?

CHAPTER 27

Austin
Texas, Present day

Austin stepped out of the house, inhaling the air after the break in the storm. He looked around at the ranch. Today, everything felt different. It was like he was in a nightmare and he needed to protect everything around him. There could be no reconciling with Joel. The thought had crossed his mind, but, to him, Joel had died a long time ago.

He walked to his truck and stepped into it. Looking up, he could see Mimi watching him. Her expression looked haunted.

Austin drove away and made the 45-minute drive to Sara's house. When he pulled up to her driveway, he caught sight of Jake playing with his friend from next door, laughing hard and unaware of the turmoil going on he was at the centre of.

He knocked on the door and Sara opened it seconds later.

Their relationship had never been about anything

more than Jake since they were teenagers. He never engaged with her about anything more than the welfare of the young boy. Who she dated and what she did with her life had not mattered to him so long as there was no influence on Jake. She stepped backwards, holding the door open for Austin to step inside.

"So, let me guess. You're being noble as ever and taking Jake to meet his real daddy."

Austin shot her a look that told her she had crossed a line.

"I am his real dad. Much more than you have ever been a mother," he snapped.

Her expression twisted. "I do the best I can."

"How has he been? Does he suspect anything?" Austin asked.

"Nope, nothing. He's just been playing with the kid next door. I told him that you are working, like we agreed."

"Good."

"So, has Mimi taken him back? Fallen back into his spell?"

"I don't know."

"You and her…what happened?"

"It's got nothing to do with you, Sara."

"I never understood why you and Joel could never find women of your own. Seems that as much as you hate one another, you have the same taste in women."

Austin tried to ignore Sara's constant jabs. The only thing that mattered right now was keeping his son safe and away from Joel. He didn't trust him and he knew he would only try and get back into his son's life to win Mimi over, to show he was a changed man, that he could be the man he should have always been.

Sara looked up at Austin. "What happens now?"

"Honestly, I don't know. I hate that asshole being at my house, but I need to keep him close to find out what he is up to. I don't trust him, and if you ever wanted to do anything right by Jake, you need to keep him away. Joel cannot know where you are."

"I may have made many mistakes in my life, but if there is one thing we can both agree on, it's keeping Jake away from Joel."

Sara wasn't a bad person. She just was not cut out to be a proper mother. She loved Jake, but she was far too selfish to give him what he needed, and by giving him to Austin, she knew he would never want for anything.

She crossed the room, her feet bare, and picked up a drawing.

"Here," she said, handing Austin the drawing. "Jake did this last night. Seems he's pretty taken with the English rose and you."

Austin studied it, making out the colourful scroll. It was a picture of Mimi, Jake, and Austin.

Austin gave her a half smile and put it on the arm of the tattered chair.

"I need to take care of things and somehow get Joel out of the way. I'll come back for Jake when I'm done."

"What are you planning to do?"

"Just please keep Jake safe. No matter what."

It sounded like he was giving her a warning. She

had never seen this side of Austin before. There was a fire in his eyes which told her right now, there was nothing that would get in the way of him and his son.

The air seemed to have been sucked out of the room with only the wrath of Austin's warning. *No matter what!*

Austin wondered what Mimi was thinking, what she was feeling. He wished she would leave Joel. He wondered if she would be able to get past all of his lies. She married a stranger. He knew Mimi was strong, but when it came to matters of the heart, he realised nobody could ever know what they would do, how they would react, how much the heart could forgive.

His mind whirled with a thousand different scenarios. He wished Joel had been killed. He hated to admit he wanted his own brother dead, but without him completely out of the picture, he posed too much of a threat to him and his world.

He must keep him close, he must make sure that he is never far away. His next move may be risky, and he may get caught, but it was worth it to keep Jake away from the man who was threatening to take his child away from him. He knew he was not thinking straight. He knew that this could cost him his freedom, but he would do what he needed to do no matter the consequences.

"Be careful," Sara warned.

Austin's gaze burned into her. He swallowed hard as her words hung in the air.

"I will."

They both knew what he was thinking, and for

the first time, Austin knew Sara was truly somebody he could count on.

***

Mimi

Mimi wasn't feeling well. She was on a cocktail of pills, and for the first time since she had been in Texas, she felt homesick. She needed the warmth of her mother's touch, her sister's silly humour, and to be in the safety bubble of her childhood home, where she was untouched by tragedy. She reached for her phone and saw she had a text message from Meg.

She had barely had any communication from her best friend since Meg left Texas. Meg would have known that she almost died, and the thought suddenly occurred to her that she had been out of the picture.

Mimi felt somewhat relieved when she saw that her friend had finally gotten in touch with her, but when she opened the message, she was confused.

Meg: Don't fall for him again, Mimi.

She wondered what the cryptic message meant and why Meg had sent it.

Meg had always been critical of her relationship with Joel. When Mimi announced she was engaged, she hadn't been met with the shrill and excitement she expected her best friend to give. Before the wedding, Meg asked her several times if she was sure she wanted to spend her life with somebody in the military.

You know what they are like. Can you really trust him when he is in another country? Can you really ever be sure you can trust him?

At the time, Mimi assumed that her best friend was just worried that she would up and leave her, move away from the UK, and start a new life in the States. She reassured Meg that she knew she was doing the right thing and she needed her love and support to move forward with the new chapter in her life.

Before Mimi had a chance to reply to the message, she heard a tap on the bedroom door.

Joel.

Mimi crossed the room, throwing her phone on the bed. Joel was now so unfamiliar to her. He looked the same, but so much had changed. She felt herself wanting to ask a thousand questions which all led to the same thing: Who was he?

"Can we talk?" he asked. She rested her body against the door frame and took in a deep breath.

"We spent the entire evening talking. I'm all talked out."

"I love you, Mimi. And I know I haven't given you any reason to trust that, but I do."

"I wish I could say I love you too, Joel, but really, who is it I love? Is it the Joel who told me he had a stupid falling out with his brother and that's why you moved away from here, or the Joel that walked out on his kid and lied to his wife?"

"You have every right to be angry with me, but things are not as straightforward as this. There is more I need to tell you." Joel paused for a second. "There is one other thing."

"Oh, what now? You got another kid somewhere or another wife?"

"Meg," he said.

Mimi froze. Why was he mentioning Meg? She suddenly thought about the message that she had just seen on her phone.

Meg: Don't fall for him again, Mimi.

"What about her?"

"I slept with her." He blocked his arms over the door to stop her from pushing past him. "It was once and it was at the very start, when we were not even sure there was an us."

He tried to defend himself, as if giving some form of justification was going to save him from taking another fall.

"When?" Mimi shouted.

"It was the night you asked me to take her home."

"The day before you met my parents?" Mimi hissed. "And you were not sure if there was an us?"

Things kept going from bad to worse. She felt betrayed, and somehow this even felt worse than when she found out he had a child. She could give him an excuse for being a stupid teenager, but this was something else. Meg was her best friend, the person who was with her when she was grieving over the death of her husband, the woman she had grown up with and trusted like a sister.

Her mind flashed back to the day that she was in

Meg's Mini after Joel had "died" and she had said that he was a sexy guy. She hadn't liked it, but she shrugged it off. Now, as she imagined her hands on him, his lips on hers, there was a weight of truth behind what Meg said.

In all of this, she learned that she had been blind to so many things. She had been fooled and lied to. She refused to be a victim to this anymore.

"I can almost expect it from you. I mean, nothing you have told me has ever been the truth, but Meg? She was my best friend and you both had fun behind my back."

"It wasn't like that."

"Oh, what was it like?"

"It was just a stupid one night thing."

"You weren't drunk that night. I know she was, but you were not. So, how many other secrets are you keeping from me?"

"I promise that is everything. There is nothing else."

"I can't get past this." Tears sprang to her eyes, but not out of hurt or upset. They were born out of anger and humiliation, an abasement of her pride.

It was like she had been living another life. If she could turn back time, she wished she would have never met Joel, but, if she hadn't, she would never have met Austin, either. With Austin, she saw things clearly for the first time. She made no pretence of her feelings.

"Thank you," she said as she pushed past Joel and ran down the spiral steps. She needed to get some fresh air. She could feel herself gasping.

"What for?" Joel called after her, trying to catch

her arm.

She made it to the front door. She held it open, the humid air starting to spike.

"For pushing me into the arms of a man that is ten of you." She locked her gaze on Joel and suddenly felt alleviated and free from the burden of stress that came with struggling to be true to her heart.

"What are you talking about, Mimi?" Joel's face was twisted and just inches from Mimi's.

She turned to face him. "You are not the only one who has a few secrets," she whispered.

"What secrets?"

"I'm in love with your brother."

As the words fell from her mouth, she was unprepared for Joel's reaction. He stumbled backwards, holding his head in his hands.

"Did you sleep with him?" He grabbed hold of her shoulders, shaking her as he screamed.

Just moments ago, she felt like she had finally regained power and control of her own life, but now she was truly frightened.

"Let go of me," she screamed.

It was as if Joel could not hear her. His face was haunted, like he was possessed and out of control. She felt herself fall to the ground as he finally let her go.

She curled into a ball on the porch, crying.

Joel stood over her. He hugged his arms around his body.

"Mimi, I'm sorry."

"Get away from me!" she sobbed. Her hair stuck to her face and her body trembled.

"I forgive you, and I'll fix everything."

"You forgive me? There is nothing I want your forgiveness for. I'm not sorry. I don't care if it hurts you. I love Austin and I'm glad all of this led me to him. Don't you get it, Joel? We can't come back from this. Hiding the truth made me fall for somebody who wasn't real."

"Don't you understand how much I love you?" Joel sobbed.

Mimi pushed herself back onto her feet.

"Were you loving me when you lied to me about Austin and why you fell out? Were you loving me when you slept with my best friend?"

"I can't live without you."

"You have to." She finally found her voice. She had spent too long giving him excuses, reasons, but she couldn't do it anymore.

"What are you saying?"

"I'm saying it's over. I want a divorce."

"Mimi, no. We can get past this. It can all be undone."

He moved close to her, trying to reach out to her, but she wriggled away from his grip.

"Mimi, please. I'm begging you."

"Joel, I've let you go."

She had no idea what to do. Her thoughts whirled around her head. She had no idea when she became so fearful.

"Austin is not who you think he is."

"Oh, and who is he? He's the man looking after your kid, he's the man that told your wife the truth, and if you are going to try and tell me that he is the reason that your father is dead, save it. Just save it. I know everything. Unlike you, he's honest."

Mimi's pulse raced as she waited for Joel to speak.

"I won't let him have you."

"You don't have a choice."

"I won't let him. No, just no."

Joel shook his head. Perspiration beaded on his forehead, running in rivulets down his face. The heat bounced off the wooden porch; the blue sky lay still in the humid air.

Suddenly, there was silence. It was a moment where only the sound of their breathing could be heard. They stared at one another. Mimi had given her heart away, and she wasn't going to try and give it back to the man who had betrayed her over and over again.

"Joel, you have to let me go."

"I don't want to. I can't."

He began crying. There was a small part of her that wanted to reach out to him, to take the pain away, because despite how much he had hurt her, no matter how much of the version he portrayed himself to be was in front of her, it was too late to give him any comfort.

"What now?" Joel said.

"Now you leave, and I'll file for a divorce."

"Just like that? We let us go, without even trying?"

"I don't love you, Joel. The person I thought I was in love with was nothing but a fictional character you created. I don't want to live in a world of make believe. I want a real marriage. I want the truth, even when it hurts. I want the whole story, warts and all. I want real love with a man does not sleep with my best friend, somebody I can trust and depend on."

"But it's okay for you to fuck my brother?" he spat.

"I didn't. I made love to him, and I'll keep on doing that because he's the one I want and he's more of a man than you'll ever be. You can hide behind your big guns, your quest to go out there and fight the enemy, but the person who is your real enemy isn't Austin. It's you."

Mimi realised their love had been a battle all of its own. It had been a war. She knew love is seeing the truth in your lover's eyes and being able to accept that truth. Their relationship had been like glass. It was broken and it was better to leave it broken than to try and put it back together.

***

After the words were out and there was no reconciling, no way back, Mimi asked Joel to leave the ranch even though she knew he had more of a right to be there than she did. After all, no matter what had been said and done, this was still his childhood home.

When he tried to claw back to her, she had kept strong. She told him that if he really loved her like he said he did, he would leave and give her a true chance at being happy. Into the early afternoon, Joel went back into the house and gathered all his belongings, packing them into the same bag he had arrived with.

Mimi had no idea where Austin was, but she hoped he wouldn't be back before Joel left. She needed some distance to grieve the end of her marriage once and for all and clear the way for her crash landing.

Although it was her choice to let go, she still felt a sorrow inside her. There was one last feeling left. Joel had been the man that she had chosen. She had married him, and although she could barely look at him for all the things he'd put her through, he was once her love.

Even if she would never hear his voice again or see those eyes again, and no matter how hard it was for her to say goodbye, she knew it was time to truly let him go.

Her life ended the day she was told her husband had been killed, but it wasn't because he hadn't kept his promise that he was coming back to her. It was because it was the day that led her on the journey to find the truth.

She could hear Joel fumbling around, his feet heavy on the floor above her. The knot in her stomach tightened as she thought about what had just happened. In a short amount of time, Joel would leave and this was born out of her own choice. She thought of Meg and was tempted to call her, to tell her exactly what she thought of her, but what would be the point?

Her life back in the UK was a distant memory. She would always be a part of her family, and she knew that she didn't need to be physically there.

It had been the longest time without Joel, but she knew she was missing a man who wasn't real. He was riddled with secrets and lies. She thought she couldn't live without him. People told her it would get better in time.

In her dreams, he had come back to her, and there were too many times she had woken up in an empty room, his place next to her cold and empty.

Now she was sending him away for reasons she knew were right, but somehow it didn't make things any easier. Austin had been real to her, he had been honest, and that was what she needed. It was what her heart wanted.

The sunlight flooded the kitchen. Joel walked in, and he looked crestfallen. Mimi couldn't meet his gaze. She felt something she couldn't explain.

"I know you've made your choice, but I promise, if you give me one last chance, I'll spend the rest of my life making it up to you." He kept a respectful distance from her as he spoke.

"I wish you nothing but happiness, and let this be a lesson learned with whomever you give your heart to next. Be honest with her and never hide anything because sometimes the truth will hurt, but lies will wreck things."

"I've told you the truth. You know everything now, Mimi. You think you know my brother, but you don't."

Mimi shook her head. "Stop, Joel. Please, just stop."

She knew he was trying to sway her, to give her doubt in her mind. Everything she ever believed her husband to be was a lie. He was a master of deception, and she almost died following the path to find out the man he was.

She reminded herself that she had been deceived by the two people she had trusted most in her life—her best friend and her husband.

Joel hoisted the heavy bag over his shoulder.

"So, this is really it? You're letting us go."

Mimi lowered her head. Her heart felt like it would explode out of her chest. Suddenly, tears were falling from her eyes.

"The truth is, we were never ever really together. I married a stranger. You made me believe you were somebody you weren't."

"This is for you." Joel handed her a crumpled photograph of herself. "This is the photo that pulled me through the darkest of days in Afghanistan. It was you I lived for."

"Not Meg?" Mimi spat.

"I was stupid. I know I should have never have slept with her. I regretted it, and I hated that she stood there with us on our wedding day. I'm sorry. Really, I am sorry for everything. If Austin is the one that makes you happy, then…"

Her head jerked up. "I almost died, you almost died. We have to trust that all of this happened for a reason, Joel. We both have a path to follow, only it isn't with each other."

"I love you. I'll always love you."

He moved toward her and gently kissed her on the lips and turned to leave.

"Where will you go?" Mimi asked.

"What does it matter? Just make sure he makes you happy."

Joel realized he must pay the price for everything he had put Mimi through. No matter how hard it would be to walk away from her, he knew he loved her enough to give her what she wanted, even if that meant giving her to the man who had constantly picked up the pieces of his mistakes.

"Look after yourself," Mimi whispered.

"I'll get a lawyer and take care of the formalities," he said. Mimi felt her hands tremble.

Joel didn't say anything else. He wriggled his solid, white gold wedding band off his left finger. It clinked as it hit the marble kitchen table like a bomb, the sound of it deafening.

CHAPTER 28

Mimi cried until there were no more tears left to cry. She closed herself off into the solace of the guest room and curled tightly into a ball, using her hands to support her head. It was dark outside with only the sound of crickets to be heard. Choices had been made. She followed her heart, only it didn't make saying goodbye any easier.

Mimi was angry at Meg. She wondered how she could betray her like that. She had written a thousand text messages since, but she deleted them all. Somehow, she couldn't find the words to say that would express the weight of the pain Meg caused.

Mimi thought back to any signs she may have missed, but the thing that scared her more than anything was she hadn't suspected a thing and even now, looking back with a fresh pair of eyes, she was still confused. It worried her how many other times Meg would have betrayed her. After all, she kept so much hidden.

The sound of footsteps interrupted her thoughts.

The door gently pushed open. Her eyes were swollen and burning from the salty tears.

Austin slowly walked to the bed and gently ran the palm of his hand through her hair.

"Mimi, are you awake?" he quietly asked.

"He's gone."

"What happened?"

She pulled her body up, the moonlight catching the dried streaks of tears.

"I didn't know him. He wasn't the man I thought I married and then I found out that he slept with my best friend. I just…"

"Wait, slow down. Do you mean Meg, the girl that you came here with?"

Mimi nodded. Austin leaned his head forward and exhaled. He felt angry. His brother's deceit just kept coming, and he couldn't understand how he would jeopardize somebody so beautiful.

He tried to think of words to say, to tell her that she made the right choice, but he knew that if he said that, it would only sound like it was for his own self gain, and right now, this wasn't about him. It was about two innocent people—Mimi and Jake.

"What have you decided?"

"I told him I want a divorce."

"Is that what you really want?"

"We had a fight, out on the porch, and I said some things that maybe I didn't even truly realise until today," she paused, suddenly feeling nervous. "We fought about you."

It was hard for Mimi to look at Austin. She felt so exposed, so vulnerable. She twisted her body and stood up, moving toward the window.

"I told him I'm in love with you, and you are the one who has my heart."

There was silence. She gripped her fingers onto the window sill, trying to steady herself.

"Is that the truth?" Austin said. "Or were you just trying to get back at him?"

Mimi spun on her heel to face him, shocked that he had just asked her that. She looked at him, wide-eyed. "What do you think?"

"Truthfully, I don't know what to think anymore. This is every inch of fucked up."

"Did you mean what you said when you told me you loved me?"

Austin's face was serious. He hung his head forward and exhaled. "I am in love with you, but I don't want to be your second choice or your revenge to Joel for the things that he has done."

She spoke slowly. "Joel was my husband, and I married him because I loved him, but coming here, I uncovered the truth about him. The more I learned, the more I realized that I didn't know him. And then there is you. Austin, there are so many things that have blown me away—finding out about Jake, almost dying, thinking that Joel was dead and then he wasn't, and now finding out my best friend betrayed me. In all of this, you have been the one to catch me."

"But if I didn't send you away that day, you would have never been in that car wreck. That's my fault."

"You didn't know. I don't blame you for that."

Austin looked tired. His eyes were heavy and his body looked strained. He sat on the edge of the bed, silence filling the room once more.

"What now?" he muttered.

"Now, you need to decide if you still want me to stay."

Mimi held her breath, waiting for Austin to take her in his arms, to tell her that it was all going to be all right, that he would look after her, but when he stood up to leave the room, panic came over her.

A thought entered her head, one that she had never considered before. Did she really know Austin? Less than a couple of days ago, he was practically down on a bended knee telling her how in love he was with her. And now, when she said she wanted him, he was silent.

Suddenly, she wondered if Austin was still angry at Joel and used her to get back at him. Had she missed yet another betrayal right in front of her?

Mimi seemed to have lost her trust in everybody; nobody, it seemed, was true to her. She sat still, afraid to move. She was trying to read between the lines, but she knew she couldn't see anything clearly anymore.

"I do love you," he said.

Mimi sucked in her breath. "Then why are you about to leave the room?"

"Because I need you to be sure."

"I am sure," she protested.

She crossed the room, putting her arms around his waist.

Austin turned to her, his face difficult to read. Mimi pulled him close to her. He didn't resist but he didn't hold her back.

"I wish I'd met you first. I wish this was just

normal, but there are so many things to consider. I just don't know how to handle any of this," Austin said.

"Don't leave me tonight. Please, just stay with me."

He took her by the hand, leading her out into the brightly lit hallway, and closed the door of the guest room behind him.

"Are you sure it's me you want and I'm not just the version of Joel that you crave?"

She lowered her head and then met his gaze. "I've never been surer."

He took her by the hand and led her into his bedroom. Then he slowly moved toward her mouth and kissed her. She fell into him, letting out a sigh.

Letting Joel go had been hard. She had almost felt guilty, but now that she was once again in Austin's arms, she felt safe, and she felt like she was home.

***

Mimi woke up next to Austin. He was already awake, his arms tightly wrapped around her.

"Hmmm, what time is it?" she asked, her voice throaty from sleep.

"Just past 10 a.m.," Austin said, pulling her tighter. She wasn't sure where his body started and hers ended. She couldn't seem to get any closer to him.

Austin stroked her left hand, noticing the whiteness of where her ring used to be.

It was all over. She had made her choice and she

was now with Austin. In the light of day, things felt different to him. The heavy weight of Joel seemed to have been lifted and, for the first time, he saw hope and a future with Mimi.

"Cast comes off in a few days," Mimi said. "I was thinking I'd like to go out today, away from the ranch. Maybe go out to lunch and do what normal couples do."

"You mean you want me to take you on a date?" he said, his voice playful.

"Well, yes. Seems like we have leapt forward into what most couples would have in the depths of a serious relationship. I want to have some fun with my boyfriend, so yes, you can take me on a proper date."

"Boyfriend!" he laughed. "Been a while since I was called that, but I like the sound of it, girlfriend."

Mimi snuggled into his shoulder, content with the decision she'd made. She knew she needed to contact her parents and tell them everything. Then there were the details of finding a lawyer, the complications of a divorce. But today, she didn't want to think about the heaviness she had carried for all the months since this craziness happened. She just wanted to be in the moment with Austin and relax. Her body was craving it.

She reminded herself she almost didn't make it. She could so easily have died in that car wreck, and now she would spend months, if not years, under the close watch of doctors because of her heart. It was as if she had been given a second chance at life. She had stared death square on and given it the big

F-U.

"How long will Jake be at Sara's?"

"A week or so. I want things to settle down. I think he will be pretty stoked that you are here. He drew a picture at Sara's of the three of us."

Mimi smiled. "That's really sweet. I love that kid."

"And I love you," Austin said, cradling Mimi's face in his hands. Austin exhaled slowly. He hadn't realised he'd been holding his breath.

Mimi turned to him, her face close to his. She gently bit her bottom lip, tossing a long strand of her dark hair over her shoulder.

"Do you want to tell me something?" she asked.

"It's quite scary how well you seem to know me already," he said with a forced smile.

Mimi let out a half-hearted laugh, holding her palm flat against her chest.

"I'm hardly the best judge of character, am I?"

Austin pushed his body up on his elbow and laid to the side.

"Actually, there is something." His tone had dramatically changed. Instinctively, Mimi pushed herself upright. Her shoulders instantly became rigid. Her cheeks flushed hot.

"Come on, then. Out with it."

"I don't want to keep anything from you."

"Just say what you want to say, Austin!"

"When I thought there was a chance Joel might want to be in Jake's life, I freaked out."

"That's understandable," Mimi said, a lump filling her throat.

Austin took Mimi's hand and squeezed.

"If Joel had told Jake he was his real father, it would destroy him. I couldn't let that happen." Austin paused for a moment, hung his head, and inhaled. "So, I had a plan."

It scared Mimi to see Austin looking so shaken. She lifted her hands away from him and moved them to her head, running her fingers through her scalp.

"I was going to take money from the ranch from underneath him and go. I had planned on burning this place to the ground to get the insurance."

"That's it?" Mimi said, her tone high pitched. "That was your big plan? I thought you were about to tell me you hired a hit man or something to kill him."

"Burning down my family's legacy is hardly something to be proud of!"

"Maybe not, but a father that will do anything to protect his son *is* something to be proud of."

"So, you don't hate me?"

"Hate you? How could I?"

Mimi placed her middle two fingers underneath Austin's chin and lifted his head. He gently opened his eyes. She put her lips to his and whispered, "Thank you for being honest."

"Thank you for choosing me."

"For today, lets focus on us." She winked.

"You're saying it's time to lighten the mood around here?

"That's exactly what I am saying."

"Right, I'm going to jump in the shower. I've got a hot date," he said as he bounced out of the bed and moved into the en-suite.

Mimi heard the hiss of the shower and giggled to herself as Austin hummed. Her mind suddenly flashed back to Joel on the first drive during their honeymoon. She quickly caught herself before she let her mind go there.

She got out of bed and felt slightly off. A sickness came over her in a hot wave. She missed being a normal, healthy person. She reminded herself that she must make contact with the hospital to talk about the next stages of treatment.

Once the nauseous feeling passed, she stood up once more and made her way to the guest room. Her phone lay face down in the same spot she had left it the night before.

She pushed the button and the phone came to life. She clicked her messages and looked at the last message from Meg.

Without thinking, her fingers took on a life of their own as she typed out a message and hit send before she could second-guess herself:

Mimi: Know you slept with Joel. Thank you for making my decision to let you both go.

A few moments later, the phone started vibrating.

She answered it without saying a word. Meg's panicked voice was at the other end.

"Mimi, I'm so sorry."

"So it's true?"

"Mimi, it was a stupid drunken mistake. It meant nothing. Please, forgive me."

Mimi took a deep breath. "I forgive you, Meg,

but I need you to do something for me."

"Anything," Meg said, her voice desperate.

"Never contact me again."

"Mimi, please…"

Without listening to another word, she ended the call. Their lifelong friendship was over. She would no longer invest another second in her, nor would she bring her into her fresh start with Austin. Then she went into her phone book and called her parents. It was late into the afternoon in London. Her mother would be settling in after walking the dog. She could picture, play by play, what her dear, sweet mother would be doing.

The phone rang. It was a long, drawn out sound. Her mother answered breathy at the other end.

"Mama, it's me. Are you sitting down?"

***

Simon and Kanchana

"I could kill her, that bloody cow! I knew she was a no good piece of jealous trash. And to think we let her here in our home when her own bloody mother wouldn't take care of her, and she does this to our Mimi!" Simon complained, parking himself in the armchair as Kanchana told him what happened.

"She's chosen Austin," Kanchana said, her voice strained. She settled herself next to her husband, shaking her head.

"Well, we have to support that, love. Bloody hell, look at what Joel put her through. If I could get my hands on that dick."

"I do support it, of course I do. It's just…"

"She's a grown woman, love. We have to let her make her own choices."

"Oh, I know, I know. I guess I never imagined she would be living so far away from us, that's all."

"Love, even if she'd stayed with Joel and none of this had ever happened, there was every chance she'd be living in America."

"You're right. I just feel so emotional about it all. First we think Joel's dead, then we think Mimi might die, then Joel's not dead and now we find out he slept with her best friend and she's chosen to be with his brother." She looked at Simon, wide-eyed.

"Like bloody Eastenders," he joked.

Kanchana managed a smile and threw a cushion into his stomach.

Simon stood up and knelt next to his wife. "Let's just be grateful that she made it, yeah, love?"

"You're right. It still won't stop me from picking up the phone to call Meg and telling her exactly what I think of her."

"You're gonna have to beat me to that!" He reached his arms out and Kanchana fell into them.

As parents, they always knew their daughters would grow and make their own way in life, only they hadn't expected things to be as dramatic as they had turned out to be. All they had to do was remind themselves they did the best they could by both of their daughters and they would always be there to support their decisions, even if it meant they would live with an ocean dividing them. They just wanted to know that their girls were happy.

***

Mimi

The wind blew through Mimi's hair as Austin drove his truck along the windy roads. The fresh air made Mimi feel alive and in the moment. She promised herself that today would be a good day. She would leave her worries behind and enjoy the start of the rest of her life.

Every so often, Austin looked at her and smiled. She reached across, taking his hand in hers. She loved how easy he looked, how the worried scowl had disappeared. He looked younger, fresher.

They pulled over when they reached the nearby town. It hit Mimi that life moved on as normal for other people going about their day-to-day business with nothing much changing in their lives, but for Mimi, everything had changed. She had spent so long living in a fog of one disaster after another. It was nice just to feel like a face in a crowd.

She and Austin walked hand in hand. There were a few glances and suspicious smiles from people that he knew, like they were desperate to know who the girl with the long, dark hair was.

"People will talk," Austin said.

"Will you tell them?"

"Nah, none of their business."

They took a seat on an outside seating area. A waitress with too much makeup and big hair quickly came to them and handed them menus.

Mimi looked at the specials. The smell of steamed fish got caught in her nose as a plate of it drifted past. The same wave of nausea that she felt earlier that day came back. She felt her mouth fill with water.

"You okay, Mimi?"

"I feel really sick," she said, holding her hand to her mouth.

"Do you want to leave?"

"No, no. I haven't really eaten much these past few days, and I think it's suddenly caught up with me. The pills that I'm on are meant to be taken with food, so I guess that's why I feel crappy. I think if I eat, it will do me some good."

"Excuse me, ma'am. Can we please get a basket of bread?" Austin said to a passing waitress.

"Sure thing."

"I like how you look after me," Mimi said when the bread arrive. She took a bite and chewed slowly, hoping that it would absorb the acid in her stomach and allow her to enjoy her first real date with Austin.

"I'll always look after you. Now, I hate to have to bring things up, but we need to talk about how this will all work. I mean, how long are you allowed to stay in the States before I have immigration knocking at the door?"

Mimi suddenly looked at him, wide-eyed. "Oh my God, you're right. I mean, I never thought about that."

"We'll take care of it. Don't worry. As it stands right now, doctor's orders say you can't travel, so I think that will make for a pretty good case."

"I was thinking about things. And I love it at the ranch. It feels like home to me."

"Mimi, are you asking me if you can live with me? Usually, my first dates don't ask this sort of thing," he teased. Mimi suddenly felt her cheeks burning. "I want you to," he said, taking her hand in his and raising it to his lips. He kissed her fingertips.

"I have to warn you, I can be a real pain in the ass to live with. I mean, I'm really messy and I..."

Austin cut her short. "I don't care. The thought of losing you cut me up real bad. You can be as messy as you like, so long as it means I have you."

Mimi smiled, but there was still a part of her thinking about Joel, wondering where he was, what he was doing. It was as if her heart had been split in two. She felt like a drug addict on a high and low. Her stomach kept knotting every time she thought about the end of her marriage, but when she looked at Austin, she felts a strange sense of comfort.

They ate lunch together and talked about the future. It was a refreshing change from looking backwards, into the past. Austin playfully joked with her. She liked the less serious side of him—the playful, carefree spirit that, up 'till now, she hadn't seen.

Mimi looked at a bird on a nearby rooftop; it flew off, stretching its wings out wide, gliding freely and effortlessly into the sun-drenched sky. That's how she saw herself in that moment, free to fly and explore her new life, leaving the old one behind.

"You look dazed," Austin said.

"Oh, sorry...I guess I was just deep in thought. Just ignore me. Are you ordering dessert?"

"Um, no, I don't really have much of a thing for sweet things." He looked at her for a while and then said, "You are so beautiful." He smiled, shaking his head. "I can't believe you're mine."

For a moment, she got lost in Austin's eyes, and then she remembered how lost she used to get in Joel's.

Mimi's hair flung forward. He reached toward it, brushing it gently away from her face, and then softly asked, "Mimi, *are* you mine?"

Her gaze met his. "I told you, I chose you. I'm just feeling scared. I love you, I know I do, but I'm feeling so overwhelmed by everything right now, and I feel guilty."

Austin's face drained of colour.

Mimi quickly tried to redeem herself. "I mean, I'm not like him. I can't just switch myself on and off."

"Look, Mimi," he paused, taking a sip of water, "I don't expect any of this to be easy, and I'd be lying if I told you I didn't feel jealous every time you have that faraway look in your eye because I know that means you are thinking of him. Let's take this as it comes. I know I love you, and I want to be with you, even if that means things are not quite as straightforward as I'd like them to be."

He pushed his plate away, and the sweet aroma of sticky barbeque chicken wings hung in the hot air.

Mimi didn't say anything. Her eyes filled with tears. She gently rubbed her index finger along his lips.

"When this thing comes off, I'd like to ride

again," Mimi said swiftly, changing the subject, jolting them straight out of the intense moment between them.

"Really? I'm not so sure. You and moving objects are a bit of a dangerous mix."

"What is it they say? If you fall off the horse, you have to get right back on."

"We'll make a real Texas girl out of you yet. Ah, you are funny, Mimi Mimi."

She stopped dead, looking at him like she had just seen a ghost

Mimi Mimi.

Of all the things he could call her, he used the exact same affectionate words as his brother. She couldn't hide her shock. As she opened her mouth to tell him not to call her that, the waitress came over, bright and bubbly, interrupting her.

"Can I get you anything else? Maybe some more drinks?"

"Um, yeah. I'll have another jug of water please," Mimi said. She needed to wet her mouth, to banish the dryness and stop her tongue from feeling like sandpaper.

She thought twice about admitting to Austin why she had just been so startled, so she said nothing, but Austin wasn't about to let it go.

"What did I say?"

"Nothing," she replied, too quickly, too sharply.

"Bullshit."

"You called me Mimi Mimi," she said.

Austin looked at her, confused. "…And?"

"That was what Joel always called me. It was like a pet name."

Austin tried to hide his anger, but it slowly uncoiled. "I'm not fucking Joel."

His anger was natural. She understood it. She would have hated to be compared to another girl all the time, but his outburst still upset her. She wasn't used to Austin's temper. He was always so controlled and so cool.

"I know you're not. I just thought you should know why I don't want to be called that. Would you rather I just lie to you?" she snapped.

Austin lowered his head. Tiny beads of sweat clustered on his hairline. "No!"

"Good," Mimi said. "This is all new to us both, like you just said, so let's take it as it comes…yeah?"

"Yeah, you're right. Now, since we are laying our cards out on the table, is there anything else I need to avoid so I don't get compared to or remind you of him? I know we look a lot alike, but I can't really do anything about that."

She gave an awkward laugh at his attempt of humouring a bad situation.

They interlocked their hands together. Mimi sighed.

"Horses. That's our thing, you and me. Let's focus on that."

"Quite hell bent on riding again, aren't you?"

"Uh huh."

"Let's get that cast off first and speak to the doctor, and when they say you can ride again, I'll take you. Is that a deal?"

"Deal." She lifted herself off the seat, leaned her body over the table, and kissed him on the lips, a long, sensual kiss that left him breathless.

CHAPTER 29

Joel

Joel glanced up at the sign flashing Gate 19 boarding to London at the airport. People moved past him, pushing luggage and rushing around like bees around honey.

Every sound around him startled him. The roar of a plane overhead made him duck for cover. The yell of an older man screaming for his wife to forget the shops and move to the gate gave him a flashback of Afghanistan, yelling to take cover, only he had to remind himself that he was no longer in a war zone. He was not a Marine in combat. He was a civilian, dressed not in camouflage but in regular blue jeans and a crisp white t-shirt. The only thing that he still wore were his dog tags. They had become as much a part of him as his own skin.

He reached for his pocket and took out his phone.

"It's me," he said. He could hear her breathing at the other end of the phone. "Don't pretend you can't fucking hear me, Meg."

He strained to hear what she was saying, but the interference on the call made it difficult. He pressed his finger in his ear and lowered his head, moving across the airport floor to try and get at least a couple of bars of signal.

A speaker announcement boomed above him. He dropped the phone and crouched down, raising his hands above his head. Passers-by stopped and stared and two kids pointed and laughed. Everything around him seemed like it was moving in slow motion. It had been like this ever since he returned from Afghanistan and now, with the stress of losing Mimi, he felt like he was out of control, like he was crazy!

He managed to bring himself back to his feet and he found a fountain, where he splashed water across his face. He hung his head over the stainless steel bowl and watched the water swirl into a tornado and drain away.

Everybody around him had a purpose, a reason for being at the airport. Whether it be the janitor cleaning the bathroom, travellers going on vacation or on business, or pilots ready to fly planes…every person around him knew where they were going. As Joel stood, watching the world turn just as it always had, he realised for the first time that he was truly alone.

He needed to get back on the ground again and do something, but he knew that was out of the question. Medical orders, or so they called it. He should be back in London, back with Mimi, but she was with *him*.

He'd told Mimi it was just once, and Meg too had stuck to that, but neither of them had told her that there was a time after that and another time after that. He hadn't considered it an affair as much as he considered it somebody he was just seeing.

Each time he had left Meg, he would always say that it couldn't happen again, only it did. He seemed powerless to stop it, although he wanted to. Every time Mimi would arrange nights for them to all go out to dinner with whichever guy Meg happened to be seeing at the time, Joel would always make his excuses and say that he had to be on duty.

On the rare occasions he had seen Meg in a group, he always insisted it be at a pub or a nightclub, somewhere he could disappear off into a crowd and not feel on edge the whole time, fearing that Mimi would somehow guess.

"Last call for Gate 19 to London, Heathrow."

He quickly came to his senses and started running as fast as he could. He pushed past people, beads of sweat dripping from his lower back.

When the sun hit him as the glass doors slid open, he looked across at a busy line of taxis and mini buses. He weaved his way around to get to the front of the line.

An overweight, bald man pulled him by his shoulder, getting too close to Joel's face, and said, "There's a line here, buddy."

Without thinking, Joel pushed him backwards, knocking the man to the floor. His wife kneeled by his side, wide-eyed and startled.

Joel stood over the man who was holding his hand to his chest, gasping for breath.

"I'm sorry, man. I'm sorry." Then he jumped into the waiting taxi.

"Where to?"

"Eastleigh Ranch, out West."

"That's too far, man. I—"

Joel reached into his pocket and pulled out several hundred dollars.

"Buckle up," the driver said, turning his body to face the road. He flipped the indicator on.

Tick tick tick.

Joel squeezed his eyes shut, reminding himself it wasn't the sound of a bomb about to explode. The driver gripped his hands on the steering wheel and pulled out. An oncoming car slammed on its breaks. The sound of the car horn was deafening. Joel felt his body go rigid. He kept his eyes closed until the tires were in motion, and then he let out a sigh.

"You just get back, man?" the driver asked, looking into the mirror.

"What?"

"You're a soldier, right?"

"US Marine, sir."

He watched the driver's head bob up and down, sweat creased into the folds of his neck.

"Thought so. I see it. I've seen that look so many times."

He pointed his index finger up to his eyes. Joel ignored him and looked out of the window. He was determined to get back the woman who belonged to him.

***

Mimi

Mimi tore out the pages of the journal containing the letters she had written to Joel. Once again, the threat of another headache loomed and the wave of nausea that had been coming and going for days seemed to be getting stronger.

She reached into her bag containing the bottle of her pills. A pack of tampons fell out and scattered at her feet. She bent down to pick them up. As she rose, her mind started calculating the last time she had a period.

Her fingers brushed over the blue tampon box. She reached into the inner zip of her makeup bag and found the negative pregnancy test that she had taken before she had come to Texas. Shortly after that, her period had arrived.

At first, she told herself that with everything her body had been through—the accident, the heart failure—there was no possible way that she could be pregnant. She dismissed the idea, putting it down to stress, and quickly dressed in a white cotton dress, which illuminated next to her dark brown tan.

She found Austin out on the porch looking out onto the hazy early morning sun.

He smiled when he saw her and pulled her in close. "Cast matches your dress," he joked.

"So glad this is finally coming off today."

"Yeah, kind of feels like I've always known you with it."

"Appointment is at ten. How long will it take to get to the hospital?"

"Around thirty minutes, so I was thinking, since

we have some time, do you want to maybe go back upstairs for a little bit?" He raised his eyebrows and smiled.

Mimi took him by the hand, moving into the house and up the stairs. She wrapped her fingers around the door knob of the bedroom door. When she pushed it open, her hand quickly flew to her mouth. She ran into the bathroom, slamming the door shut behind her. As she fell next to the toilet bowl, her head hanging, her body trembling, something told her she needed to take a test.

"Mimi." Austin tapped his knuckles against the door. "Honey, are you all right in there?"

"I'll be out in a minute," she shouted.

He stood at the door, waiting for her to emerge. When she did, he put his arm around her.

"Good thing we're going to the hospital. Maybe we can ask them about this sickness?"

"Austin, I think I know what might be wrong."

He looked at her, waiting for an answer. She coyly moved across to the bed. She didn't meet his gaze. "I think I'm pregnant."

The blood drained from Austin's face. He tried to steady himself against the door, but he was caught completely off guard. "Is it his?"

"No, it's impossible."

"You're sure about that?"

"Certain."

His eyes widened. "Wow, we are moving fast."

He paced to the balcony adjoining his room. He turned back to look at her. "Well, we will need to get this confirmed."

"Austin, if I'm pregnant, it's yours."

"I don't mean that. Jesus, Mimi, I mean we need to find out if you are actually pregnant."

"If I am?"

She suddenly felt deeply insecure. She hadn't had time to think how he might react and she wasn't sure she was even ready to be a mother. This was never how she planned to have children. She needed space to think. That was something she realised since this all happened that she hadn't had.

"If you are, then I am here for you and we are in this together. How do you feel about this? Is it something you want?"

She turned to look at him. This man in front of her, a man she had not planned to fall in love with, her brother-in-law, may very well be the father of her unborn child. The reality of the situation weighed heavy on her. She shrugged her shoulders.

"I don't know. This is so sudden, I don't know how I should feel."

She felt as if she were drowning, sinking, unable to swim to shore safely. Nausea whirled in her stomach, a niggling reminder that she could be carrying a life. She wasn't sure how she was meant to support another person. How could she if she didn't know who she was?

She felt like a boat on dry land.

"I'm not going to pretend that this isn't a shock to me, Mimi. Far from it. But none of this has been easy, and somehow I feel like everything that is happening is just pulling us together. Or am I just kidding myself?"

He ran his hand through his hair. In the glowing sunlight, it looked fairer and his eyes looked greener. A needling of anxiety began at his brow. He wasn't used to being so out of control. He always had a hard exterior, and no woman had ever been able to get past it, not since Sara and not since he became Jake's dad.

He didn't always like the vibe Mimi gave off; it made him so unsure. Mimi's eyes were glassy, and she wasn't in the moment with him. He didn't know if he should move closer to her or keep a distance. He was finding it increasingly difficult to gauge her wants and needs.

Dazed, Mimi turned to Austin and held her hand out to his.

He moved toward her, and without saying another word, he pulled her up and into his arms, wrapping his arms into a tight grip around her hips.

He took in the sweet scent of the shampoo she'd used that morning. Her head rested gently on his shoulder, the softness of her breath warming his neck.

She had no idea where her life was taking her. She felt disconnected from all reality around her, lost in a sea of thoughts, and the pressure of constantly processing was making her tired.

Mimi could not escape the feeling that Austin felt reassuring to her, but every so often, doubt would take over. Was she just upgrading Joel?

***

When Mimi stepped out of Austin's truck, the heat hit her like the opening of an oven door. She had always been a lover of the summer. She hated winter and craved the tropical warm days and swimmingly cool nights.

She could see the heat waves modulating off the pavement. Her cotton dress was damp from sweat. Her flip flops clattered against the soles of her feet as she made her way to the entrance of the hospital. She glanced up at a plane, the tips of the wings gliding freely like a bird.

Her mind drifted back to when she had been on a plane, making her journey from London to Texas. Meg had set next to her. Mimi had been so unaware of her betrayal and thought her best friend had been nothing but a pillar of support in her time of need. She wondered why Meg had travelled with her:

Perhaps out of guilt?

Sometimes she wished she could have seen what was going on right under her nose, but in another way, she determined that ignorance was bliss. Being a fool was easier than heartbreak, and then there was Austin. If all of this hadn't happened, he would have never happened. He was like her angel, a blessing that had come to her when everything else around her had fallen to pieces.

As the automatic doors sprung open, Austin took Mimi's hand and squeezed it tight. "No matter what, you have me," he whispered into her ear.

A wave of affection came over her. His voice was tangy and reassuring, deep, but soft, and although she felt nervous, with Austin by her side she knew she couldn't fall.

Ahead, there was a directory crammed with information. She tried to search for Department 17, where she was due to report to. Austin pulled her toward the elevator.

"Up a level," he said.

When they entered the lift, Mimi glanced at the swollen belly of a pregnant woman. She didn't look tired or fed up, like so many of her pregnant colleagues in the past. She looked like the picture of contentment.

Austin caught Mimi staring at the lady. She quickly averted her eyes to the floor. They both were thinking the same thing—in just a few short months that could be her.

When the doors opened, they stepped out onto the busy ward. Mimi felt panicky. The sterile smell of the hospital walls seemed to get caught up in her nose, bringing back a memory of the accident. A flashback of the collision haunted her mind.

They took a seat in the waiting area. Mimi gently rested her head against Austin's shoulder. He raised his arm and wrapped it around her.

"How are you feeling?" he asked.

"Excited to get the cast off," she joked, avoiding the real reason he asked the question.

"Mimi Marcus," a nurse called.

They both stood, moving toward the consult room.

"Wait here," she said, pushing him back. It took him by surprise.

He said nothing. He simply stepped back and turned away to sit back down. Although she knew she had pissed him off, he did his best to contain it.

Mimi was relieved to see a female doctor sitting in the room. She was older and stand-offish. She flipped through papers on a clipboard.

"Can you confirm your name, please?"

"Mimi Marcus."

"It says here you are a Mrs. Is that right?"

Mimi started tugging at the hem of her dress. "Yes, that's right."

"You can ask your husband to come in with you," the nurse said.

"Oh, um, no, it's fine. Actually, I wanted to ask…"

The doctor looked up, her eyes gazing over the top of her dark framed glasses.

"Um, what happens, I mean, when the cast comes off?"

"Well, you may still have some bruising. That's normal and actually we expect that. Now, to start with, your arm may feel a little weak. You have to remember that there will be loss of muscle, and we expect that you will still experience pain for around another ten to fourteen days."

Mimi nodded, pursing her lips together.

"So, will I need an x-ray?"

"Yes, I'd like to do one to make sure that we are happy to go ahead and remove the cast for you today."

"I need to tell you. I think I may be pregnant."

The doctor remained expressionless and not at all phased. Mimi felt strange saying the word *pregnant* out loud to a stranger, and one with no bedside manner, not even a thread of one.

"How far along do you think you are?"

"I don't know. I mean, I kind of lost track after a series of unexpected life events."

"I see. Well, we can carry out a quick urine test.

Emily, will you quickly see if Sandra has any?"

The nurse disappeared out of the room. The doctor turned to Mimi. "Will this be your first?"

"Um, yes."

"Where are you from?"

"London."

"Are you here visiting?"

"My husband, he's Texan."

Mimi felt like an imposter. Joel was her husband, but her boyfriend was the one outside in the waiting room and she was waiting to find out if he was about to be a father.

Silence filled the room once more.

The nurse handed Mimi a small plastic container. "Just take this to the bathroom, first door on the right, and bring it back to us."

Mimi took the cup in her palm. Somehow, she felt humiliated. This was never how she imagined becoming a mother. It felt so clinical, so emotionless.

When she came back into the room, she handed the cup that she had covered in a grey paper towel. The nurse dipped a strip into it. Mimi could hear the blood rush to her ears as she awaited the fate for the rest of her life.

"Negative."

"I'm sorry, what?" Mimi said. She had been so sure, so certain, that she didn't know how to feel. She had convinced herself that she was pregnant. She hadn't considered the possibility that she wasn't.

"We can arrange for you to have a blood test, but since you are not sure of the date of your last period, it's up to you. Maybe wait it out a week or so."

When the doctor finished her examination on Mimi, she gave her the all clear to get her x-ray, and then she would be able to have the cast removed.

Mimi pushed the door open. She saw Austin waiting for her, slumped forward. As soon as he saw her, he stood up, searching her expression for an answer.

"I'm not pregnant," she said.

He pressed his back against the yellow wall behind him. "Well…how do you feel about that?"

"Relieved, but also a little disappointed. I don't know."

He gave her a half smile. "Let's just have fun together for now, and when the time is right, maybe we can plan things properly."

Mimi felt her heart flutter. "Let's get this thing off. I have to go to another department."

***

Austin drove up the crackly driveway. Mimi had the truck window down, letting the wind flow through her hair. When he pulled the truck to a stop, she opened the door and let her bottom slide off the leather seat.

The air smelled of dirt and fresh cut grass. The cattle smells wafted in the light breeze. She tucked her hospital notes under her arm and drifted toward the house. When inside, she caught a scent so familiar to her, it stopped her dead in her tracks.

"Everything okay?" Austin asked.

"Yeah…I think…I think I'm just really tired."

"Still feeling sick?"

"No. That seems to have passed."

He placed his hands on her shoulders, rubbing them. She started to feel the stiffness soften and the tension melt away every time he pressed his fingers into the depths of her muscles.

She turned around and met his gaze.

"I'm a mess," she said, tears stinging her eyes.

"Let me fix you." His words were clear.

Slowly, he brought his hand to her cheek and she ran her thumb along his bottom lip. She kissed him, a hard, open-mouthed kiss, desperate and passionate. He felt a rush of intense longing for her. She was like an addiction that needed to be satisfied. His breathing quickened and she tugged at his t-shirt, ripping it away from his body. He could feel her pulse quicken. He promised himself that he would never lose her ever again.

He pulled her dress up, running his hand along the inside of her thigh. "I love you," he said as he buried his face into the nape of her neck. She didn't say anything. She simply looked deep into his eyes, pulling him in closer, kissing him harder.

After, he rolled onto his back and Mimi caught her breath next to him.

"Fancy that horse ride?" He laughed. "Or are you too tired?"

She inhaled deeply.

"Tomorrow. Right now, I just want to snuggle."

"Snuggle?" he said, pulling a face. "I don't really snuggle."

She playfully punched his arm. "Of course you

do, cowboy."

"You sound sexy when you call me that."

"Come on, let's go snuggle. I want to spend the entire afternoon being lazy with you and eating too much ice cream and binge-watching stuff on Netflix."

"It may have escaped your mind, but I actually have some work to do."

"You're the boss, right? Therefore, you can take a day off."

"If you insist, my Mimi." He paused for a moment, raising his eyebrows. "I can call you that, right?"

Mimi turned to her side, pulling her dress off the floor and covering the bareness of her chest.

"Yes…you can call me that."

She ran her fingers along his jaw line, specked with stubble.

They spent the afternoon with the balcony doors wide open, snoozing, laughing, and making love. For the first time, the freshness of the wounds from Joel being at the ranch and finding out about Meg seemed to have less of a sting. The thoughts still crept into her mind every so often, which was quickly met with a sinking feeling in the pit of her stomach, but she knew it was all a process. She must go through the motions to come out of it on the other side.

"Tell me about your childhood. You know all about mine," Austin said. The sunlight had long given way to the darkness that filled the room.

"It was simple, I guess. I had good, hardworking parents and the most amazing sister, Larna."

The mention of her love for her sister made Austin's eyes dim.

Somehow, talking about a sibling always brought them back to Joel. It was as if Joel would come up and slice through the foundations of their relationship. She found herself needing to catch herself, careful not to hurt Austin's feelings.

When she thought of her childhood, bam, smack in the middle of it all, was Meg. She still hadn't addressed the feelings she felt about her betrayal. She sometimes found herself wondering if the woman she'd called her best friend, who she had shared so much laughter with for so many tears and so many firsts, felt any regret over what she had done.

Mimi didn't hold back when she told tales of herself growing up, and she forced herself to mention Meg in all of this, although her name seemed to get lodged in her throat. She was like a taboo subject, but she still pressed on, giving Austin pieces of her life.

***

Mimi flicked the light on in the hallway. It was just past twelve in the morning and she couldn't sleep. She made her way down the stairs and opened the front door, her bare feet crossing the porch. She sat on the swing, allowing her foot to push her backwards and forwards. She breathed in the cool air, letting it fill her lungs. She liked how it was so peaceful and calm with nothing but the starlit sky to look up to, the landscape drowned in darkness. She needed the solitude, a moment to herself.

She hugged her arms into her middle and closed her eyes. On the inside of her eyelids, she thought about Joel. She wondered where he was, what he was doing.

The images of him had become crumpled. She wondered if she had ever truly known him; she wondered if she had ever known Meg.

Her throat was choked with tears. She had been betrayed by the two people that she had trusted the most, and although she had now found solace in Austin, it still didn't mask the fact that her perception of Joel and Meg were just a good show of smoke and mirrors.

It was only in the darkness of her life that she was able to see truth.

If Meg had been with her when she found out about their affair, she would have grabbed her, shook her, and screamed, but she hadn't been there.

She hoped that her happiness at the ranch would be enough to push the entire episode behind her. Maybe it all really was a blessing in disguise. She allowed her mind to creep to where it wanted to go, letting her tears flow freely like a river down her cheeks.

She needed to come to terms with what happened and finally put the nail in the coffin. Only she knew there was still more to come. A divorce lay ahead of her, legal documentation that would end their marriage, and that would sever the ties that bound them. It had taken the chain of tragic events to lead her to the place she was supposed to be.

Behind her, the orange glow of light fell over the porch, followed by footsteps.

"What are you doing out here?"

"I couldn't sleep." She managed a sleepy smile.

"You've been crying."

"Just thinking."

She didn't want to lie to Austin. She had been lied to and she didn't want to become the person that kept secrets. If she was going to go into this new chapter of her life with him, she needed to be an open book.

CHAPTER 30

Joel

He lay in the darkness, the ceiling fan swirling above his head pushing the hot air around the room. Outside, he could hear a horn of a speeding truck drown out into the distance on the highway. The vacancy sign flickered on and off, lighting up the worn carpet next to the bed. He was a few miles away from the ranch, out toward the city.

He ignored the broken mattress springs stabbing his back. The interstate that the taxi driver needed to take to get to the ranch had been closed because of an oil spill, so he stopped off at a motel to rest and gather his thoughts.

When he closed his eyes, he could see Mimi. He knew she would be with him right now. He could feel the blood rushing to his head, and his heart felt like it was going to thud out of his chest. He was so angry, but mostly he was angry at himself for making so many mistakes by keeping so much from the one person who had believed in him the most.

When he thought of Mimi, he saw her standing on the edge of a cliff top in Yosemite. He remembered the moment when she had been so afraid to climb the face of the rock, but with his reassurance alone, she had made it to the top. It broke him into a thousand pieces knowing he wouldn't be that voice, her man, that would pull her through in life.

If he had just been honest with her from the onset and kept away from her best friend, he knew he would be the one holding her right now.

He walked into the bathroom and let the cool water run from the sink. He splashed his face and held the basin on either side, staring back at himself. A rage filled him. His anger shot to the surface. He was filled with a jealousy that could not be tamed, like a lion that was thirsty for blood.

He would sell his soul if he knew he could win Mimi back. He was driven by a force somewhere deep within him that knew he had survived because he had something to fight for. He couldn't let Austin keep her. He would do whatever it took, anything, to have her with him again. He was sorry for everything he'd done, but that was not enough to let her go. He needed to be the one to make her happy. He couldn't get past it. He wouldn't let his brother be the one to keep her heart.

The digital clock read 2 a.m. He gazed out of the window. The sky was tar black. The large clouds gathered fast and furiously. Soon, the gentle specks of rain flicked against the window. As it grew heavier, the tarmac on the car-park soon turned into a black river. He saw a man quicken his pace and slip into a beaten old truck.

He opened the door, letting the rain fall on him, drenching through his clothes. He moved out into the stormy weather, needing to wash away the hurt that lay inside him.

He remembered having this feeling once before, after the death of his father. It was then that the divide between him and his brother had become even greater. It had torn them apart, ripping them at the seams. Austin had stolen Joel's father, and now he was taking his wife. He had no control over the first time, but he swore he wouldn't let Austin win this time.

Blood pounded in his ears. He was still at war, but this time with himself.

The wind started to pick up, whipping through his body. The rain battered him like sharp blades. He needed to feel alive. Since he had left the ranch and left Mimi, he had become a ghost, weaving in and out of memories, and it was as if she couldn't see him, couldn't feel him, no matter how much he had begged her to give him one last chance.

When she told him about Austin, he had suspected it. He saw it in her eyes. He knew it was beyond Jake, beyond Meg even. There was something that had changed, and he saw it when he saw the way she looked at Austin. Still, the confirmation of her saying the words out loud was deafening. It felt like he had taken a bullet through his heart, which had exploded inside him on impact.

Her words, "He is ten of you," echoed in his head ever since. She had cast him aside, and he couldn't claw his way back to her. He was living a nightmare he was desperate to wake up from, like when he had woken in Afghanistan. Back then, he had been rescued. It seemed that nothing could rescue him from the fire around him now.

He squinted through the rain and his tears. He hadn't cried in years, not even when his father had died and he had seen his body still and lifeless.

For the months and years since losing his father, Joel had thrown himself into combat training. It gave him power. He was able to let out the demons of grief that lurked deep inside him, but now they couldn't be suppressed.

His life without Mimi was nothing.

When she had said that their marriage had ended, it was as if all the life he had held onto had been sucked out of him.

The world around him seemed so slow.

He noticed the glow of a cigarette coming from the truck. Gentle puffs of smoke drifted out of the small crack of the window. He moved toward it. He stood next to the driver's side.

A man opened the door. His skin was weathered, his eyes bulging. It was as if he had lived his life out on the open road, bouncing from motel to motel along the way. Joel noticed a pile of empty soda cans, cigarette boxes, and a *Penthouse* magazine peeking out from the glove compartment, the stale fog of smoke clinging to the fabric seats.

"What the hell do you want?" the man asked, his voice gruff and low.

"I need a ride."

"Do I look like a taxi? Fuck off."

"I don't think you heard me. I need a ride."

The man pushed open his door and his boots splashed into the puddle beneath his feet. He was at least three inches taller than Joel.

"I don't think you heard me, boy. Now get the hell away from my truck or I'm gonna bust your sorry ass."

He pushed Joel backwards. Joel raised his hands in the air and started to turn his body as if he was about to walk away, but then he swung back, connecting his iron fist to the man's face. He could see him wincing in pain.

The man started to get up, but Joel kicked him in the stomach, and then again and again until he couldn't stop. The sound of explosions echoed in his head. He could hear gun fire. His body may be in Texas, but his head hadn't truly left Afghanistan.

When the man lay still, he searched his pockets and took the keys. He could see he was still breathing. He dragged his body under the canopy of the reception roof. Then he ran toward the truck.

His hands shook as he tried to put the key in the ignition. As soon as the truck roared to life, he backed out and turned the steering wheel quickly. The tires screeched along the surface of the road. The windscreen wipers swished furiously against the windscreen. He kept driving, his eyes fixed on the road ahead.

He hit the brakes too quickly and the truck shook from side to side. Passing drivers honked their horns furiously. He squeezed his eyelids together several times to try and take the blur out of his vision and steady his focus.

He looked down and saw that blood had splashed

back on his t-shirt. The colour red brought back unwanted memories. The truck soon started to steam up with condensation on the inside, so he turned the fan up high to expel it, but it didn't work.

He leaned over, popping the catch of the glove compartment open. Inside, he found a grease-stained rag. When he pulled it out, the clunk of the shiny steel metal toppled out, falling onto the stained car seat. He recognised it immediately—a weapon that seemed to be waiting for him, almost as if it was all planned.

He kept his eyes on the road ahead. When he saw the exit for Eastleigh, he told himself that he would get her back, no matter what it took.

CHAPTER 31

Mimi sat out on the porch long after Austin had left her with her thoughts. He had given her a respectful space to think. She sat there long enough for the weather to change. The wind rustled through the trees. Thunder rumbled in the far distance followed by a flash of lightning. The dry soil hit by the rain filled the air with a musty dampness.

After she returned back to the house, she crawled into bed next to Austin. His breathing was even as he lay in a peaceful slumber.

The room felt too hot. The single sheet clung against his body. She slipped in slowly, careful not to wake him. She lay in the dark, the storm beginning to draw in closer.

She sunk her body into the softness of the mattress and gently reached her arm across Austin. He stirred, pulling her into him and gently kissing her on her forehead, and then drifted back to sleep. She loved how he made her feel so safe. As she nestled her head onto his chest, she fell into a deep, dreamless sleep.

After a couple of hours, Mimi was startled awake by the sound of a bang. She jolted upright, her skin clammy, her eyes not yet focused, and her heart pounding because of the unexpected sound.

The rain fell heavy, lashing against the balcony door, which had flung open. She quickly rushed to close it. The curtain blew over her face. She caught it and bunched it up in her hands.

As she grabbed the door and pulled it closed, she could see a figure standing under the large oak tree. She was rooted to the spot. Her mouth felt dry. The room seemed like all the air had been sucked out of it.

He watched her, his eyes sad. They appeared to gleam in the flash of simultaneous lightning. He appeared to reach out to her, his body bloody and wet.

Mimi remembered a dream that she had a few months before, the night before she had been informed that Joel had been killed, only this wasn't a dream. She was awake and he was standing in front of her.

She felt the blood drain from her face.

"What is it?" Austin asked.

"It's Joel. He's…he's outside." Her voice trembled.

Austin leapt out of bed. He saw his brother standing out in the pouring rain. He felt a wave of anger, followed by fear. Joel looked like a ghost—lost, broken—but the way his body stood rigid told him he needed to worry.

"I'll go talk to him," he said, pulling on his jeans that were draped over a chair sitting in the corner of the room.

"No, don't. He looks crazy," Mimi said, her voice high-pitched.

She'd never ever been fearful of her husband. He had never given her reason to, never any doubt, but in the darkness of this stormy night, something inside was telling her she had cause to panic.

"Just stay here, all right."

"Austin, please don't go out there," she pleaded "Let me go…I'll talk to him. It's me he's come for."

Austin swallowed hard. "Actually, Mimi, I think it's me he's come for."

Mimi was rooted to the spot as she kept her gaze fixed on Joel.

Austin appeared, walking toward him.

She saw Joel run away. The rain seemed to pour harder, making a clear view almost impossible.

She decided that she needed to face Joel. She needed to find out why he came back.

As she quickly dressed, she took another look outside of the window only to see that both Austin and Joel were no longer under the tree. They had both disappeared. Her eyes frantically searched the grounds, but they were nowhere in sight. She turned and raced out of the bedroom door, her heart thudding as she went down the stairs in a hurried pace.

When she opened the front door, the wind howled into her face, like an angry beast.

"Austin!" she yelled. The rain soaked through her dress immediately.

There was no answer.

She felt sick. She knew that no good would come of them being together.

"Austin, answer me!" she screamed.

She could see the glow of a light switched on in the barn in the far distance. She ran as fast as she could, but her feet sank ankle-deep in mud. She struggled to plough forward.

"You think you can fucking have her, but you can't!" She heard Joel growl.

She edged her body forward, peeking through the cracks of the barn door. She was careful not to let either of them see her, as she realised that she would be the fuel to the fire already burning between them both.

"She was your wife. You hid your kid from her and you go and cheat on her with her best friend. What gives you the right to still think she should be with you?"

Joel took a swing at Austin's face. He didn't fall, and blood dripped from his bottom lip, which began to swell on impact.

"Does the truth hurt, brother?" Austin said, his voice deep, low, and honest.

"And she should be with you? Does she know you left our father to die?"

"It was an accident and you know it. You can blame me all you want, but he would have died even if I'd gotten help a few moments sooner."

"Bullshit," Joel said, his eyes narrowing.

"Do us all a favour and get the hell out of Mimi's life."

"Fuck you," Joel spat. "I'm not leaving tonight without her. I'm not giving up on her."

"She's given up on you," Austin yelled.

Joel threw his body toward Austin, grabbed him by the throat, and pushed him into the dirt. Austin groaned as Joel punched him hard on his shoulder.

"You can't have her! I won't let you have her," Austin yelled.

He managed to push Joel off him, stumbling backwards. He curled his fist, ready to fight back if Joel lunged again.

Joel was enraged. Everything he'd been through in Afghanistan rose to the surface. For a brief moment, he stepped back and locked his gaze on his little brother. In that moment, he knew he was willing to do anything it took to get his wife back, even if he knew he was not truly deserving of her. No matter what, he knew his heart was only beating because of Mimi.

"You had a beautiful son and you turned your back on him, and then you have a beautiful wife and you manage to fuck that up. You're a total screw up, Joel. You think you're a fucking hero, off fighting in wars and being some goddam hero, but you're a fucking coward."

"What did you say?" Joel spat.

"You heard me. You are a coward."

The next sound was a bang…

Mimi's entire world spun in slow motion. Her vision became a foggy blur.

She ran in, throwing her body next to him as he bled.

"What have you done?" she screamed. "Austin! Austin! God, no. Please, baby, don't. Don't leave me, please."

Her hands were covered in a deep crimson thickness, a red river of pain draining his body of life as the blood pumped out of his neck.

She pressed her hands against his wound, trying to suppress the bleeding. She felt so helpless. Nothing she was doing could slow the inevitable. She couldn't focus. Every moment, however brief, with Austin flashed in her mind.

The air felt like it had been vacuumed out of the barn. She couldn't catch her breath. She looked around, her eyes frantically searching for something, anything, she could use to snatch him away from death, which lurked in the shadows.

Just as she was about to rip her dress in a last ditch attempt to stop the bleeding, she felt Austin's hand on hers, the hand where her wedding ring once belonged.

Austin's eyes were fixed on Mimi. "Tell Jake I love him," he whispered.

"No, don't you dare leave Jake. Don't you dare leave me!" She choked on her tears. Everything around her was spinning.

"Mimi, I love…" Austin's words trailed off.

"Call a fucking ambulance," she screamed at Joel.

But it was too late. He squeezed her hand one final time before he took his last breath.

Joel watched. He saw his wife holding his brother and he suddenly realized what he had done. The grief of watching his wife cry over another man was too much for him to take.

He knew she would never, ever be his.

"I'm sorry," he said, and then he turned the gun

onto himself.

CHAPTER 32

Mimi
Six Months Later

Looking up to the sky, Mimi stood on the porch of the ranch, reminiscing, putting together the events in her life that had led her to where she stood now. She had taken this journey to feel close to the man she loved, the man she said, "Till death us do part," to, but it wasn't Joel after all. It was Austin.

The moon was full and the stars were twinkling bright.

"You see that one there," Mimi said, pointing up. "That one is your daddy and he's watching over us both."

"I miss him," Jake whispered.

"I know you do, honey, I know you do, and so do I. But you know what? He'd want you to be happy and to be the best little boy that you can be."

"I want to live here with you," Jake said.

"I know you do, but that would make your

mummy really sad. Mummy says you can come here whenever you like, though."

"Am I having a brother or a sister?"

Mimi stroked her swollen belly. "You're having a brother. I told you that already."

"I know. I'm just checking. So, what will he be called?"

"Austin, after your daddy."

The End

ACKNOWLEDGMENTS

This book was born out of a very special sign given to me one winter's night. It was a journey that started with a different manuscript entirely. I faced unexpected twists and turns, which led to me writing the story you are about to read. A wise person once said that obstacles are put in our way to see if what we want is really worth fighting for.

There are so many special people who have made my journey possible. First, I'd like to give a special thanks to my parents for both their encouragement and unwavering support. My mum has always given me the determination to see this through to the end. I want to thank her for believing in me and believing in Mimi.

I know I can always count on my sister, Johanna, and my brother-in-law, Andrew. They are my close friends, friends that happen to be family. To Will and Philippa for the laughter in the sunshine of Florida and beyond. I am very grateful for my darling friends, Natalie, Caz, Sharon, and Poppy, for not letting me give up. These girls are my best cheerleaders. I want to give special thanks to Melanie Bundock, the manifestation queen and the woman who helped me smash the barrier. You rock, Mel!

A very big thank you to the MDG Family for the love, laughter, and encouragement they have given to me and to one another. There is a very special lady that is no longer here, but she lives on in spirit and in my heart—my Nonna. I know she is always watching over me.

I want to thank the team at Limitless Publishing for the favourite gold star on my Twitter pitch, #pit2pub, that led to me getting my publishing contract. I will forever be grateful to them for making my dreams come true.

And finally, to my husband and my son. This book is dedicated to both of my boys. For better or for worse, my husband, Adam, will always have my back. He is the one who listens to my crazy insomniac ideas at 3 a.m. He's the one that is always by my side. He's the one who is my partner in life, no matter what.

I love the life we have made together and the crazy pets we share it with. There is a little boy named Lucas. He stole my heart and calls me Mama. There is nothing more inspiring than those big blue eyes!

ABOUT THE AUTHOR

Cristina has always been a bookworm, rarely seen without a pen and paper in her hand, she loves delving into a literacy fictional world of her own.

At the age of 11, her junior school teacher told her mother that she would be wasting her life if she didn't become an author. Throughout her teenage years and beyond, her parents spurred her on to keep writing. She later began a career in commercial real estate, working in London's West End, a corporate bubble where she was unable to fuel her passion to write.

It was on her Californian honeymoon in 2012 that the bug to write was becoming increasingly difficult to ignore. After visiting Yosemite National Park she was inspired by the natural beauty of the land that surrounded her. Holding a special place in her heart, Yosemite would later be written into her debut novel.

She finally gave up the *'big smoke'* when her son, Lucas, was born in October 2013.

When Lucas was a newborn, Cristina was told to sleep when the baby sleeps. She never could. There was a calling inside her to write. After getting to grips with her new role as a mother, she began working a psychological thriller, but she couldn't fully connect to the characters she created. She ditched the manuscript and started ***Till Death Us Do Part*** (Limitless Publishing, 2015).

Cristina is married to Adam, who runs a successful business; together they share their Bedfordshire home with their son, crazy white

German Shepherd and three spoiled cats. They can be found trekking through woodlands, or around the many shops Cristina loves to explore. As a family, they love to travel frequently, the United States being a firm favourite.

Facebook:
https://m.facebook.com/cristinasloughauthor?ref=bookmarks

Twitter:
https://twitter.com/cristina_slough

Website:
http://www.cristinaslough.com/

Lightning Source UK Ltd
Milton Keynes UK
UKOW01f0608140216

268258UK00002B/12/P